LAST
ONE
ALIVE

BOOKS BY H.K. CHRISTIE

VAL COSTA SERIES

Gone by Dawn

Don't Make a Sound

Hidden in the Dark

THRILLERS

A Permanent Mark

The Neighbor Two Doors Down

MARTINA MONROE SERIES

Crashing Down

What She Left

If She Ran

All She Wanted

Why She Lied

Secrets She Kept

What She Found

How She Fell

Her Last Words

Who She Was

How She Escaped

Lies She Told

Echoes of Her

H.K. CHRISTIE

LAST ONE ALIVE

bookouture

Published by Bookouture in 2025

An imprint of Storyfire Ltd.
Carmelite House
50 Victoria Embankment
London EC4Y 0DZ

www.bookouture.com

The authorised representative in the EEA is Hachette Ireland
8 Castlecourt Centre
Dublin 15 D15 XTP3
Ireland
(email: info@hbgi.ie)

ISBN: 978-1-80550-257-9
eBook ISBN: 978-1-80550-256-2

For Trish

PROLOGUE

The road ahead was dark and daunting. There was something eerie about being alone on a country road, the pitch-black night broken only by the beam of my headlights. Driving late at night always made me nervous—not that I'd ever had any trouble since I'd moved up north. I hadn't planned to be out late, but when I was offered a double shift at the bar—extra money I could desperately use—it was too good an opportunity to pass up. Work had been busy and exhausting, leaving me a bit weary this late at night. I turned up the volume on the stereo to perk myself up. I certainly didn't need to run my car off the road—mostly because I couldn't afford the repairs or the medical bills.

It had been a rough year. After breaking up with Jed, I thought moving to northern California where I didn't know a soul was a sure way to make a fresh start. With only five hundred dollars in my bank account, I was lucky to find a studio apartment above an old couple's garage. A couple who were fine about me moving in without a security deposit or first month's rent. They must have sensed my desperation and taken pity on me. Maybe that was why the highway seemed so unsettling. It magnified how alone I was. No boyfriend, no family, a dead-end job, and living in someone's backyard above a garage. It wasn't how I had pictured my life. My dream was to be an artist, a painter. I thought moving to a place surrounded by hills and forest would be peaceful and that nature would inspire me. I'd even had a blue-and-purple butterfly tattooed on my right wrist to symbolize my transformation into a new person. A person who didn't let their circumstances define her, someone who could start over and live creatively.

I'd planned to paint when I wasn't working, but I hadn't imagined it would be so difficult to find a decent-paying job where I only needed to work *one* shift a day to pay for food and rent. The dashboard clock read midnight. The commute home was only fifteen minutes, but at this hour it felt longer. Two lights suddenly appeared in the rearview mirror, catching my attention. I was no longer alone. Was that a good thing?

The car behind seemed to be closing in on me at an alarming rate. My adrenaline kicked in, and I shifted my mind to full alert. They were coming awfully fast. Was it my imagination? Could they see me? I was probably just being paranoid—surely, they'd slow down or pass me. Heart racing, I readied myself for them to overtake when I heard a loud *womp*. My car swerved and I corrected it just in time to pull off to the shoulder. At a complete stop, I muttered, "Dang it!"

The sound and disarming lack of control was familiar. I had a flat tire. Frustrated, I pounded the steering wheel until I could calm myself. What on earth was I going to do now? There was no way I could afford a tow truck, and I was miles from home. *Just my luck.* Reaching for my cell phone to call for help, I stopped when I realized I had no one to call. No one to help me. Angry tears spilled as I thought of all the events that had led me to here. Crappy parents. Two-timing boyfriends.

A knock on the car window broke me away from my pity party and swung me into full panic. My heart pounded as I turned my head toward the sound.

There stood a man. He must've seen the terror on my face because he smiled and said, "Looks like you got a flat. Need a hand?"

I hesitated, then shook my head at myself for being silly. This was the country. People were nice here. People stopped to help with flat tires. I still wasn't used to it. Everyone I had met in town had been friendly. Maybe it *actually was* my lucky night.

I opened my car door and stepped out. The man was tall and lean, with bright blue eyes and sandy hair. Handsome. His megawatt smile was illuminated by his high beams, still on behind him.

"Yeah, I think so."

"I've changed a thousand tires in my day. I've got a jack. Do you have a spare in the trunk?"

A spare? I wish. After my last flat, I hadn't had the money to replace the spare. This man couldn't help me after all. I'd likely be walking home or back to the bar since it was only a half mile down the road, maybe one of my coworkers could give me a lift home. "I don't."

"Let me take a look. It might just need a simple patch. I've got a kit in my trunk. I might be able to fix it for you."

"You can do that?"

He nodded. "I'm a mechanic by trade. I carry quite a few tools with me."

He knelt to inspect the tire, pressing his palm against it. "Looks like I should be able to repair it."

Relief washed over me. "Seriously?"

"Sure. Where are you headed, anyhow?"

"Just home. I work at Joe's Tavern."

"That's funny—I was just eating there. Maybe that's why you look familiar."

"Oh, really?" I didn't recall seeing him, and I had been the only server tonight.

"Best patty melt I've ever had."

We did serve a great patty melt. But... still... "Oh, okay."

"Let me grab the patch kit. You from around here?"

"I moved here about six months ago."

"Yeah? Got family in town?"

Was he trying to learn if anyone would miss me? "No." I said, before adding, "Just a few friends I'm staying with." To let him know I would be missed by someone if I didn't show up that night. Would Mr. and Mrs. Fletcher notice if I never came home?

"Cool. I'm Dom. Nice to meet you."

He extended his hand. I hesitated, then shook it. His hands were warm and strong. I told myself I was letting my anxiety get the better of me. Standing by my car, I watched as he opened the trunk of his and pulled out what looked like a small case.

"Here it is."

I wasn't sure what was in his hand. He had said it was just a patch, but I didn't see any tools. Maybe he didn't need a jack or anything like that. He strode back toward me with a smile.

"Got it. I'll just pull the nail right there." He pointed and I looked down at the tire. But before I could squint to get a better look, I felt something prick the back of my neck.

The last thing I saw were his arms catching me as I collapsed, and everything went black.

ONE

VAL

Head in my hands, I tried to stop the tears from streaming, to keep my body from rocking. I had to remind myself it was only a dream. The nightmares had nearly stopped, until recently. Until I'd received the last note from the Bear, the serial killer who'd captured me nine months ago, when I was supposed to be hunting him. He'd kept me for nearly two days before my team found me. Everything in my gut screamed that he'd been tracking me and watching me since I'd moved back to my home-town after my rescue, and when I'd got that note on Sunday night—after we'd closed the last case, after Brady and I had shared our first kiss—there was no longer any doubt in my mind it was true. The Bear was in Red Rose County. And he wanted me to know it.

I'd called Kieran almost immediately, but like the other notes the Bear had left for me at crime scenes and in my moth-er's mailbox, there were no fingerprints, no trace evidence, and no touch DNA. There was no surveillance outside the restau-rant. There were no clues to his identity or current location.

Kieran, my old boss at the FBI, had assured me he'd do everything in his power to catch the Bear, but with nothing to go on, the FBI's hands were tied. Of course, he'd flown out immediately to talk to me face-to-face, but there was no proof it was actually the Bear who had tucked the note underneath my windshield wiper blade. He could have hired someone to place it there, like he'd done in the past. But call it instinct or gut feelings or whatever. I *knew* it was him.

I shook my head and wiped my face with the back of my pajama sleeve. I hadn't told Mom or Brady that the nightmares were back in full force, that I wasn't sleeping. Although I suspected they knew. I'd started wearing makeup to cover up the dark circles, but they both saw right through me. And I hated it.

I hated that the nightmares had returned and that they affected me like this. I needed to be strong.

I needed to find him.

I took a deep breath, then exhaled until my lungs were empty. Climbing out of bed, I trudged into the bathroom. I stared in the mirror, trying to remember who I used to be before the Bear had taken me, before he'd marked me. I pulled off my shirt, damp with sweat, and stared at the scar he'd carved into my chest.

He'd put his mark on me. Made me his.

There was only one way to be free of him forever, and that was to ensure he was locked up or dead.

But for the first time in my life, I had no idea how to move forward. I needed to end this. But I had nothing to go on. *No leads.* I had lost control of the situation and I hated myself for it.

Before the Bear, I was unbeatable. Nothing could take me down. He'd taken that away from me. *Oh, what I would give for another shot at him.*

Shaking off the thoughts, I focused on getting cleaned up. I grabbed a tissue and blew my nose and returned my gaze to the mirror. My brown eyes were rimmed with dark circles and my hair was wild and damp from streaks of tears and sweat from the nightmares. It had been nine months since my captivity, yet each night I dreamed of it, it felt like it had happened only minutes ago.

Stripping off my pajama bottoms, I turned on the shower. The water wasn't warm yet, but that didn't bother me. I got into the shower, hoping the shock of the cold water would wash away the memories of my nightmare. Soon, the warm water streamed through, and I began to relax.

I knew what I needed to do. It was what I would tell anybody in my position. Mumbling to myself I said, "Call your therapist. Increase the number of sessions. Get help. There is no weakness in asking for help."

It was so much easier said than done.

I hopped out of the shower, got dressed, and pounded down the stairs for coffee.

Julie greeted me with a smile. "Good morning, Val. How did you sleep?" Her question trailed off as she took in my face. I hadn't put on makeup. *The jig was up.*

"Good morning, Julie. Not great."

"I've made coffee."

"Thanks, Julie."

"Morning, Val. Nightmares?" Mom's voice was gentle.

I suspected they hadn't believed a word I'd said about being fine, about sleeping through the night, and I didn't have it in me to pretend anymore. I nodded. Julie handed me a steaming mug of coffee, and I joined my mother at the dining table.

"It's been like this all week, hasn't it?" Mom asked.

My mother—the retired sheriff of Red Rose County and, apparently, expert in all things me—had suffered a stroke eight months earlier. She'd made significant progress in her recovery and was now able to walk a little around the house with the help of a quad cane. Her friends, Julie and Diane, were almost permanent fixtures in our home—my childhood home—since the incident, helping take care of her and, quite frankly, taking care of me, too.

"It has. I think it's time I maybe increase my therapy sessions."

Mom nodded. "That's a great idea, Val. And you know if you ever want to talk, I'm here. I know this can't be easy for you."

"It's not."

Julie sat down at the table with her own mug. I hadn't even touched mine. I glanced down, inhaled the rich aroma of fresh-brewed coffee, and took a sip. It was great.

"Mom, did you ever feel, when you were still in law enforcement and investigating a case, that you hit a wall? That you didn't know where to turn next when you ran out of clues?"

"Unfortunately, more than once. Some cases stick with you. And honestly, you have to learn to live with them, grieve them. There's so much that's out of our control, Val. I mean, look at me—I was fit, healthy, then I had a stroke and couldn't even walk or take care of myself."

She was right. There was so little in life we could control. The fact that we thought we could was an illusion. We couldn't stop all bad things from happening. Sure, we could be cautious —look both ways before crossing a street, wear our seat belts, don't drink and drive—but there were too many forces at play. Too many instances of chance, of bad luck, and of good luck.

How was I forty-six years old and just now learning this? How had I missed it all these years? "What if I can't live with it, Mom?"

Julie looked at me, her green eyes sparkling. "Living with it, Val, doesn't mean forgetting about it. It means learning how to keep going and to keep getting up each morning, going for a jog or a hike, and visiting with friends and loved ones. You carry on. You *never* forget."

It made sense, I supposed.

Julie patted my shoulder. "You'll get through this, Val. The women in this family? I don't think anything can break them."

I looked over at my mom. I knew that was true of her—and of my sister, Maxine, a captain in the US Army, a trained helicopter pilot. I supposed we had been raised to be tough, which made it even more difficult when we didn't feel tough. When we felt more like gooey, weak pudding.

Julie interrupted my thoughts. "How about some breakfast, Val? Your mom and I already ate. But I can whip up some eggs and toast. There's fruit salad, too."

I didn't feel like eating, but I knew better than to argue. And if I were giving myself my own advice, I'd insist I needed my strength.

As Julie got up and headed toward the stove, Mom said, "I got a text from Harrison."

"What did he say?" I asked, smiling.

"Just telling me good morning and that he loves me."

Warmth filled my insides and I wondered if he had texted me too. I hadn't even looked at my phone this morning, too distracted by the nightmares.

Julie called over from the stove. "That boy of yours, Val, he's quite the young man."

I grinned. "I tend to agree." My son was nineteen years old and in his first year at MIT. He was smart, caring, and empathetic. I was blessed to have him.

"Speaking of wonderful young men," Julie said, "do you have any plans with Brady?"

"We talked about a hike this weekend. But tonight, I'm going out with the girls."

Sally and Lucy were my closest gal pals in Red Rose County.

Mom said, "Well, that should be fun."

"I think so. Sally met some new guy, and I'm dying to hear

about him. She went out with him over the weekend, but with everything going on, I haven't been able to touch base."

"Love is in the air," Julie sang.

A knock on the door silenced our conversation.

"Expecting anyone?" I asked.

Mom shook her head. Julie did the same.

I stood, realizing I had no weapon on me. "Stay put." I raced upstairs to my room, unlocked the safe, and grabbed my gun. The knock on the door sounded again. I ran downstairs. Who could it be? *Whoever it is, I'm ready.*

TWO

VAL

Weapon firmly by my side, I looked through the peephole, and my body instantly relaxed. I opened the door and a chill floated inside, but the sight before me stirred a warmth in my chest. There stood Brady with a five o'clock shadow, hair mussed, and in uniform.

"Hey. I wasn't expecting you."

"Can I come in?"

He was seemingly all business. "Of course."

He stepped inside and glanced down at my hand and the weapon in it.

"Let me put this away."

He gave a slight smile and nodded. I ran upstairs, shaking my head at how foolish I'd been. Of course the Bear wouldn't just walk up to my door and knock. I could have checked the monitors before assuming the worst, but instead I let fight mode take over, and I hadn't thought rationally. Hopefully I wasn't losing my mind.

With the weapon secured, I ran back downstairs to find Julie chatting with Brady, trying to convince him to come in for coffee. Then, I heard my mom call out, "Brady, is that you?"

Brady gave me a knowing look, and I tilted my head toward the kitchen. He nodded, understanding there was no escaping Elizabeth Costa or her pal, Julie.

"Good morning, Elizabeth."

"Good to see you, Brady. Were we expecting you?"

"No, I guess Val hasn't checked her phone. I've been trying to get a hold of her."

I noticed the expression on Brady's face. This wasn't a social call, then. "What is it, Brady?"

"We need to talk privately. It's an active investigation."

Julie folded her arms. "Well, technically, we're all civilians here."

Julie had become like a second mother to me. She and my mom were thick as thieves and wanted to know every detail of every case I had worked since I'd been home in Red Rose County—and Brady knew it.

Brady exhaled. "True, but it's a bit of a sensitive situation, and..." He met my gaze. "We need Val's help."

A chill ran down my spine. Another murder.

"Another investigation for you, Val. That'll get you back to your old self," Julie said, knowing that a new case usually perked me up when I was feeling down. But something in my gut stirred. I wasn't sure that was the situation here.

Brady said, "It's good to see both of you ladies, but I have to request that I speak to Val alone, if you don't mind."

"Of course we don't mind. You two do what you do," Mom encouraged.

I led Brady into the living room, out of earshot of my mother and her friend. "What's up?"

"Well, first of all, how are you doing?" He studied my face.

"Nightmares. I'll get through it."

"If you ever need anything—ever. Even just someone to yell and scream at, someone to listen—I got you, Val. Anything. You know that, right?"

"I do. Thank you. I'm fine, really." As much as I adored Brady, I hated that our relationship had started with me dumping all my problems on him. Our first kiss should've been the beginning of something magical. Instead, it had been tarnished immediately by another note from the Bear. I wanted so badly to wrap my arms around Brady and forget everything else, but did he even want to be with me anymore? I'd understand if he didn't. Wherever I went, trouble seemed to follow. He had moved back to Red Rose County for some peace and quiet, not to get caught up in serial killers.

"Are you sure? I've barely heard from you since..." Our kiss. The note.

"I'm sorry. I didn't know if maybe... you'd changed your mind about us. And I didn't want to put you in danger."

Brady's jaw dropped ever so slightly. "Val. I don't think I could change my mind, even if I wanted to."

My skin tingled and heat bloomed on my cheeks. "Oh."

He reached out and touched my hand, his warmth comforted me. "Now, are we okay?"

I nodded. He took on a serious tone. "Good, because I'm afraid I have some disturbing news."

I stepped back, ready for the worst. "Oh?"

"Three hours ago, a man in Hectorville was walking his dog near an old abandoned property."

As I processed the information, my body temperature rose. My heart pounded. Sweat began to trickle down my temples. Brady touched my arm and led me to the sofa. "Breathe with me, Val. Inhale. Exhale."

After a moment, I put my hand on his and looked into his eyes. "I'm fine. Keep going. What did they find?"

He hesitated but relented. "A body. Inside an old barn."

"Male or female? Homicide or accidental?" I asked the questions, but I already knew the answers.

"Female. Homicide."

"Any suspects?"

His lips pressed together. For a moment, he said nothing. Then quietly, he said, "The sheriff requested your services, like before, to help us solve the case. I told him I wasn't so sure it was a good idea. You've been through a lot. If you're not up for another investigation right now, it's perfectly okay. You deserve a break."

As if I had a choice. The timing was too coincidental not to think it was connected to the Bear. "I want to help. Do you have photos?"

Brady paused, and averted his eyes. "I do, but they're hard to look at."

He was avoiding something. Avoiding telling me a detail that my body already knew.

"She was cut up pretty bad," he admitted. "It's probably best you walk the scene. They're expecting you."

He was right. The scene would be better than photos. *And to think just minutes ago, I thought I had no more leads, I had no control, and may never find him. I was right about one thing—I wasn't the one in control right now, but if it was the Bear he'd just given me another clue and I would find him.* "Okay." I stood, ready for the challenge.

"And Val," Brady said. "There was a note."

I lowered my head, processing the information. The Bear was here. In Red Rose County. *I knew it. I'd felt it.* I had no proof, but the signs were there. "I need to call Kieran."

"I talked to the sheriff. If it is the Bear, which I told the sheriff it could be, he knows the FBI will want to be involved."

"If it's him, the FBI will take over."

"Let's take this one step at a time. It might not be him."

Not likely. "Where's the note?"

Brady pulled it from his jacket, sealed inside a clear evidence bag. Not that there would be any clues on it. No fingerprints. No touch DNA. That would be too easy.

On the outer envelope, in all caps: VALERIE COSTA. Just like the others.

The note card inside, written in bold black letters:

THINKING OF YOU. UNTIL WE MEET AGAIN.

—S.

Glancing up at Brady, I said, "It's *him*."

THREE

VAL

Armed, I headed to the crime scene with Brady, but not before Julie had packed me an egg sandwich to go and insisted that Brady take one too.

We didn't talk much on the drive. We just ate quietly and sipped coffee while my mind buzzed, tangled with too many thoughts at once. I knew the Bear was here for me, but now the reality of it settled over me like a black cloud. What did he have planned?

Adrenaline was racing through my veins and I was ready. Especially knowing that my instincts had been correct. I didn't need physical evidence—other than the scar he'd left on my chest—to know he'd been tracking me, watching me, and that he was in my hometown. *And now, he'd taken another life.*

I knew the only reason why he killed her—other than his sick pleasure—was to send me a message. He had used this poor woman to get to me. I knew there wouldn't be any physical evidence that would lead us to his whereabouts, but the scene might provide some clues.

We arrived at the abandoned property—one of his favorite places to work, to abduct, and to kill. A place where he could listen to his victim's screams without interference. There were half a dozen sheriff vehicles, the crime scene unit, the sheriff himself, and now reporters were gathering. Deputies lined the perimeter and crime scene tape sectioned off the area. It was my nightmare coming to life.

We exited the car without a word, marching toward the sheriff. His expression was ashen. "Morning, Val. We're glad you're here."

How could he be glad? There wouldn't be a crime scene if it weren't for me. "Hi, Sheriff. I want to take a look and then I'll call my former supervisor at the FBI."

"Go ahead."

I ducked under the crime scene tape, nodding silently at some of the sheriff's deputies I had gotten to know over the past year. I covered my shoes with booties and walked toward the scene. One of the techs was crouched down beside the body.

As much as I feared what I'd see, I forced myself to look. The woman had been brutally attacked. She was young, with a pretty blue-and-purple butterfly tattoo on her right wrist that he had left unmarred. The rest of her had been brutalized. My eyes locked onto the carving on her chest—an "S", one that was nearly identical to my own. It was consistent with the previous murders we had attributed to the Bear. Most of the "S" markings were sloppier than the one I'd received, and his earlier markings resembled more of a zigzag or a long curved slash, making it difficult to see the connection at first glance, but I was the one who had put together the pattern. With the FBI, I had linked eleven murders across four states. My abduction had been the last one attributed to him—until *now*.

I knew he wasn't done with me.

I glanced around the barn. The scene was eerily similar to my own abduction. The Bear had used a variety of locations for his crimes, but they tended to be abandoned properties—sometimes the kills were inside old houses that had been left vacant or outbuildings, but only one other barn. The one I had been held captive in.

He had nearly replicated my own crime scene. The only difference was this woman didn't have a chance. She hadn't had a team searching for her when she went missing and she had no idea whom she was dealing with. And unlike my attack, he had been able to complete his ritual.

He enjoyed inflicting pain and suffering. He got off on it—the power and the control. All likely because in his earlier years, he'd had none, or he was a sociopath with narcissistic tendencies. The Bear had stolen this young woman's life, her power and her control. And I had every intention of taking his.

Brady exhaled. "What do you think, Val?"

"It's definitely him."

Brady hadn't seen my crime scene photos, but he knew what had happened to me. He knew about the scar on my chest and that I'd been held in an abandoned barn. He had seen the notes the Bear had left me in Red Rose County. He knew this *display* was for me.

"Do we know who she is?" I asked.

"She's been identified as Linda Castillo, a twenty-three-year-old woman who lives in Hectorville. She worked at Joe's Tavern and was last seen leaving work close to midnight two days ago. Her landlord reported her missing. Her car was found abandoned on the side of the road—flat tire."

"Does she have family in the area?"

"None that her boss or the landlord knew of. She moved here six months ago, and mostly kept to herself."

"Did they recover her cell phone?"

"Yes. Contacts are limited. When she was reported missing, they checked it for relatives, and they found her car fairly quickly."

"He'd likely been stalking her."

Brady tipped his head and I stepped out of the barn, trying

not to lose the egg sandwich I had just eaten. After a few deep breaths, I called Kieran. He answered the call after one ring. By now, I think Kieran understood that if I was calling it was serious.

"What's up?"

Trying to remain calm, I said, "It's him. He's here."

"What's happened?"

Pacing, I explained the situation. "A body was found a few hours ago. It's nearly identical to my crime scene. An 'S' carved on her chest. And he left another note for me."

"Are you at the scene?"

In a low voice, I said, "Yes." But I wished to God I wasn't. I wished that none of this had happened. That Linda Castillo hadn't lost her life because of him.

"What does the note say?"

"It says: 'Thinking of you. Until we meet again. S'."

Kieran's voice hardened. "Okay, I'll have the team out in thirty. Stand by. Tell the sheriff not to touch anything. The FBI is taking over. That includes you, Val. I need you off this."

My hand balled into a fist, my nails digging into my flesh as I fought the urge to scream into the phone. "Kieran, I can't *not* be part of this."

"First of all, you're no longer a member of the FBI. Second, you're not law enforcement. And third, you're one of his victims. You can't be anywhere near this if we're going to get a prosecution, if we're going to get this guy. Do you understand?"

There was no way I was backing down. I couldn't step back and do nothing while the monster that was trying to end my life was running around my town killing my neighbors. Kieran should have known better. We'd worked together for nearly my entire career at the FBI.

"Val?"

"I understand, Kieran."

"Good. I need someone from the sheriff's department to notify us officially."

"Hold on."

I lowered the phone and turned to Brady. "He needs an official notification."

"Should I get the sheriff?"

"Are you the lead?"

"Yes."

I handed him the phone.

"Hi Kieran, this is Brady Tanner with Red Rose County Sheriff's Department."

As Brady and Kieran talked, I stared at the barn, my mind racing. There had to be something—some clue that could lead me to him. I needed something pointing to him, because there was zero chance I was going to stand down from this case.

FOUR

HIM

Perched in a grove of trees, I concealed myself nicely. I wished I could get closer because I'd love to have seen the look on Valerie's face when she saw my message—the note and my gift —a memory for her, a reminder of our time together. Did she need a reminder? Probably not. But I'd been coy until now. I needed her to know I was close and that soon we would be together again. Was she as excited as I was?

Truth be told, I felt like a fool, hiding in trees, peering through binoculars. But I wanted to be part of her world—or rather, I wanted to know all about hers so that I could create a world just for the two of us. I wasn't sure how long that world would last. Typically, time spent with my new friends only lasted a few days, but with Valerie Costa, I wanted more. How long? I wasn't sure. A week, two weeks, a month? Years? Wouldn't that be something.

She already bore my signature—my mark. But there was so much more we could do together. So much more we could *be*. Could she feel it?

I raised the binoculars again and watched her. There she was, with *Brady*. Her so-called love interest. That would end soon, I would make sure of that. He wasn't worthy of her. Far from it.

There was only one man who should be in her life, and that was me. I *owned* her. She just didn't know it yet.

She looked fired up, waving her hands around, her expression sharp and intense. Brady nodded like a robot, lifeless and weak. Valerie didn't need a robot. She needed a real man. Someone who could put her in her place. And I was just the man to do that.

The sight of her reminded me of our first meeting. She had actually surprised me. That didn't happen often—if ever. I was setting up for my next adventure with a new friend, someone I'd been stalking for weeks. My tools were ready. The barn was set up. Imagine my surprise when, just as I was slipping on my mask to go retrieve my new friend, Valerie appeared right around the corner. I chuckled lightly at the memory. *She came to me.*

Imagine my surprise once I knocked her out, chained her up, and found her FBI credentials in her wallet. *FBI!* That was a close call. I knew the FBI didn't work alone and therefore Valerie and I didn't have much time together. It was disappointing, but also concerning. Somehow, they had found me despite how careful I'd been. But how? I knew about forensics—who didn't? Every other television show, and every true crime podcast laid it all out. You'd have to be a fool to get caught these days. But somehow, she had done it. Somehow, she had found me.

Because of her, I had to change things up. From what I'd read, they probably had a full profile on me. That meant I had to alter my ways. It was a warning and I had taken it. All thanks to Valerie.

Normally, I liked to get up close and personal once my new friends and I were alone, but because she was FBI, I never let her see my face.

Of course, that would change.

Before, I knew I didn't have much time with her and I savored every moment. With each second passing too quickly, I knew I wasn't ready for our encounter to end but I didn't want to rush things. Valerie wasn't like the others. She was different. She was special.

She was willing to fight me to the death. A true contender. Maybe even a partner.

When she was chained up, her screams had been different. The others screamed in fear, but she... she knew what I enjoyed and soon, *too soon*, quieted. She talked to me. The others didn't know anything about me. Valerie knew me. And that changed everything.

Valerie wouldn't give me what I wanted—not then. But she would when we were reunited. And we would be reunited because I had planned this carefully. But Valerie was careful too. I had been watching her for months. Keeping tabs. Tracking her routine. Who she talked to, who she went out with. Her two friends Lucy and Sally. Sally I was quite fond of. And she was useful too—for now. And of course there was Brady. *That guy.*

Sudden movement down on the property drew my attention. I pulled up the binoculars once again. The FBI had arrived in Red Rose County.

Who was this? *Oh yes, this must be an old colleague of Valerie's.* I had seen him at her house earlier in the week. Perhaps her previous supervisor. It looked like he was being stern with her. She shook her head and gesticulated, before storming off. Have they told her she can't be part of the investigation? My Valerie would not like that. There's Brady, trailing behind her, trying to calm her down. As if he's enough for her. Not even close. There's only one person for Valerie. And that's me.

She'll see that in time.

Six agents stood there, all wearing their jackets with the gold FBI logo emblazoned on the back. The older, sturdy, burly man—the one I had seen at her house earlier in the week—approached Valerie again, clearly trying to reason with her. She shrugged, and the two of them walked away together.

Sorry, Brady. I smiled. Poor sap. Doesn't he realize he's not needed here?

I watched Valerie with this other man—this agent. She seemed... calmer.

As they turned and walked back toward the barn, a new thought crossed my mind. I'd assumed Valerie would lead the investigation, but maybe the FBI had other plans. I needed to ensure Valerie would get to play too, but the FBI might need a few nudges of encouragement to let their star shine. After all, this was a game for Valerie and me. It wasn't for the Feds and it certainly wasn't for the sheriff's department of Red Rose County.

No. This is all for you, Valerie. Don't worry, I'll make sure you get to play in the big game.

FIVE

VAL

Kieran studied Linda Castillo's body without saying a word and I wondered if he was remembering my crime scene photos. The scene was a match for my own, not exact, but close enough. It was difficult to look at her body, but I forced myself to in case the Bear had left me any more messages on the body or at the scene. There wasn't anything obvious, but I would examine the photos later to make sure I hadn't missed anything. Breaking the silence, I said, "Is Jordan coming?"

"He is. He was working another case, but he should be here any minute. I've reassigned him back to the Bear task force. This will be his, and our, top priority. Until we get this guy, we're not leaving."

It was reassuring to know Jordan and the old task force, plus a few faces I didn't recognize, would work the case. Jordan was the one who had actually found me—rescued me. He had been part of the team tracking the Bear into Nevada all those months ago. He'd realized by breakfast the next morning that I was missing and then figured out how to get into my computer by working quickly with the tech team back in Quantico. My mind flashed back to the moment our eyes met in that dilapidated barn. Jordan was tall, a bit lanky, with a brilliant mind. Stoic, usually. You know, the intellectual type—a runner with focus and determination. I had never seen him break his usual demeanor, but when he saw me—when he saw that I was alive —there were tears in his eyes. Relief washed over my battered body as he rushed to unchain me. Quickly the logical part of my brain kicked in and I stopped him. "Take pictures first. There could be clues." He hesitated, but I assured him, "I can handle another minute. Please, take photos. We have to get him." Jordan took photos on his phone and swiftly removed the chains by picking the lock. The other members of my team showed up shortly after. When they saw I was alive and standing up, with the help of Jordan, they froze. I managed to croak out, "Hi," and watched as Jordan commanded the scene beautifully, telling them not to touch anything without gloves, and to be cautious where they stepped, before he directed them to collect anything and everything that could be evidence. He wasn't in charge but he took charge, and I appreciated it.

It would be good to see him again and to see his reaction to this new scene.

Kieran pulled out his phone and held it up to his ear. "Kieran Fox." And then, "Yes, we're in the barn."

He slipped his phone back into his pocket. "He's here."

Good.

Kieran hadn't outright said that I could work the case, but I think he understood that I had to at least consult on it. The Bear was after me. He was targeting me. There was no way I could just stand back, go binge-watch TV with my mom, or visit Harrison at MIT. I couldn't just disappear until they found him. From what I knew about the Bear, he wasn't going to stop. He'd come here for me. If I left, he would too. This wouldn't end until he and I came face-to-face and finished this sick game— once and for all.

I turned toward the entrance of the barn, and there he stood —Jordan.

He was in his late thirties with piercing blue eyes, and dark curly hair. He was exactly as I remembered him. I couldn't help but smile, and neither could he.

"Good to see you!" I said, as he stepped inside.

"You too, Val. I wish it was under better circumstances."

"So do I."

"But this time, we're going to catch him."

"Yes, sir."

We stood silently as he studied the barn, the chains, the body, and the brutality the Bear had inflicted upon this poor young woman.

"Has the medical examiner been here?" Jordan asked.

Kieran said, "We told the sheriff's department that we would handle it. Our team is on their way."

"Sally—I mean, Dr. Edison, is a great medical examiner. She's solved cases with me since I've been in Red Rose County. She's top-notch. She could help."

Kieran eyed me. "It might be nice to have backup. I'll consider it, but for now, our team will handle it. They'll collect evidence, remove the body, and bring it back to our local lab."

"Okay," I said. "But I don't think the Bear is done. He's not going anywhere without me—I'd bet my life on it. You may need the extra hands."

Jordan and Kieran exchanged a look. Motioning to the body, I said, "What do you think of the scene, Jordan?"

"There is a strong similarity to his last crime scene," he said quietly.

My crime scene. "Other than the extra carvings and likely fatal stab wounds, I'd say he was re-creating it."

"That's my thought as well. And Kieran said there was a note. What did it say?"

"'Thinking of you. Until we meet again, S'."

Jordon nodded. "I agree with Val. He's not leaving without her. We need to make sure she's protected at all times."

"And I need to work the case, right?"

Jordan glanced at the body, then at Kieran, then back at me. "Let's go outside."

We walked out without hesitation. I didn't need to see the body any more than I already had—for now.

"All right, Kieran, what are you thinking? You're not really going to keep Val on the sidelines, are you? She knows him better than anyone," Jordan said.

"She's not even FBI or law enforcement. And she's a victim."

Surely they could reinstate me, or hire me as a consultant, or Red Rose County could. That would be quicker and I'd legally be part of the team. My proximity to the case could cause legal troubles, but I highly doubted the Bear would let us take him alive. *Fine by me.* "I'm a survivor. But I will be a victim if you don't let me help on the case. He's after me. And if you sideline me, he's going to know. I don't know how he knows, but I'm pretty sure he's been watching me. He could be watching the scene as we speak..." My adrenaline spiked. "He's likely watching the scene right now! We need to have people searching the perimeter—anything within viewing distance."

Kieran said, "We'll send out teams. Red Rose County can help."

Practically vibrating, I said, "I'd go out a mile, but start closer—a hundred yards, a quarter mile, half mile. Anything that's viewable with binoculars."

"All right. I'll talk to the sheriff." Kieran ran off to talk to Sheriff Phillips.

Jordan said, "I'll gather the team and send out pairs—quickly."

"Go."

With that, a flurry of activity erupted and I ran over to

Brady who was standing with a few patrol officers. "What's going on?" Brady asked.

"I think he's watching the scene. He's close."

He glanced over his shoulder, then scanned the area before his eyes landed on me. "We need to keep you safe."

"I appreciate that, Brady, but not now. We need to get this guy. It's not going to end until we do."

The sheriff and Kieran jogged over to us. Kieran said, "We're doing a full perimeter search. The sheriff called in for extra help. Pairs are going out. If he's here, we'll find him."

With a slight nod, I surveyed the property. "The house. It's about a hundred yards away and surrounded by trees. With even a cheap pair of binoculars it would give him a direct line of sight. Brady and I will head for the house."

Kieran quickly said, "I think you should stay back, Val."

"Not a chance. If he's watching, he knows what's going on, and he's going to be on the move. We don't have time to waste." Without waiting for a reply, I pulled my weapon and sprinted toward the house.

SIX

VAL

As I rushed toward the house—roughly a hundred yards away, weapon clutched by my side—I heard boots running alongside me. I could just about kick myself for not thinking of it sooner. *Dang it.* The location near the residence was a perfect hiding spot. He could be inside the structure or he could be in the thick of trees next to it. I should have thought of it earlier. The realization hit me hard, screaming in my mind that we were probably too late. As we approached the dwelling, I slowed, listening. Brady did the same, quieting his radio.

Then—the sound of a car engine. Tires squealing on gravel.

I yelled, "The road!"

I sprinted toward the road, sweat running down my back. By the time I reached it, there was only the faint outline of a vehicle. And then it was gone.

He's gone.

He was right here. *I knew it. I felt it.*

Why hadn't I thought of it earlier? If I had, we could've caught him. Instead, we were stuck here, chasing shadows.

Brady exhaled sharply. "We're gonna keep looking."

"He's gone, Brady. It was him. He was in that car. He was

watching. As soon as he saw the commotion he knew we'd realized he was here—and he left."

I was breathing heavily, exhausted from the sprint. It was a reminder that I needed to get back to my routine after slacking off this week due to the lack of sleep from nightmares. It was foolish to slip from being at the top of my game; I had to be prepared at all times. Kieran and Jordan ran up, stopping beside us. "What's going on?"

I turned to them. "He was here. He got away."

"You saw him?" Jordan asked.

"I heard the engine. That's why I ran to the road. He's gone."

"But you didn't actually see him?" Kieran pressed.

"No, but I didn't need to, Kieran. I've been right about him all along. He's been stalking me. This was a message. *For me.* Of course he'd want to see my reaction." With a sinking feeling, I knew that he'd likely watched me at other crime scenes too. Like at the Nelson crime scene, he'd left a note and then the mysterious fire that led to us solving the case, followed by another note. At the time, my intuition had told me it was him, but without evidence it could have been any psychopath. After the Nelson case I should have pushed harder to find him. Considering that after the end of the first case I worked in Red Rose County, the Scarlett Douglas case, he'd left a note. And then during and after the Nelson case, and one after the Cramer murders. He'd been following my every move. *Without me even realizing it.* I shook my head, frustration and rage clawing at my chest. I should've known the second I got to the scene he was close by. I could kick myself.

Kieran turned to Jordan. "Tell the others we still need to check the perimeter. Maybe he left something behind. He does have a penchant for notes."

I knew there wouldn't be any because, as much as I hated to admit it, the Bear and I were connected. It was like I knew him, but at the same time, I didn't—not completely. But I knew enough to recognize his unpredictability, and I understood that we couldn't underestimate him. I loathed that we had this connection. *But I knew one thing for sure—that tie between us will be severed, once and for all.*

SEVEN

HIM

Speeding down the highway, I thought, *that was a close one.* Who had figured out I was there? Was it Valerie?

It probably was.

She could feel me like I could feel her.

I chortled. *Don't worry, Valerie. We'll be together soon.*

Good things come to those who wait, and I could be patient. This game was too much fun to show my final hand just yet.

I guess I just can't help myself because I love watching Valerie in action.

EIGHT

VAL

With a push of the front door, I stepped inside and turned back to face Kieran. "Okay, I'm home. As soon as I shut the door, I'll activate the security system."

"This is for your own protection, Val, and to make sure we get this guy."

He'd already lectured me the entire drive from the crime scene back to my house. He escorted me himself, claiming he wanted to make sure I got home safely, but I knew it was to ensure I actually went home. How could Kieran not see that this was killing me? That I couldn't stand by and do nothing. Not only that, but I knew that the Bear wouldn't stop until he had me.

Sure, we had some of the best profilers in the world working on the case—but I wasn't included. Not anymore. I was no longer with the FBI. But Jordan was right. They had a strong team, but they didn't know him like I did.

And I knew that the Bear was a threat. To me. To my mother. To her friends, who were always around the house. Now, I had to break the news to them—that the serial killer who had once captured me was in town, and he wouldn't leave until he had me.

"I get it, Kieran. Good luck with the investigation."

"This doesn't have to be adversarial, Val," Kieran said, his tone softening. "I can keep you updated on what's going on. I just can't have you present at the crime scenes. I can't have you being part of the investigative team. Tell me you understand."

"I don't. You could hire me as a consultant. It can be above board."

He was about to argue but changed his mind. "How are you sleeping?"

"Fine," I lied.

"Really? From what I can see from the dark circles and how out of breath you were after you ran toward the house, you're not. I don't think you're ready to be in the field chasing him. I think your emotional wounds are still healing. It can cloud your judgment, and I don't want anything to happen to you."

My judgment isn't clouded. I'm fine.

Kieran continued, "Look, for now, I need to keep you safe. The team will find him. Do you understand?"

No. "Yeah."

An SUV pulled into the driveway. I turned to see who it was. Brady.

Kieran followed my gaze. "Were you expecting him?"

I hesitated. "Brady and I are... friends."

Kieran's expression didn't shift. "Okay. Well, he and the sheriff's department will likely be helping out with the investigation since we might need local resources to assist."

Brady stepped out of the SUV and strode toward us. He and Kieran exchanged one of those quick, professional nods.

"Brady," Kieran said.

"Kieran," Brady returned.

Kieran adjusted his stance. "Are you here in an official capacity?"

"No. Just came to check on Val and Elizabeth."

"All right, then. Remember what I said, Val. I'll be in touch. See you later, Brady."

I stepped aside and waved Brady inside.

With the door shut, Brady said, "How are you holding up?"

"Not great."

How could I be? I'd been stalked for months—being watched by a serial killer—and I hadn't even noticed. *That was the worst part.* But I could handle myself if he came at me again. There was no way he'd win that fight a second time. But what lengths would he go to, to get to me? That was what frightened me.

He'd already killed an innocent young woman just to send me a message. I was sure of it.

"I'm assuming you haven't told your mom yet? Or Julie and Diane?"

"Just got home."

"I can talk to them with you."

"Okay."

The television sounded in the living room, a tell-tale sign that was where Mom and Julie would be. Sure enough, they were sitting on the couch, drinking tea, watching *The Great British Baking Show*.

Mom, ever perceptive, paused the TV and turned to me with bright, eager eyes. "Well? What's the case?"

That familiar gleam was in her eyes, like she expected another thrilling investigation for Val Costa and the team at Red Rose County. I hid my exhaustion and took a seat next to her, motioning for Brady to sit as well. He chose the chair across from us, his expression neutral but tense.

Looking between my mother and Julie, I steadied myself. "The body of a young woman was found today. There was a note at the scene... for me."

Mom's excitement dimmed. "Another note?"

"That's not all, Mom." I took a breath, then pushed forward.

"The crime scene was almost a re-enactment of mine—when I was taken. It's the Bear. He's here in Red Rose County. He's likely been here for months, watching me. The body was a message."

Mom gasped, turning to Julie. I added, "He's sent notes to the house. He knows where we live."

Silence settled in the room.

They knew what that meant.

If a serial killer was after me and willing to kill an innocent person just to send me a message, then my mother, her friends, anyone close to me, was in danger.

"So, what's the plan?" Mom asked, ever stoic.

"I'm not part of the investigation, but Kieran and the task force are here in Red Rose County. They're not leaving until the Bear is in custody."

Julie's voice was tight. "But what about the threat to you? To Elizabeth?"

I rubbed my temples. "We could move to a safe house. Or... we could be vigilant. He hasn't gotten inside. There's security all around the house. I just have to stay on high alert."

Mom frowned. "What about when you're not here?"

My mother was still recovering from her stroke. It was miraculous that she could walk around the house with just a cane, but the stairs were still too much for her. She needed to keep going to physical therapy to continue her progress. If we put her into hiding, there would be no more sessions. I couldn't let the Bear derail her progress.

"I'll start taking you to physical therapy, Mom. Nobody goes anywhere alone."

"What about Diane? She's coming over later today."

Brady spoke up. "The sheriff's department is willing to put surveillance on the house. We can also escort Julie and Diane when they're coming and going. We're taking this threat very seriously. I have volunteered for the first shift. Anything you ladies need, I'll have someone get it for you. If you need an escort home, Julie, it will be provided. I'll also accompany you on any errands including visits to the physical therapist. Nobody will get to you. I'm here until another deputy arrives tomorrow night."

He hadn't told me this, but I wasn't surprised. Frankly, I was a little relieved. Mom looked at the two of us. "Val, are you okay with this?"

I'll have to be. "I am. I can't think of a better solution, Mom."

I hated not having all the answers. I wanted to be in control, but I knew I wasn't. The Bear had left me a clue he was in Red Rose County but nothing else. That led me to only one conclusion, and that was whatever sick plan the Bear had to get to me wasn't over. And the deep dread in my gut told me that this whole thing was just getting started.

NINE

VAL

Later that night, under twinkle lights in the backyard, Lucy, Sally, and I had just finished a hearty meal of ravioli, a garden salad, and homemade garlic bread. Mom and Julie had convinced me to have them over as opposed to canceling altogether. Julie had offered to serve us for an "authentic al fresco" dining experience. At first I was hesitant as I didn't want to put my friends in any danger, but considering the Bear had been following me, he likely knew they were my friends. Both Sally and Lucy loved the idea and accepted the invitation.

Unsurprisingly to everyone, the dinner conversation had revolved around the case. We were on our second glass of Merlot when Lucy sighed. "Crazy day."

"Sure was," I agreed. Glancing at Sally, I added, "I was surprised you weren't at the crime scene this morning."

"Oh, that? Yeah, I didn't get the message until the FBI had already arrived. I was, um preoccupied this morning..."

"Preoccupied?" Lucy said.

A smile spread across Sally's face, her eyes shining like the lights above. "Yes. I had a visitor."

I said, "Okay, we could all use a little reprieve from serial killers, crime scenes, and constant surveillance talk. Sally, you gotta dish."

Lucy added, "And don't leave anything out!"

It was so nice to have a distraction from the feeling of powerlessness. From the sense of being watched. From knowing my family and friends were at risk. From being sidelined, not being able to act. Not knowing how to catch the Bear. As much as I hated to admit it, he was the one holding all the cards. And I had this ominous feeling that he had mapped out exactly how he wanted things to play out.

Sally tucked her fire-engine red hair behind her ear. "Well, we had dinner last night. He came over to my place, and I cooked for him."

Lucy scoffed. "You cook?"

"I can cook! A few things anyways. You know, I can do other things besides cutting up dead bodies and determining cause of death, thank you very much," she said with a smile. Clearly, the second glass of wine was kicking in.

"Okay, and then?" Lucy pressed.

"And then, after a bottle of wine—apparently my weakness —we had our first kiss, and it was magical. He has these lips, and these hands, and his shoulders. He's tall... Boy, was it my lucky day when he walked into the restaurant and sat across from me."

"And this was just last week that you met, right?" I asked.

"Yep. I was having lunch by myself at Drake's. He's new in town."

"New in town? And you've never seen him before? Not around town, grocery shopping, or anything like that?"

"No, never."

"And you said he's a hiking guide?"

"Yep. It keeps him really fit. And he is fit, I am happy to announce." Sally giggled. "If you know what I mean."

Just then, Julie walked out onto the patio. "Can I get you anything else? More wine?"

Lucy said, "Why not? We have a ride home and tomorrow is the weekend—no work for us."

"Unless something else happens," Sally said quietly.

I said, "If something else happens, it's the FBI's job."

"Unless they need help," Sally added. "The sheriff said they may call us in for backup at any time."

Lucy shrugged. "Guess that's no more wine for us, then."

Not that I needed it. I needed to stay alert. But at the same time, I wondered if I needed to forget, to let go, to relax.

"Okay, then, if no more wine, I did make some dessert," Julie said.

"Oh? What did you make?" Lucy asked.

"Well, I made little mini carrot cakes. I know it doesn't really go with Italian food, but Elizabeth and I have been watching baking shows, and I just had to try something delicious. And well, I love carrot cake. What do you think?"

We all nodded enthusiastically.

"Okay, coming right up." Julie headed back into the house, closing the glass slider behind her.

Lucy said, "This was so nice, Val. We should do this like every week, or every other week, or, you know, more often."

"I agree. It's so peaceful here, and the weather is getting warmer. The spring air is magical," Sally said.

Lucy smirked. "And love is all around."

We laughed. It felt so good to have something to smile about. Not that I didn't have my own budding romance to be happy about, but I also had a dark cloud shading the sunlight that was fighting to break through.

"So, back to this guy, Sally. What do you know about him? You said he just moved to town."

"Just recently, yeah. He's originally from Washington. He's one of three kids. His mom and dad are still in Washington. He used to work in a testing lab, which is convenient because he kind of understands the science. He's totally fascinated by my job and thinks it's really cool. Let me tell you, before, when I dated, men were really intimidated by the work I did or thought I was weird for being a medical examiner. They thought it was morbid or strange. I mean, not that I'm not strange sometimes, but I think giving a voice to the dead isn't weird at all. I feel like I'm helping the dead—helping to get justice for them."

Lucy nodded. "That's why I like my job too. And you too, Val? I mean, we all work in law enforcement—or, well, you did work in law enforcement for a long time—to do what's right. For justice."

"It is." Although, I wasn't currently working. But then again, we just closed a murder investigation a week ago.

"So what's your guy's name?" Lucy asked.

"His name is Dominic. He's very handsome—if I didn't mention that before. There's just something about him. He's got this calmness, you know? I can be a little highly strung, but he's got this demeanor like he's unflappable. I don't know if it's his lifestyle but he's just... he's just like that hiker you see on a trail, you know? He's got the cargo pants with all the pockets, the hat, the stick. Real rugged and outdoorsy. But he cleans up well." She grinned as she took the last sip of her wine.

She liked him. I supposed that was a good thing. "And how about you, Lucy? How are things with Jonathan?"

She sighed joyfully. "Things are wonderful. No complaints here."

"And how's the new house?"

"Great. I love living with him. I just can't believe I found my other half—you know, my person."

Sally and I both let out a dramatic "aww" at the same time. Lucy threw a napkin at us. "Oh my gosh, what are we, fifteen?"

"Do you remember being fifteen?" Sally said.

"What were you like in your teen years, Val? I heard you were a little bit rebellious."

"I wouldn't say I was totally rebellious, but I liked to push the limits a bit. Brady was always the one trying to keep me on the straight and narrow," I said with a small smirk.

"I can totally see that," Lucy said.

"Well, other than having a serial killer in town, seems like you're doing really well," I said and laughed at the ridiculousness of the statement. "Cheers to that."

Lucy grew serious, pushing her giant glasses up her nose. "They'll get him, Val. Nobody in this county is going to let him get to you. *We won't.*"

As if on cue, Julie came out with Brady, both of them carrying plates of carrot cake for us.

"Apparently, I've been promoted to server," Brady said with a wink.

Lucy grinned. "Talk about full service."

"I'm here to serve," Brady said. "Enjoy," he said before heading back into the house.

Lucy checked her phone. "Oh my gosh, have you seen the time? We've been out here for three hours! Can you believe it?"

And I realized this must be how my mother felt when Julie and Diane were over. Since her stroke, they visited regularly and helped take care of her. They had this incredible female bond, more than just a friendship, almost like a sisterhood. They lifted each other up even in the darkest times. It made me think that maybe, despite this looming threat, this huge monster on my back that I was trying to get rid of, I also had a great life that I had been building in Red Rose County with Brady, Lucy, Sally, and my mom. A community. That was what had been missing from my life for so long. *And I wasn't going to let anybody destroy that—certainly not the Bear.*

Before I could even comment on the amazing cake, Sally

was already moaning in delight. "This is amazing. I love cream cheese frosting."

The slider opened, and Brady emerged. This time his expression was grim. He let out a breath and said, "There's been another body."

"Already?" Sally asked.

Even I was surprised. "Same MO?" I asked.

"No, it's different. I'll spare you the details. It was recent—maybe earlier today. Not particularly consistent with the last scene, but..." Brady looked at me.

"But what?"

"There was a photo at the scene. *Attached* to the body."

"A photo?"

Brady handed me his phone, and I stared at the screen. My breath caught in my throat. I gasped and then looked up at Sally and Lucy.

TEN

VAL

On the screen was a photo of the three of us sitting on the patio, *where we still sat*, with wine glasses in our hands. Part of me didn't want to tell Sally and Lucy that the Bear had been right here. Likely shortly after they had arrived. That didn't necessarily mean he'd actually been on the property. I knew telephoto lenses could reach up to half a mile and still capture clear images—crisp, clean, as if the person were standing right there. If leaving the photo at a crime scene was meant to creep me out, it worked.

Sally leaned in, her voice sharp with concern. "What is it?"

I took a deep breath. "The Bear left a photo of the three of us at the crime scene."

Sally gasped. "Like... from tonight?"

"Based on the photo..." I handed the phone to Sally. Lucy scooted closer to Sally to take a look. "It had to be when you first got here. We had just sat down with our first glass of wine. It was still light out."

I glanced back at Brady. "What did Kieran say?"

"He'll be here any minute. He wants to talk to you."

"This is exactly why I need to be working the investigation."

"You won't get an argument from me," Brady said. With a warm smile, I thought, *And I adore you for that.* Brady was right, he wasn't the one I needed to argue with, it was Kieran. Didn't Kieran see there would be more bodies until I was actively working the case?

Sally handed back the phone, and I passed it to Brady.

"That is so creepy," Lucy commented.

"I know. It shouldn't have happened. I didn't even hear anything—or see anything. I mean, I was... I guess, preoccupied with wine and the two of you. But I think we would've seen something—or at least heard something—if someone was close enough to take a picture."

Unfortunately, it was now pitch-black aside from the lights on the patio. I tried to think of what vantage point the Bear had used when he'd taken the photo. He could've easily been across the street, but to get the angle in the photo he would've had to be perched up in a tree. Was there really a serial killer perched in a tree looking down at my house? "Let me see the photo again."

Brady passed me the phone without hesitation.

I studied it. The angle was at a downward trajectory—he was higher than we were, which made sense. That's how he was able to see over the fence. The only way to have gotten the photo was to have climbed a tree and waited. *That's unsettling.* I stood up and looked around the yard. I couldn't see much, but I knew it like the back of my hand. I'd lived here most of my childhood—and for the last nine months of my life. There were so many trees surrounding the house, he could've easily been hidden if he wanted to be.

I turned back to Brady. "You hike rather regularly, right?"

"Yes, on my own and I've got my hiking club too."

"How many people do you know who could climb one of these trees, take a telephoto lens with them, and go undetected?"

Brady shrugged. "Probably more than you think. I mean, a lot of people grew up in these woods." He paused. "Is it possible the Bear grew up here?"

"I have no idea, Brady. He could be anyone. But now, based on this? He has to be someone familiar with—and comfortable in—the outdoors. Someone who could climb a tree and take a photo of us. And then hurry off and kill someone."

"Or," Lucy added, "he could've hacked into your security system. I'm guessing you have cameras pointing right at us?"

"That's a good point." I grabbed my phone from the table. "Let me check to see if I received any notifications of a new login."

I turned it over, opened my email app, and scrolled through, looking for a notification from the security system's automated messaging system. There were none.

"No new logins. But maybe there's a flash on my surveillance footage that will tell us when he took the photo."

Lucy's eyes lit up. She was the tech expert at Red Rose County, formerly with the NYPD. She knew all things tech inside and out. Both she and Sally were experts in their field.

Before I could speculate further, I saw a looming figure reflected in the sliding glass doors. It was Kieran. He stepped outside. I waved and then introduced him to Lucy and Sally.

Kieren nodded at them. "I've heard a lot about both of you. Apparently, if we need extra hands, you're the two we should talk to."

He turned slightly toward Brady. "You too," he added, almost as an afterthought. But since they'd already been working together, maybe it wasn't meant as a slight.

"What are you thinking, Kieran?" I asked.

"Our team thinks it's a message."

Obviously. "I think so too. He wants me working the case. And I think if you don't put me in it, more bodies are going to pop up—as a message for me."

Kieran's gaze sharpened. "What can you tell me about the photo? When did he take it?" He studied the table. "Was it tonight?"

"Yes. We need to review the surveillance footage. See if there's any indication of a flash or anything to help determine the exact time. We think maybe he was up in the trees and took it from a downward angle."

"How long have you been out here?"

"Just over three hours," I said.

Kieran shook his head in disbelief. "That means, he took your photo, hit the trails, and likely killed the first person he encountered."

Silence fell over the table.

I felt sick.

"What do you know about the victim?" I was surprised they'd already found them.

"Seth Wallace, aged sixty-seven. He was reported missing by his wife, said he shared his route before he went out, and was late by fifteen minutes. She said he was never late and she was worried he'd been hurt. From first look, he died pretty quickly."

Despite growing up in the area, I didn't know Seth Wallace. But it proved that the Bear wasn't just after me or young females. He liked to kill. It didn't matter who it was. That's what made him different. Unpredictable. He just wanted to inflict pain. To hear the screams. That's what he loved. Part of me wanted to understand him—find out where he grew up, what kind of childhood had turned him into the monster he was. But I'd just as easily settle for him being dead and unable to hurt anybody else. Although that wouldn't bring back his previous victims.

"What's next?" I asked pointedly.

"The team is still collecting evidence and will analyze the paper the photo was printed on. It's not high quality; it's standard white paper, probably from a home printer. Most likely untraceable. But we'll do what we can to see if it'll lead us anywhere. If you can provide the surveillance footage from your patio we can match up the photo time stamp. It'll start the timeline."

"Where are you with the Linda Castillo case?" I asked.

"Still collecting and processing evidence. The medical examiner will finish up the autopsy and give a report."

"Any insights into what he's likely to do next?" I asked in a tone that told Kieran I knew exactly what the Bear was likely to do next. He started to answer and then hesitated. "We'd like to bring you in as a consultant. You'll be partnered with Jordan."

Thinking back to my conversation with Kieran earlier that day, I assumed Jordan had pushed for it. He was very sharp and likely knew more bodies would be found if I wasn't included, and *fast*.

With a satisfied grin, I said, "I accept."

ELEVEN

HIM

What a day. Hopefully the FBI and their little friends at the Red Rose County Sheriff's Department understood my message, otherwise I'll have to send more. *I want Valerie to see what I've done. To collect the clues. To be led straight to me. This is our game to play—not theirs. They were trying to take it, and I wouldn't stand for it.* If the Feds didn't wisen up soon enough, I'd have to be clearer next time. All of this was to build to a grand finale and I won't let them steal it from us.

It had been fun climbing that tree to take photos of Valerie's backyard soiree. I'd planned to just drop by, leave a little memento... but thanks to Sally, I knew I'd get a glimpse of her and brought my camera along. Sally Edison was one of my favorite women. It was going to be a shame to lose her. *What a dazzling rose she is.* And she had been dazzling—probably one of the most interesting women I'd met. The more time I spent with her, the more I saw it.

She had a darkness like I did. Of course, she used her proclivities to cut up the dead—to look inside, see what killed them. As opposed to me... I liked to start on the outside. Watch their reaction as they died slowly. It was like we were two sides of the same coin.

It almost pained me to get rid of her. Maybe I wouldn't. I'd never had two at the same time before. But that didn't mean I couldn't. That would take further planning, though. My Valerie would call that an escalation. With a small smile, I thought back to an article I'd read about serial killers. Apparently we escalate. *Boy, had I escalated.*

Sitting up in that tree waiting for the ladies to arrive, I had time to reflect how much Red Rose County felt like home. The trees here breathed the same way the ones back home did—silent, watchful, never judging. Just waiting.

My parents hadn't belonged to regular society, and neither had I. I hadn't even known society existed until I was older. It wasn't like today where kids are on leashes or tracked by AirTags. After morning chores, we were free to go. No school. Nobody looking for us or telling us what to do.

We'd spent hours—whole days—out in the woods, making forts and traps. The forest had been our kingdom, and I had ruled mine with cleverness, patience, and a fascination with death.

I remembered the first time I took a life—I had been with my old man.

He liked guns and wanted me to be a proper hunter—to shoot to kill. After a single shot between the eyes, I had watched my father gut a deer on the dirt floor of our shed, skinning it with long, methodical strokes. I liked the cutting, but I had found the death too quick. Not satisfying. So I started experimenting on my own. First it had been insects. Then small animals. Then bigger ones. I chuckled quietly at the memory.

I had been amazed at what creatures did—how they reacted under that kind of stress. I had been mesmerized. It was my favorite pastime to play with them. I thought it was normal. But on one outing with a few kids from a neighboring property, and my brother and sister, I showed them one of my experiments. With a grin on my boyish face, I marveled at my handiwork. My sister had vomited. *Can you believe that?* How I had been in the same family with such weaklings, I'd never understand. I hadn't been one of them. I *wouldn't* be one of them.

Perhaps I had been more like my old man. He hadn't taken guff from nobody or nothing. If something got in the way of what he wanted, he eliminated it—or put the fear of God into it. That had usually been enough to get what he wanted.

It had been enough for my mom. Enough for my sister. Enough for my brother.

And I had learned the hard way a few times, but I survived. And eventually he got what was coming to him. He was easy after I'd had my first real taste. *You never forget your first.* I had been fifteen. A tourist—Hannah. Pretty little thing. A girl with curly blonde hair, too much sunscreen, and a camera hanging around her neck. She had wandered off a trail while her parents were preoccupied. She had gotten lost somewhere between the creek and the ridge trail. I had spotted her from a bluff— watched her twist around in circles like a deer that sensed it was being hunted. It had been a perfect opportunity. Our time together was brief, but I still thought about her. She reminded me of Valerie in some ways.

Valerie had come to me. So had Hannah. Valerie had fought me. Just like Hannah did.

But Hannah had been much weaker. When Hannah and I met, I had been nice to her and offered to help her back to the main trail. I hadn't gone on the attack right away. At first, I had just wanted to know what it was like to kiss her. To touch her skin. She hadn't liked that. That was when I'd had to get a little rough.

Regretfully, I hadn't had much time with her either. But when it was over—when the act was done—I knew right then what *my purpose* was. What I was meant to do in this life. And that was to be there—to be that person who watched as their souls left this Earth. They hadn't found Hannah's body for several days; I'd read about it in the news. Law enforcement never came knocking at the door and I was never a suspect. Maybe my memories of Hannah were what drew me to Valerie, that, and to have learned she'd been studying me. *Hunting me.* It was fascinating. I very much looked forward to being with Valerie again. To touching her skin with my blade. To touching her lips. Unlike my encounter with Hannah, and my first encounter with Valerie, the next time we were together I was going to take my time.

TWELVE
SALLY

I stood at the kitchen window, my fingers wrapped around a mug of coffee that I now realized had gone cold. Across the street, the Red Rose County patrol car sat parked like a reminder I hadn't asked for, but couldn't turn down.

Val and Brady had insisted that both Lucy and I have patrol cars outside our homes until they could be sure we were safe. I knew the Bear was after Val, not us, but once a serial killer has taken your photo and left it at a crime scene, you don't argue.

In the brightness of the morning, though, the deputy's presence felt less like protection and more like a reminder that there was a killer on the loose in Red Rose County—and they knew who I was, or at least I figured they did.

Not that I was afraid. Not exactly. Just... unnerved.

Unlike Val and Brady, I didn't think the Bear would come after me. But considering my profession, I knew what people were capable of. I'd seen the atrocities humans committed against each other. And I was vigilant. *Always.* Like Val, I had a security system, and I knew how to fight. Even before I'd worked within the darkest corners of the world, I had learned self-defense. I was a woman, after all, and too many men seemed to believe they could take whatever they wanted. I started self-defense training in my first year of college, right after an attempted sexual assault. It had happened on campus. I was lucky a small group of students approached right as he had his hand over my mouth and an arm around my midsection. The presence of the three students, two men and one woman, had scared him off and he'd fled. That moment defined everything that came next. I vowed I would never be a victim again and I'd learn how to defend myself. I decided I would never be easy prey for someone lurking in the shadows ever again, and ever since then I hadn't been.

My phone buzzed on the counter. Glancing at the screen, I saw it was a text from Dominic.

Still on for today? Found a hidden gem of a trail. Quiet, beautiful, no tourists. You'll love it.

I smiled in spite of myself. I'd only known him for a week, but there was something about him that grounded me. It was like he and I existed in a parallel world, one where nothing could hurt me.

A second ping.

I hope dinner at your friend's place was fun.

I was about to reply but stopped. Had I told him I was at Val's last night? I scanned my memory and I quickly recalled the pillow talk that involved discussing plans for that night and the weekend. Shaking off the unease, I realized the whole Bear thing was making me paranoid.

I typed back. *It was good. A little heavy. Looking forward to some fresh air.*

I didn't mention the deputy outside. Or the photo of me that had been attached to a dead body. If I told him, would he look at me in a different light? Would he think it was too dangerous to be near me?

His reply came almost immediately.

Great. See you soon.

I answered with a smiley face emoji.

One hour later, Dominic knocked on my door. I rushed downstairs to answer it, butterflies swarming in my belly. I opened the door and there he was—handsome and rugged in hiking pants and a zip-up fleece.

"Good morning," he said, flashing that killer smile.

Cheeks flushed, I said, "Good morning."

"Are you ready?"

"Not quite. Let me grab my backpack."

He nodded and waited on the step as I dashed back inside and grabbed my day pack from the dining table and hurried back to him.

I couldn't help but smile as he led me to his jeep and opened the passenger-side door. As I glanced down the street, I spotted the deputy watching me from the patrol car.

"Give me a second," I said to Dominic, and jogged over to the very obviously parked sheriff's department cruiser beside my house.

I leaned down and greeted him. "Hey, Baker. I'm heading out for a day hike. Should be back by five."

His gaze lingered on Dominic before he said, "Okay. Have fun."

As I walked back to the jeep, I figured Deputy Baker would likely run Dominic's license plates. But I wasn't worried. I climbed in and said, "All set."

"What was that about?" Dominic asked as I buckled my seatbelt.

"Oh, that? It's the sheriff's office being overly cautious. We've had two murders in the past few days."

"I read about that in the news. Terrible," he said, reaching over to give my knee a quick squeeze. "Let's forget about all that stuff and have a beautiful day. What do you say?"

"I'm in."

He turned up the radio, and hummed along to Bruno Mars as he drove us north toward the hills.

He parked outside the gate that blocked a narrow dirt road. As he led me toward it, he said, "Don't worry. I've been here a few times. It's breathtaking. They only have the gate because the rangers don't want cars blocking the fire trail."

"Cool. Let's go."

He winked at me before sliding his sunglasses on. He was charming, for sure—but what I liked most about Dominic was that it didn't feel like he was trying too hard. He was confident in a quiet way, like he had nothing to prove.

The beginning of the trail was wide and well-worn but narrowed quickly as we veered off. The higher we climbed, the quieter the world became. The only sounds were birdsong and the soft swish of tree branches swaying in the breeze.

"Did you spend a lot of time in the woods growing up?" I asked, brushing a branch away from my face.

"Yes. I grew up in the woods. Literally. My dad was one of those doomsday prepper types—off the grid. I could build a fire and catch a fish before I could read."

"Wow. That's weirdly impressive."

He snorted. "Thanks. How about you? Did you grow up hiking and camping?"

"No, not too much, but I love the outdoors. It's one of the reasons I settled in Red Rose County."

We reached an overlook, and he hadn't oversold it—it was

stunning. The trees opened up to a broad ridge. The valley stretched out below us like a painting in beiges and soft greens.

At the edge of a small clearing, he set down his backpack and pulled out a thermos and two tin cups.

"Coffee?" he asked. "Thought the mountain air might make it taste better."

"You're an angel," I said, accepting the cup.

He smiled. "You earned it."

We sat on the ground for a while, drinking quietly. The silence felt comfortable—not the kind you have to fill.

Then he asked, "What's it like working with the dead?"

I glanced over at him, surprised by the question. "Honestly? Mostly clinical. It's procedure. Patterns."

"But you see things others don't," he said. "The aftermath. The truth."

Something in his voice made me pause. "I guess."

"Have you ever had a case you couldn't let go of? One that stuck with you?"

I set my coffee down. "More than one. But I don't usually talk about them. It creeps most people out."

He leaned in slightly. "Not me. I'm okay if you want to talk about it. Sometimes the dead have more to say than the living."

That stopped me cold. I couldn't tell if he was being poetic —or creepy. "You're giving me serial killer vibes right now," I said with a chuckle, trying to lighten the mood—and change the subject.

He laughed, but the smile didn't quite reach his eyes. "Not to worry. If I were a killer, I wouldn't waste a view like this on a victim."

I startled.

He nudged me with his elbow. "I'm teasing. I'm sorry. I didn't realize you were so sensitive due to the recent murders. That kind of surprises me considering your profession."

"Oh no. I'm just not used to being with someone who can

joke about the macabre. I'm fine, really. Here—I'll show you." I leaned over and gave him a quick kiss on the lips, trying to steer the conversation away from murder. *It worked.* After a few lingering kisses, we packed up the coffee cups and headed back toward the trail. Shaking off the niggling paranoia, I told myself I was overthinking things because of the photo of us taken by the Bear. My gut stirred and I thought, *Or is it that I'm not thinking enough?*

THIRTEEN

VAL

Brady greeted me at the entrance of the Red Rose County Sheriff's Station on a bright but chilly Saturday morning. After a stern conversation with Kieran the previous night—and again early that morning—it was decided Brady would be the liaison to the FBI and work with the task force to find the Bear. He'd serve as the go-between for the Bureau and the sheriff's department, which we needed, especially since the FBI deemed the Redding field office too far for comfort. Kieran had made arrangements with the sheriff to have a conference room set up at the Red Rose County Sheriff's station.

With a slight grin, Brady said, "Good morning."

My nerves were on overdrive. Knowing how close the Bear had been—and the fact that we'd found two bodies in less than twenty-four hours. I was back on the case, officially, as a consultant. So if the Bear was watching, I hoped he could see it and he'd stop killing people just to get my attention.

"Let's hope so."

We walked into the familiar, comfortable space. That old smell—stale coffee and dust—shouldn't have been comforting, but it was.

"Amen to that," he said as we walked. "How are you? Did you get any sleep?"

"A little. I'm in fight mode, so... more a storm of thoughts with brief breaks for naps," I said. "You?"

"A little. I received the report that it was quiet at your house, but after the photo, I was still on edge."

"Understandably. I was too. But I need to keep my head clear. Mom, Diane, and Julie are safe, and I think as long as I'm working the case, it'll stay that way." I paused. "I know it's me the Bear wants. Not my friends and family." *Or so I hoped.*

"Coffee?"

"Always."

We headed toward the machine in silence, not saying or doing what we really wanted to. If we weren't in the sheriff's station, I'd have wrapped my arms around him and thanked him for always being there. I was glad he was working the case with us. Not just because I liked having him around, but because he was a great detective and had good instincts.

Coffee in hand, Brady escorted me to the FBI's makeshift conference room. Inside, I waved and received a few nods and mumbled good mornings. Kieran stood up. "Brady. Val. Good to see you," he said. "Most of you know Val, but this is Deputy Brady Tanner. He'll be our liaison to the sheriff's office. Anything we need, he's your guy."

"Happy to help," Brady said.

"I've worked a few cases with Brady since I've been back. He's good. Don't be afraid to lean on him. Use him as a second set of eyes or ears."

After a brief round of introductions, we sat down. Jordan handed me a folder. "It's the ME report on Linda Castillo and her missing person's file."

"What about Seth Wallace?" I asked.

"Not done yet."

While the rest of the team busied themselves—I wasn't sure

with what exactly—I read through the file. Then I turned to Brady. "Did you work the Linda Castillo missing person investigation?"

"No, but I read the report."

To both Jordan and Brady, I said, "It sounds like the most likely theory is she had a flat tire shortly after leaving Joe's Tavern. Everything was left inside her vehicle. Door wasn't locked. She likely got out, and someone either offered her a ride or grabbed her as she walked back toward the bar."

Jordan nodded. "Tox screen shows ketamine in her urine. And there was a tiny puncture wound at the base of her neck."

"Sounds like he drugged her," I said, "and took her to a secondary location—the barn. And then he tortured and killed her." Just like he'd wanted to do to me.

"A chance encounter?" Jordan asked, but it didn't sound like he thought that. I suspected he was testing me to see if I was still on top of my game.

"No. Not based on the photos of the tire. He likely stalked her and set a trap."

"She wasn't random?" Brady asked.

"Or she was at first," I said, "and then he chose her, stalked her, and sprang into action."

"That's what I thought too," Jordan said.

So, it was a test. Great. They invited me back, but they weren't sure I could do the job.

Kieran slid another file across the table. "Patrol report came in this morning. Thought you'd want to see it."

I opened the folder and Sally's name jumped out immediately. My chest tightened as I read.

Sally had left her house that morning with a man named Dominic Savage. Around nine. About an hour ago. An officer ran the plates on the vehicle—a jeep—registered to Savage in Washington State. He had a driver's license, a clean record, and had recently updated the DMV, the Department of Motor

Vehicles, with his address in Red Rose County. No priors. No red flags.

I was relieved they'd checked out Sally's new love interest. She had told us she had a hiking date with him today and I was glad she wouldn't be alone. Even with the check into Dominic's background, I wasn't entirely sure about him. I'd never met him, and he seemed to have popped out of nowhere. "Will the team dig further into his background? Check his employment and school records, that kind of thing?"

"Do you think we need to?" Kieran asked.

Was I being paranoid? "Well, he just showed up in Red Rose County," I said. "It's a little coincidental."

"But you've been getting notes from the Bear for at least six months, right?" Brady asked.

He was right. "True." I pulled out my phone and quickly typed a message to Sally. *Happy Saturday. Give me a call when you can. Have fun today.* No need to freak her out. But I'd feel a lot better when I heard back.

I stared at the screen for a bit too long. No reply. Understandable, I told myself. She was out hiking. She was probably fine.

"Let's talk strategy," Jordan said quietly.

I nodded, not trusting myself to speak.

An hour later, I stood in front of the evidence board. Two victims. Two crime scenes. Two messages.

The first: Linda Castillo. A crime scene that eerily mirrored my own. Believed to be picked up after getting a flat tire on the side of the road—charmed, perhaps, or forced. Either way, she ended up leaving with him. The message: *Thinking of you.*

The second: Seth Wallace. Found on a narrow hiking trail near Bell Ridge. A quick kill. The message left at the scene was far more personal—a photo of me, Sally, and Lucy, laughing just hours before he died. The message: *I'm watching you.*

To Jordan, I said, "It's a conversation. And I'm the one he's talking to."

Jordan stepped beside me, his arms folded across his chest. "I agree. But the second message... I'm not sure I totally understand the full extent of it. He's watching—yes. But why a picture of you with your friends?"

That was what I couldn't figure out either. "I know he wants me on the case," I said. "But is it more than that? Would he take one of them just to send a message?" I didn't like that idea one bit. "Maybe the friends don't factor in this at all. Maybe it's just a reminder that he's talking to me. Like a friend would."

Jordan tipped his chin toward the photo. "You're smiling. Having a good time. Maybe he's saying he wants to play too."

With a shiver, I said, "He wants me to play with him."

"It fits."

I nodded, but the unease in my chest didn't lift. I couldn't ignore the feeling. This was more than him watching me. It was one thing to be targeted, it was another to have him watching me when I thought I was safe in my own home.

A man walked into the room, likely a tech. He looked in his mid-twenties and new enough to still seem intimidated by the team. He headed straight for Jordan.

"Hi, Troy," Jordan greeted him. "This is Val Costa. She was on the original Bear task force. She's now consulting and working with me to lead the investigation. Val, this is Troy. He's in from Quantico. He'll be helping the team process all forensics."

"Good to meet you," I said.

Troy nodded and held out an evidence bag and a file. I took it without a word.

The bag was small and thin. Inside was something metal. I turned it over, squinting at the object.

"Where was this found?" I asked.

"This is from the Seth Wallace scene," Troy said. "The item was found encased in plastic inside the victim's mouth."

My stomach turned. I studied the item more closely. It was a button. Worn around the edges, about the size of a dime. Matte black. Lettering painted across it—barely visible now.

Jordan leaned in. "Is that from...?"

"FBI tactical jacket," Troy said. "We checked. It was discontinued ten years ago. Issued to field agents on special assignments."

Jordan looked at me. "Could it be yours?"

My mouth went dry. "I don't know."

Turning to Troy, I asked, "Was it checked for fingerprints or DNA?"

"It was," he said. "And we got a hit."

FOURTEEN

VAL

The prints wouldn't be from the Bear. He wasn't that sloppy. And considering he encased the item in plastic to preserve it, I knew, my body vibrating with fear, the prints belonged to someone else. Someone who, chances were, was no longer part of the living.

"Who is it?" I said.

Troy replied, "Thomas Ingram."

Stunned, I could barely comprehend the implication. "That's not possible," I said. "He wouldn't... he's not—" A memory surfaced. Thomas wearing the jacket, proud, like it meant everything. "Thomas wore his until it nearly fell apart," I added. "He said it reminded him of where he came from."

Kieran eyed me. "You knew him. He was your training officer. Could he be involved?"

Anything was possible. But I thought it highly unlikely. We hadn't seen each other for a while. He'd reached out a few times over the past year, mostly checking in on me after my captivity, but we never spoke for more than a few minutes. The idea that Thomas could be linked to the Bear left me grasping for how to even begin to answer.

"Did you look him up?" Jordan asked.

Troy nodded. "We tried contacting him. He's not answering his phone, and no one at Quantico has heard from him since he retired two years ago."

Kieran's voice rose slightly. "Have you heard from him, Val?"

More memories surged forward. Thomas had announced his retirement rather abruptly. It was right before the Bear task force was formed. Right before I put the pattern together—that it wasn't multiple killers, but one. "It's been a few months. He calls to check on me and Mom."

Thinking back, the timing of his retirement had struck me as odd. But Thomas couldn't be the Bear. I would've recognized him during my captivity. All I knew of the Bear's physical description was blue eyes, approximate height and weight. None of those matched Thomas. Thomas had deep brown eyes with weathered skin and wasn't quite as tall and the build was wrong. Could he be an accomplice? We hadn't been terribly close since his retirement, but we had history. He'd trained me at the FBI and had sharpened my instincts. He gave me my first big assignment when others thought I was too green. I owed him more than I could put into words. Could he have really worked with a serial killer?

It didn't fit in my mind, but maybe the years of hunting killers had changed him. All the cases. All the victims we couldn't save. Maybe it had got to him. "Did you check his property records?" I asked.

"Property deed lists a remote cabin in the Cascades," Troy replied, tapping on his tablet. "Washington State. North of Skykomish, close to Stevens Pass. No cell reception out there right now."

"Not during the storm," Jordan added. "How long to get there?"

He was thinking what I was thinking. Whether Thomas was an accomplice or not, he could be in trouble.

Troy said, "Let me check. Give me a minute."

He returned his attention to the tablet while the room fell silent. My heart pounded loudly in my ears.

Troy sucked in a breath. "The only road up to his cabin is currently closed. Storm dumped almost a foot of snow yesterday—and it's still going. Forecast says it'll stop tomorrow. It'll take maintenance crews a day or two to clear it."

Of course he had a mountain cabin. Thomas hated noise. Hated crowds. He always said solitude was where clarity lived.

"Until the road clears, we sit," Kieran said, his voice laced with tension. "And we figure out how to get ahead of this guy."

We were all likely thinking the same thing. The Bear had already proven he liked to play games. This was calculated. We wouldn't find him just hanging out in Thomas' mountain cabin. My instincts told me this was part of the Bear's plan—a single piece in the twisted puzzle he'd created. Was it a clue that was meant to lead us closer? Or was it a diversion?

Was he testing our response? Or was he testing me? He likely knew it would take days to investigate Thomas and that it would drag us out of Red Rose County.

My gut screamed that we were two steps behind. But we had no choice. We had to follow the breadcrumbs the Bear had left for us.

FIFTEEN

VAL

Over the last two days, we'd come up with a plan to try to get ahead of the Bear. And I was finally able to catch up with Sally, who said she'd had a lovely time on her hike with Dominic at the weekend. It was good to hear her voice. To know she was safe. That it was just my paranoia—that this new man in her life didn't have an ulterior motive or, worse, wasn't actually a serial killer.

I knew that anything was possible, but Dominic's background hadn't turned up anything suspicious. No flags. No criminal history. That was a relief.

The truth was, I hadn't slept for more than a few hours in the past forty-eight hours, or if I'm being honest since they found Linda Castillo's body three days earlier. I'd tried, but my mind kept drifting back to Thomas. His laugh. His deadpan humor. The way he used to look at crime scenes like he could already hear the killer's whisper. He had a way of understanding them. At the time, it was impressive. Now, it was unnerving.

Thinking back to our conversations, I suspected there were clues I hadn't seen. Like the pauses in a conversation when certain names came up. Questions he never answered. I never pushed, assuming it wasn't that he couldn't answer, but that he didn't want to. Painful memories, maybe. Part of the job. I shoved these thoughts into the darkest corners of my mind, because it was easier than contemplating the alternative: that someone I respected might've been part of something unspeakable.

When the storm finally passed, we loaded into the FBI's SUV before the sun came up to get to the airport, I sat in the back, lost in thought, gripping the armrest.

Once we'd landed, and were in our rental, Kieran drove in silence while Jordan kept an eye on the GPS as it flickered in and out through the patchy signal. None of us said it out loud, but we knew we were likely heading into a crime scene. There was still snow on the roads, making the conditions a bit hazardous, and at times, the SUV fishtailed slightly on the narrow road, tires crunching over packed ice. It was as if winter had hung on, not wanting to let go. If we weren't hunting a serial killer, the views would've been breathtaking—frost clinging to every branch like the forest had been dipped in sugar.

"There's more snow than I expected," Jordan said, breaking the silence.

"It's pretty typical for this altitude," Kieran said. "It melts during the day, freezes at night. Cabin's just over 4,000 feet. Could stay this way well into May."

"Remind me not to move up to 4,000 feet."

I barely registered the conversation. My eyes were locked ahead, where the tree line broke and a clearing came into view. We had arrived.

Thomas' truck sat parked at the edge of the clearing, half-buried in snow. No fresh tire tracks. No footprints.

"Doesn't look like anyone's been here in a while," I said, but then again, the snowfall would have erased any signs of recent activity.

Kieran brought the vehicle to a stop, and we stepped out into the biting air. I kept one hand close to my holster, the other wrapped tightly around my flashlight. Our approach to the cabin was slow, deliberate—every step calculated. Weapons drawn.

As we neared, I saw the front door was slightly ajar.

Adrenaline surged. My body tensed. I was ready to go in.

Jordan glanced at me, then nodded. "You want point?"

Of course I did. I gave a short nod back and advanced. The door creaked open as I pushed it. The cold inside hit harder than the air outside. It was deep, untouched, and heavy with something that didn't quite feel natural. There was no heat source. No fire. Just that kind of lingering chill that seeps into the walls and never leaves.

We cleared the main room first, then moved into the kitchen.

There were no signs of a struggle. A half-used roll of paper towels. Canned food still stacked on the counter. A coffee mug, half full, now frozen solid, on the dining table. And sitting in front of it... was Thomas.

He was slumped in a kitchen chair, his body angled slightly toward the window. One hand rested near the mug, the other hung limp at his side. His head lolled at a wrong, final angle. A neat, round hole marked the center of his forehead.

I sucked in a breath and forced myself to remain composed despite the rage and sadness brewing within me.

Kieran moved in, checking his pulse. "He's cold. Stiff. He's been gone a while. It'll be hard to tell for sure. The low temps preserved him."

There was no bloating. No smell of rot. Just the faint, metallic trace of dried blood.

His skin was pale, waxy in places, with subtle marbling along the jawline and neck. His lips had darkened. His eyes were sunken but open—seeing nothing. Suspended in time. Frozen in death.

Jordan stepped toward the window and narrowed his eyes. "Val," he said. "Look at this."

I moved beside him. In the lower corner of the window-pane, the glass had shattered in a tight spiderweb of precise cracks. The outer screen was torn.

"He was shot from outside," Jordan said. "Sniper round. Clean. Deliberate."

"He never saw it coming."

I looked back at Thomas, still sitting there like he'd been waiting on something. Or someone. His expression was almost peaceful. *Almost.*

"He didn't just die here. He was executed. And then left on display."

My gaze shifted to the envelope resting in his lap. Plain white. My name printed in block caps. VALERIE COSTA.

Of course. I picked it up with gloved hands. Inside was a single white notecard, like the others.

Welcome back, Agent Costa. Let the game begin.

Signed with the same single, "S."

I swallowed hard. This wasn't impulsive. It wasn't reactionary. Thomas had been dead for at least a week. The Bear had planned every step. Planting the button when he wanted us to find it. When he wanted to lead me here. This message was: *I'm in control.*

"Let's check the perimeter," I said, forcing the words out. "Inside and out. Don't miss anything. Collect anything that could be evidence."

Jordan nodded and headed outside. Kieran moved deeper into the cabin, sweeping the remaining rooms.

I stayed with Thomas, trying to put the pieces together. Why him? Why now?

What game was the Bear referring to? Had Thomas been involved? Probably not. If they'd been working together, the Bear could've walked right in. They could've had a conversation. He could've shot him point-blank. But he didn't.

He killed him from a distance. Because he knew Thomas would've been armed. Would've been ready at the first sign of a threat. How did he know? Because the Bear had been watching him, just like he did with his other victims. *Most* of his victims. Had Thomas sensed it was coming?

Jordan returned, holding a sealed evidence bag. "Found this in the trash bin out back. This was stuffed inside."

Inside was a jacket made of dark cloth. The tactical jacket was missing a button. Why toss it in the trash? Was it a sign of disrespect or an attempt to conceal evidence? What else would we find?

Over the next hour the cabin swarmed with agents. The air buzzed as they collected evidence and photographed everything. As the team worked, I carefully studied every inch of the cabin. Nothing seemed out of place, and it wasn't messy which made my job easier. It was sparsely outfitted with minimal furnishings and there wasn't much decor or any obvious attempt to create a cozy or homely space. He either didn't get many visitors or they were close enough to him that they understood his lack of need for those types of things.

Jordan came up behind me as I stood staring at a wall, lost in thought. The past week played like a reel in my mind. The bodies, the messages, and the latest victim, *my training officer from the FBI*. How had the Bear known? Had he gone through newspaper clippings or broken into the archives? It seemed far-fetched, but anything was possible. I glanced at Jordan. "What's up?"

"The team is just about done."

"They find anything interesting?"

He shook his head and then eyed me. "You seem unsatisfied with that."

"I am." I exhaled, my breath visible in the frigid air. "I hadn't talked to Thomas for more than five minutes at a time over the past few years, and I know he hadn't spoken to anyone at the Bureau since he retired, according to Troy. Do you remember anything about his departure? When I asked him why he chose to retire, he didn't want to talk about it, but his retirement seemed out of the blue to me. I don't recall a party or any type of celebration. Did anything happen at the Bureau that caused him to want to leave quickly?"

"There were some rumblings. From what I heard, back then, I guess he wanted to be put on a task force, but with his age and years of service, they were kinda encouraging him to retire."

It made sense, I supposed. Thomas was in his sixties. He should've been behind a desk. But I doubt that would have suited him. I froze, stunned by a thought.

Was it possible the lack of evidence *was* the evidence? I glanced back at the wall, stepping closer. I looked up and to the right, then down. There were four tiny holes. Like something had once been hung there with pushpins. I walked over to the adjacent wall. Also clear of art or wall coverings. But another hole... and another. Four more. There used to be something tacked up there. And then, like a lock sliding into place, I hurried over to the closet. It was filled with clothes, but at the bottom, there was a rectangular spot about the size of a banker's box. Undisturbed. Just an outline of dust.

Jordan stepped up beside me. "What is it?"

"What if he was working on something? There was definitely something tacked on both of those walls. Large enough to be... I don't know maybe an investigation board. And look here." I pointed to the bottom of the closet. "There was clearly a box here. I think the killer took it all. He took whatever was on the walls, and the box that was in the closet."

"What are you thinking?"

"Maybe he was working a case. But if he was, why would the Bear take the boxes and the evidence?" I paused. "Thomas wasn't the type to simply walk away from anything. It's possible he wanted to be on the Bear task force. He lived for his work. And if the Bureau was pushing him out and wouldn't let him work the case, he worked it on his own. Maybe he made progress and even talked to someone connected to the Bear that tipped him off. If that's the case, that could be how the Bear knew who he was."

"If that's true, the techs took photos of absolutely everything. We can put it together back in Red Rose County. If there's anything here, we'll have evidence of it."

"But it won't tell us what was on the investigation boards. Or in the box. The Bear took everything. And somehow he knew exactly what he was looking for."

"We don't know for certain the items were taken by the Bear. Thomas could've moved things himself. If you're right and he was working a case, maybe something spooked him. Maybe he moved it for safekeeping. Maybe in a storage locker, or in a family member's garage. He has a son in Seattle."

"Have you spoken to him? Do you have his current information? We should be questioning him anyway. We need to know if Thomas was acting strangely before his death. Or if he thought someone was watching him. The son might know something."

"That's a good idea. We do have his current info. We called him when we got the fingerprint back on the button, asking for Thomas. He said he wasn't at his home. It wasn't a long conversation."

"What about the ex-wife?"

"We haven't called her, but we have her info too. We can have local PD reach out to talk to them."

"No, I don't think so. We're not far, a couple of hours at most. I think we need to talk to the son ourselves. If I remember correctly, I think he may be the only family Thomas ever kept in touch with. He certainly didn't talk to his ex-wife, because from what I understood, they had a rather bitter divorce." Notifying the family was the least we could do. Thomas was one of our own.

"All right. We'll do that as soon as we finish up here."

An hour later, we were packed up and ready to leave. The medical examiner had arrived to take Thomas' body and as I watched them zip the bag, I had to fight the wave of anger rising inside me. Everything in me said Thomas was working on something. And maybe... he'd found something. Could that be the reason for Thomas' phone calls to me over the past year? They were always short, no more than a few minutes, inquiring about my well-being. He never wanted to talk about himself. It wasn't unusual, but it did seem a little odd. Did he know the Bear was watching me and so he was checking in to make sure the Bear hadn't gotten to me? Perhaps this was the clue we needed. Obviously, the Bear had some sort of game he wanted to play with me. But the first clue that there was a game was found on Thomas.

Was the Bear sending me a message? Telling me he could get to me? Just like he had gotten to a decorated, retired FBI agent? A retired FBI agent, like me. I didn't like the fact that he was willing to travel to hurt someone I knew—if that was the reason he went after Thomas. Thomas deserved better than this. He didn't deserve to be gunned down in his own home and then used as a piece in the Bear's twisted game.

As we pulled away from the cabin, I took one last look at the place Thomas had chosen to live. A quiet, isolated spot. To hide away, or to hide something? Either way, the Bear had found him.

There was no physical evidence of the Bear having been there, but maybe, in his haste to remove any evidence, he'd given us a clue. Finally, there was something we could follow.

My thoughts began to swirl. What did it all mean? As I gazed out at the passing trees, branches still heavy with snow, a quiet realization settled over me. Thomas must've known something. Something important enough to get him killed. And whatever it was, the Bear went to great lengths to make sure we found Thomas' body, but not what he discovered.

For the first time in a week, a flicker of hope surfaced. I had known Thomas for years. If he had come close to cracking the case, or if he had, in fact, stumbled upon the identity of the Bear, he wouldn't have had one file. One set of notes. He would have created a backup, and kept it somewhere whoever he was chasing couldn't get to it. Thomas was far too smart to leave it for someone like the Bear to destroy completely. Assuming it was the Bear he was investigating. Would the Bear have known he'd have hidden his evidence in another location? And if he had hidden it, where and with whom? Who would he have trusted with it? All signs pointed to his son. If that were true, he could be in danger.

As the cabin disappeared from view behind us, I felt a growing certainty. Thomas had left clues, and I believe he would've known the risk of investigating the Bear and he would've prepared for the worst. But the Bear was smart. And the trick now would be finding those clues before he did.

SEVENTEEN

VAL

On the drive to Thomas' son, Owen's, place of work in downtown Seattle, I found my thoughts drifting to my own son, Harrison. Everything had happened so quickly this week. I hadn't mentioned the Bear because I didn't want to worry him. I figured there was no way the Bear would go after Harrison since he was all the way across the country in Massachusetts, attending MIT.

But now, I wasn't so sure.

If the Bear had gone after Thomas in Washington State, what was stopping him from targeting my son, or my mother, or my friends, or Brady, or anyone else I cared about?

I needed to let Harrison know to be extra vigilant. But would doing so cause more harm than good? He was only in his first year. He lived on campus. I knew there were security cameras, but I also knew he was a teenager. He went to parties, wandered across campus, lived like he was invincible like most kids his age. That made him vulnerable. Someone could easily slip into a crowd, blend in, and hurt him.

And Harrison had such a good soul. If the Bear acted

normal, kind, even, and pretended to need help, Harrison would probably help him. The thought chilled me.

I had to warn him. But maybe I'd wait until I was headed back home, so I could give him more concrete information. I knew finals were coming up, and I didn't want to disrupt his focus. Maybe he could stay with his father, Nathan, or maybe his father could take him to a hotel. I'd have to think it through. Talk it over with the team.

Kieran drove while Jordan sat in the backseat. I turned around to Jordan and said, "The fact that the Bear came all the way out here to kill someone I knew, or someone who knew who he was, or who was investigating him, worries me. What if he'll travel again? What if he goes after someone else?"

"Someone like Harrison," Kieran chimed in.

"Exactly. I haven't told Harrison about the latest killings or that the Bear is murdering people just to send me messages. I need Harrison to be safe."

Jordan leaned forward. "We could put security on him or put him in a safe house."

"But he has finals coming up."

"We could give him a private security detail," Kieran offered. "Or maybe he's fine. Maybe just call him, tell him to be more alert. No parties right now, at least until we catch this guy."

"You really think that'll do the trick?" I wasn't so sure.

Kieran said, "If you look at the facts, Val, he likely killed Thomas a week or two ago. We're not really sure when, but probably before the storm hit. And since he's dropped two bodies this week, it had to be before that. So, if he's continuing to send messages, he'll stay local. It would take quite a bit of effort to travel across the country to get to Harrison."

He was right. It was a long shot and maybe I was worrying about nothing. Still, I needed Harrison to know what was going on, at the very least so he could be on alert. We assumed the

Bear was working alone, but the truth was we didn't really know. He'd hired people to send messages before. Like the one I received in the mailbox. He'd paid some kid to send it. What if he paid someone to mess with Harrison?

"It's a possibility, Val," Kieran said. "But you've got the resources of the Bureau. You're one of our own even if you're just consulting at the moment. Whatever you need."

"All right. I'll call Harrison and let him know what's going on."

"Keep us posted," Jordan added.

I pulled out my phone and texted him. *Hey honey. There's been some stuff going on. We need to talk. Call me when you're out of class.*

Then I texted my mom. *How are you? Everything is fine here.*

Fine was debatable, but I didn't want her to worry. Shortly after, Mom texted back, *All okay here. Stay safe. Love you.*

Slightly relieved, I told Kieran and Jordan I'd reached out to Harrison and Mom.

The car went quiet for the rest of the drive. We were all deep in thought. It was unusual, *highly unusual*, for a serial killer the FBI was actively hunting to go after one of their own. One retired agent killed. Another—me—being hunted. The Bear was making this very personal.

We had security on everyone who could be at risk in Red Rose County. So far, aside from some creepy photos and vague threats, no one close to me had been targeted. For the rest of the drive, I tried to put together the pieces of the puzzle the Bear had left behind. My thought was, *the game had begun.*

If that was true, it meant it wasn't over. Not by a long shot. There would be more bodies. More messages. But I didn't understand the rules of the game, not yet. He wasn't leaving real clues. Not intentionally, anyway. Maybe this wasn't a game for us at all. Maybe it was just a game for him. Maybe he liked watching us. He liked to see agents scrambling from crime scene to crime scene, confused and reactive. Maybe we weren't even players. We were the pawns in his game.

Parked in front of an office building in downtown Seattle, Jordan, Kieran, and I stepped out and crossed the sidewalk toward the glass facade of a well-known tech company headquarters. We'd called ahead to let Owen know we needed to speak with him.

I called to let him know we had arrived, and within moments, there he was. I had never met him before, but he resembled Thomas—tan skin, brown eyes, rugged features. He looked like a younger version of his father. "Owen?" I asked.

"Yes."

"I'm Val Costa. This is Special Agent Jordan Wexler, and this is Special Agent Kieran Fox."

After we'd all shaken hands, I said, "Is there a place we can talk privately?"

"Yes, there's a café right here in the lobby."

He led the way, and as Kieran stopped at the café counter to grab us all a coffee, we slid into a quiet corner booth.

Seated, I leaned forward. "Thank you for meeting with us at short notice. We need to talk about your dad. Something's happened."

Owen's brow furrowed, and I saw the breath leave him as I gently broke the news. "We found your father deceased a few hours ago, in his cabin. I'm very sorry for your loss."

He exhaled sharply and raked his fingers through his dark hair. "It's shocking, but... I guess I'm not totally surprised. I mean, I am, but..." His voice trailed off as the weight of the news settled over him.

I could imagine the fear he must have carried growing up with a father in the FBI. Thomas was never one to run from danger; he ran toward it. It was a trait we had in common.

"I know this is a difficult time, but the reason it was so

urgent we speak with you is that we think your father might have been working a case. And we believe it may be connected to his death."

Owen blinked. "Was he murdered?"

"Yes, he was," Jordan confirmed quietly, just as Kieran returned and set the coffees on the table.

I said, "All three of us worked with your father. He was my training officer when I first joined the FBI. We worked together for fifteen years. His loss is felt by all of us. He was a great man."

"Thank you," Owen said. "But you really think his death had something to do with a case? He was retired."

That told us one thing. Thomas hadn't mentioned the investigation to his son.

"It's just a hunch," I said. "We don't have concrete evidence. He never spoke to you about conducting an investigation on his own?"

Owen shook his head. "No, he didn't tell me about anything like that."

"Was he acting differently over the last few weeks?" I asked. "Seemed paranoid, maybe? Thought someone was watching him?"

"Not really. My dad could be reclusive, yeah, but he always called the kids on their birthdays—mine, my wife's. Holidays, too. He'd come visit. He wasn't far from us. I can't think of anything out of the ordinary except he didn't call last week. He usually calls every Sunday just to check in on us."

He paused. "Which was funny, 'cause we were always the ones wanting to check in on him. He was all alone in that cabin."

"So, when was the last time you spoke with your father?" I asked.

"About two weeks ago. He called, like he always did. Pretty much like clockwork. Now that I think about it, every Sunday.

So yeah... it's been almost two weeks ago Sunday since we heard from him."

That was fifteen days earlier. That matched our working timeline. He may have spoken to his son just before he died.

"And nothing unusual happened these last few weeks?" Jordan asked. "No strange phone calls? Unexpected visitors to you or your father?"

"Only a few days ago, when the FBI called asking if he was at our house. I guess that's why I'm not so surprised by all this. But I don't know. You get a call from the FBI looking for your dad, and you get a little worried."

I nodded in understanding. "Nothing else strange?"

He threw his hands in the air, suddenly animated. "Wait—there was something. Not with us, but I talked to my mom and she said Dad had sent her a package."

Jordan, Kieran, and I shared a quick glance.

"They don't talk at all," Owen explained. "She said it was really strange, and she wouldn't open it."

Of course. It was the perfect move. If Thomas thought he might be in danger, and someone suspected he had evidence, the last place they'd look was at his ex-wife's place. Sending it to her was strategic. It would not have been the first place I would have looked—and it wasn't.

"When did she receive the package?" I asked.

"About two weeks ago. She said she didn't want to have anything to do with it and was going to bring it by the house when we celebrated Easter so that I could give it back to him."

We needed to get that package. Everything I knew about Thomas told me there was something important in it. It wasn't meant for his ex-wife. It was a fail-safe. If I go missing... if I end up dead... that kind of thing.

We quickly wrapped up the conversation with Owen. Making our way to the car, I turned to the others. "Let's go find out what's in that package."

EIGHTEEN

VAL

An hour later, Mrs. Swenson invited us into her home and offered us a seat in her living room. It was warm and cozy, with a giant stone fireplace. On the mantel were pictures of her grandchildren, as well as framed photos of her son Owen, his wife, and a man I presumed was her second husband.

"Can I offer you anything to drink?" she asked.

"No, thank you, ma'am. We just wanted to talk to you about your ex-husband, Thomas Ingram."

She nodded quickly. "Owen called me and told me what happened. I'm sorry to hear that he died. Sounds like maybe he was working a case. I figured the package must have been something intended for the FBI in the event he went missing. I'm still surprised he sent it to me, of all people."

"Why did you think it was intended for the FBI?"

"When we were married, he'd explained that it was a way to preserve sensitive information. Information that could get him killed. He told me if I ever received a package to hide it until the FBI came looking for it. Imagine my surprise when I found it on my doorstep."

Even in retirement, Thomas had never stopped being an agent. "May we see the package?"

"Of course. It's just in the kitchen." She hurried out of the room.

From Thomas' file, we knew they had been married for ten years while Thomas worked at the FBI, so it didn't come as a surprise that he'd discussed fail-safes and worst-case-scenarios with her. She returned with a small package. There was no return address just "T. Ingram" written in the upper left-hand corner. She set it down gently on the coffee table and sat across from us.

"I assume it's from Thomas. That's how he used to address his envelopes, just 'T. Ingram.' It's funny…" She shook her head, and I noticed her eyes glistening. I wondered if, despite everything, the bitterness of their divorce and all the years that had passed, she still cared for him.

"The ten years I was married to him," she said, her voice quieter now, "I always feared that one day I'd have the FBI sitting in my living room, telling me he was dead. And now, here you are. It's just strange, you know? You feel like something is bound to happen, and then one day it does. You just never know when."

"We appreciate you talking with us today," I said gently.

"Sure. Anything I can do to help. But if I know anything about Thomas, despite our troubles, he wasn't a quitter and he never let go of a case until he'd solved it."

That was how I remembered him, as well. I nodded, glancing at the package. "After you got the package, did you speak to Thomas to ask him what it was?"

"No. But I called Owen. Owen said he was talking to his dad that Sunday. They talked every Sunday, sometimes more often, depending on what was going on. But he never missed a Sunday. I guess we should've known something was wrong."

"Has anything strange happened other than receiving the

box? Any visitors, any sense of being watched, or strange phone calls—hang-ups? Anything out of the ordinary?"

"No, no. Just the box. And that Owen hadn't heard from Thomas. I guess we should've alerted the police when he stopped calling. He could've been hurt. I just assumed he didn't want to talk. He could be a bit odd. I'm still surprised he sent me the package."

"That was probably by design, ma'am," Kieran said.

She looked puzzled, so I explained. "If there's some kind of evidence in there—something important, something that could incriminate someone—they'd be looking for it. And since you were probably the last person they'd think to search, it made sense. He wouldn't want to put Owen, a more obvious choice, in danger."

She nodded slowly, finally understanding. I slipped on a pair of rubber gloves and Kieran handed me a pocketknife.

I slid the blade carefully through the edge of the package. Inside was a small paper envelope and a folded piece of paper. I opened the paper first. It was printed with an address in Rosedale and included a handwritten note.

To Val or the FBI or whoever else finds this—probably Val.
    This is a key to a PO box in Rosedale. You'll find what you need there. Good luck and be careful.
    —Thomas

I picked up the small envelope and a bronze-colored key slid onto my palm. Engraved on the key were the numbers 6-2-4. My heart pounded. Thomas *had* found something. But what was it?

NINETEEN

VAL

A mix of exhaustion and adrenaline shot through me as I stepped off the jetway. My phone vibrated in my pocket and as I saw Harrison's name on the screen, I felt a sense of relief.

"Hi, honey."

"What's up?" he asked.

"There's a situation I need to talk to you about."

"Is everyone okay? Is Grandma okay?"

"Yes, Grandma's doing great, actually. But there's been some indication that the person who held me captive, the Bear, is in Red Rose County. And he might be targeting people I know."

I didn't want to tell him everything that had happened. One, because it was an active investigation and two, because I didn't think Harrison needed to know all the gory details. But the truth was unavoidable. I was locked in a twisted game with a serial killer who had once tried to kill me. But the more I thought about it, he could have killed me, but he didn't. At the time, I thought it was because the team had rescued me just in time. But now? If he wanted me dead, he could've done it nine months ago while I was tied up in that barn. *Easily*. Had he been surprised when my team arrived? I'd assumed he was, but what if he wasn't? What if he'd devised this game nine months ago?

A chill snaked up my spine. The events of the past nine months snapped into focus, forming a clearer picture. The Bear had been stalking me. Biding his time. Waiting to pounce. And that terrified me more than anything because I hadn't realized it. He'd always been two steps ahead.

Our only hope was that whatever Thomas had found might finally give us a slight advantage. Something to tip the scale.

"Should I be worried?" Harrison asked, his voice low.

"We don't think you're in danger. But in the past he's been known to hire people, innocent people, who don't know what they're truly being asked to do, just to get to me." I sighed. "What I'd like you to do, Harrison, and I know this is hard. You're nineteen, you're in college, you want to have fun but just for now, until we get this resolved can you promise me a few things?"

"Like what?"

"No parties. Stay close to your dorm. Don't go out late. Be cautious—very cautious—with anyone new you meet. Actually, even people you do know. Just be careful and alert. If you get any sense something is off, you call me immediately. I've been working with the FBI. We have the resources to keep everyone safe, if needed. Do you understand?"

"Mom, I'm always cautious, but okay. And you'll keep me updated on how you are, right?"

"I will. If anything new develops, I'll tell you. And let's go back to our two-times-a-day check-ins, okay?"

"Text messages okay?"

"Yes. Can you do that, honey?"

"Of course, Mom. You know I worry about you too."

My heart warmed. Harrison was everything to me. "Okay.

Well, I'm about to get into the car. We just landed—back in California."

"Back in California? Where'd you go?"

"We were in Washington. Questioning." I paused. "But you don't need to worry about that, sweetheart. I love you. Stay safe."

"Love you too, Mom. You be safe."

"Will do."

I tipped my chin at Kieran and Jordan, who were already waiting for me near the SUV. As we headed toward the parking lot, I glanced at them. "Harrison's on board. He'll be vigilant. He said he'll let me know if anything seems off, and we'll text twice a day."

"Good kid you got there, Val," Kieran said.

"Yes, I have."

"All right," Jordan said. "Let's head straight to the post office. We've got to know what's in that box."

"I'm pretty interested too," Kieran added. "I'm starting to agree with you, Val—Thomas must've been looking into the Bear. The timeline fits. He retired and started chasing something. Maybe it was the Bear task force he wanted on and the director turned him down. And the fact that he left the message for you means he must've been keeping tabs on you."

"Seems like a lot of people are keeping tabs on me," I said, wryly.

"True. But I have a feeling Thomas was looking out for you."

"I think so too." My voice softened. "I fear he may have lost his life doing just that." Not that I believed Thomas went after the Bear because of me. Chances are, he'd started investigating him the moment he retired, long before I was ever captured.

At the SUV my phone buzzed again. I opened the door to the back seat and answered. "Hey, Brady. What's up?"

"Where are you guys?"

"We just landed. We're heading toward the post office in Rosedale..." I went on to explain what we'd discovered at Thomas' cabin and about the key to the PO box. "We should be there in about an hour and then we'll head to the station to update the rest of the team."

"That's great, and I hope that gives us something to go on." He paused. "But, Val, there's been a development."

Kieran and Jordan were seated and looking over at me.

"What's the development?"

"A hiker just found another body and there's another message, for you."

My gut tightened. "We'll meet you at the crime scene. Text me the location."

"Will do. See you soon."

As much as I wanted to rush to the PO box, there were only about three hours before nightfall. I ended the call and then sent a quick text to my mom to let her know not to wait up and that I loved her. Inside the car, I said, "That was Brady. There's been another murder and another message from the Bear. Brady is texting me the location." A ping sounded, and I read the text from Brady. "And there it is." I read it to Kieran and we were off.

For a moment, a thought crossed my mind. If the Bear was here in Red Rose County killing another victim then he wasn't in Massachusetts hunting my son. That gave me some relief, but it soon vanished and my thoughts returned to the latest victim and the message. What sick note had the Bear left this time?

TWENTY

HIM

Perched high in the trees, I lifted my binoculars and peered through them. The FBI had been at the scene for a while. Red Rose County Sheriff's Department had responded first, with the Bureau following shortly after. But I wasn't watching for them. I was waiting for Val.

Would she be back before nightfall? I knew her and her FBI friends had left very early for the airport, presumably to go to Washington to find my message. Would Valerie be sad her former mentor was dead? It was quite inconvenient to have to hike all the way to his remote cabin to observe him, learn his habits, and see if he'd met with anyone. But it was necessary. I couldn't let him interfere with what I'd been planning. What I'd been planning since the day I let Valerie go. She thought she'd been rescued. Not so. The past nine months were simply an intermission.

Honestly, I'd expected them back by now, especially once they heard about my latest message to Valerie. *I couldn't wait all day.* I had plans for the evening. A much more... intimate performance. Dinner with the lovely Sally. She was cooking. Wasn't that quaint? Quite the juxtaposition, given her profession. A medical examiner who made roasted chicken and poured good wine. It was charming and refreshing to learn she was well-rounded. Almost a shame to snuff out that light. But she wasn't the main act. She was merely the opening number.

Although I had been considering keeping them both. At least for a little while longer, just to see how Valerie would react. After all, what's a game without an audience?

A dark SUV rolled up and I focused the binoculars on the license plate. *She's here.*

The car stopped. Valerie jumped out the back with her two loyal sidekicks: Jordan Wexler, the younger agent with wild curls and an eagerness he couldn't hide, and Kieran Fox, her former supervisor, stoic as ever.

I'd learned quite a bit about them since they'd arrived in Red Rose County. They'd both worked with Val on the task force to catch me, and they'd both failed.

Valerie looked exquisite, though there were dark circles beneath her eyes. I worried she wasn't sleeping well, and I needed her strong. Sharp. Ready to play.

Did she know that our game was just beginning? Was she beginning to understand I'd spent the last nine months studying her? If not, that would become clear soon enough.

I lowered the binoculars and glanced at my watch. I only had a few minutes to spare before heading to Sally's.

Looking through the lens one last time, I saw Deputy Brady Tanner, the simp, hand her my message. She must be dying to know what it said. I watched her face as she pulled out the note-card and unfolded the article I'd left for her.

Would she understand?

I swear, I could watch Valerie all day and all night. But the clock was ticking, and I didn't want to be late for my romantic dinner with Sally. *Valerie, this is goodbye for now.*

. . .

I arrived with a bottle of wine she once mentioned she liked, a cabernet from Sonoma.

Standing in the doorway, she smiled. "Hi there. Come on in."

She wore jeans and a cozy sweater, her hair in soft waves. She was perfect. Warm and bright in a way that made people feel seen. So unlike the cold cases she spent her days dissecting. A unicorn, really. No wonder she and Valerie were such good friends.

"I brought this for you," I said, handing her the bottle.

"Oh! I love this winery. This is great. Thank you so much."

I said, "You're very welcome," as I entered the home. The house smelled like garlic and rosemary. A warm and inviting smell. I hadn't expected her to be such a good cook.

"So, how was your day?" she asked.

"It was a good day, actually. Took out a hiking tour earlier and now, here I am. How about you? Did you have to go out to the new crime scene today? That's, what, three this week?"

Her smile faltered. "No, I'm not working on that case," she said, brushing it off.

Did she not want to talk about work? Or was she wondering how I knew anything about a body being found, especially considering half the sheriff's department and the FBI were at the scene? Of course, the only bodies appearing this week were mine.

Which left Sally conveniently free for me. "Well, it must be nice to have a bit of a break from all that death."

She nodded. "I'm sure I'll get others soon. I look at more than just homicides, you know."

"Of course." I smiled. "So... what did you make for dinner? It smells amazing."

"I prepared roasted potatoes, mashed cauliflower, and pan-fried chicken."

"That sounds incredible."

"I hope you like it," she said, offering a faint smile.

But I could see something was off. I'd become adept at reading people. And something about her tone, her posture, there was something bothering her. I tried to lighten the mood by not discussing anything death-related. "How's the garden coming along?"

"I have my tomatoes planted and the zucchini too. Hopefully, I'll have a nice harvest this summer. I'd love to be able to eat right out of the backyard."

"That sounds nice. Can I help set the table?"

"No, that's okay, but maybe you can open the wine?"

"Sure."

She showed me the drawer with the wine opener. I popped it open while she plated the food. She glanced over her shoulder at me, not with the same sparkle I'd seen before. Something had changed. She was watching me. Was it the latest body or was it something else? Should I ask her?

I poured the wine and set the glasses on the table. She followed behind me with plates that looked like they belonged in a magazine.

"This is amazing. Thank you so much, Sally," I said, taking my seat.

"Bon appétit."

We ate in silence. She barely touched her wine. I set down my fork, took a sip, and looked at her. "Is everything okay?"

"Yeah. Everything's fine," she said, too quickly.

I didn't believe her. "You seem on edge. Did something happen? I noticed the patrol car still outside. Are you afraid you're in danger?"

She hesitated. "I don't know. I shouldn't say anything. But they found another body today, and I guess it has me a little on edge. That's all."

I nodded, pretending to understand. "I'm so sorry. And you said this killer knows of you?"

She nodded silently.

I reached out to place my hand gently on her shoulder, and she flinched. I wasn't expecting that reaction.

She shook her head. "I'm sorry. Maybe I should've canceled tonight. I don't think I'm very good company right now."

"We'll keep it short. But you made dinner. I'd hate to waste it."

She gave a half-hearted nod. "You're right. Let's just enjoy dinner. Maybe call it an early night. I have a meeting in the morning to discuss how I can assist the FBI."

"Of course. Please let me know if there's anything I can do to help. I'm here for you, Sally."

"Thank you."

She barely spoke for the rest of dinner. Afterward, I offered to do the dishes and didn't press her any further about the latest development. I kept it light. Normal. But as I walked to the door, I leaned in for a kiss. She froze and didn't lean in. If I didn't know any better, I'd say she didn't want me to kiss her. Had our passion fizzled out already? Or was it simply her head was elsewhere and she was too stressed out about this looming threat over her? Could it be she was beginning to suspect I wasn't who I said I was? *Now, that wouldn't do at all.*

TWENTY-ONE

VAL

Fletcher's Creek Trail wound through one of the more remote parts of Red Rose County, a narrow path that followed the creek as it cut through dense forest. It was popular with more experienced hikers. We arrived to find the usually desolate area with a dozen law enforcement vehicles including the FBI, the crime scene unit, the sheriff's department, and park rangers. The park ranger's truck was parked closest to the trailhead. Standing next to the ranger was Brady. Jordan and I approached them, while Kieran went to speak to our pals in the Bureau to update them on what we'd found earlier in the day.

After a quick hello, he introduced us to Ranger Dinkle.

He said, "Nice to meet you both."

"What can you tell us?"

He pointed to a thin, nervous-looking man in hiking gear down the trail speaking to two FBI agents. "That's Rodney Pierce, a retired school teacher and avid hiker. He discovered the body approximately ninety minutes ago. About a quarter mile up the trail."

"Any idea how long the body's been there?"

"The ME estimates 12–24 hours."

Likely while we were in Washington chasing another one of his crime scenes. "I'd like to see the scene while there's still daylight."

"Go on ahead. They're expecting you. Just follow the main trail until you reach the big boulder. It looks like a turtle shell. The body's about fifty yards to the east, in a small clearing. It's surrounded by law enforcement. You can't miss it."

"Thank you."

Jordan waved Kieran over, and we headed toward the scene. I pretty much knew what we would find, but knowing didn't make it any easier.

The trail was muddy from recent rain, our boots sinking slightly with each step. The creek gurgled to our right. In any other circumstance, it would have been peaceful.

We nodded as we marched past the hiker and law enforcement and continued until we reached the boulder Ranger Dinkle had mentioned. It was a large, smooth stone that did indeed resemble a turtle shell. We turned east and left the main trail. The clearing was small, barely twenty feet across, surrounded by thick pines. An agent stood at the perimeter, talking quietly with the FBI's ME, Dr. McIntyre. Both looked up as we approached.

I said, "We're going to take a look and then follow up with you. Is that okay?"

"Of course. Techs have already photographed the scene and have been collecting evidence. And I don't need to tell you how to treat a crime scene," he said with a wink.

I nodded my thanks and stepped forward, already pulling on latex gloves. The others followed, spreading out around the perimeter of the clearing.

The body was male, middle-aged, dressed in a park ranger's uniform. He lay on his back, arms stretched out to the sides, almost like a snow angel. His throat had been cut, the wound precise and deep. But what caught my attention was his chest.

The uniform shirt had been unbuttoned and pulled apart to expose his skin, where the familiar "S" had been carved.

"Jeff Adler," Brady said, his voice tight. "One of our senior rangers."

"When did they last hear from him?" Jordan asked.

"According to Ranger Dinkle, 8 p.m. last night when the next ranger's shift started."

"Did he actually see him?"

"No, they just spoke over the radio."

The timeline matched the ME's estimated time of death. He likely was attacked shortly after that call. I circled the body carefully, absorbing the details. Unlike Linda Castillo, who had been positioned to mirror my own abduction, Adler's body wasn't staged to recreate anything specific. It was the Bear's work, but this time he hadn't taken his time. It had been quick and brutal, and he'd left his signature carving. But there was no note.

"Brady, you said there was a message."

"Techs bagged it."

Well, I'd seen enough of the Bear's destruction. I was ready for the latest note. "I want to see it." I headed back toward the agent and Dr. McIntyre.

As I approached, Dr. McIntyre asked, "What do you think?"

"Definitely the Bear. Do you have the note?"

The agent said, "I'll call the tech over."

A few moments later, a woman in coveralls ran over with a plastic evidence bag in hand. "Here it is."

"Thanks," I said as I took it from her. Through the plastic, I was surprised not to find the now-familiar white envelope. Instead it was far more disturbing. It was a copy of the front page of the *Washington Post*, dated twelve years earlier. The headline read "FBI agent cracks decade-old serial killer case," with a photo of me at a press conference. It was from the

Upstate Strangler case, the first big win in my FBI career. I'd spent two years building a profile that eventually led to the arrest of Wilson Richard Holbrook, who had killed eleven women in New York state.

Across the article, written in red block letters, were the words: "Good job, Agent Costa."

I didn't understand. What was the point of this? Was there a hidden message?

"He's been researching you," Jordan said, looking over my shoulder. "Your career highlights."

"This is from twelve years ago," I said. "I'd just made Senior Agent. The Upstate Strangler case put me on the map at the Bureau. I don't see how it fits with whatever game he wants me to play."

Brady studied the clipping. "Maybe the Bear is trying to remind you of your FBI days."

Jordan said, "He wants you to play. He wants you to investigate. He wants you to catch him."

The Bear wanted me, that I knew for sure. But he didn't want to be caught, I knew that too. "No. He wants me to find him, not catch him." And I would do exactly that, but I doubt he would like the ending.

Jordan said, "You're probably right. Let's talk about what we have so far."

"Good idea."

"The Bear likely killed Adler while we were in Washington or late last night when nobody would find the body until we were gone."

"Probably part of the plan. Get us out of town so he could leave another message."

"He's playing with us," Jordan said. "Leading us exactly where he wants us to go."

I thought back to the body, anger building inside me. Jeff Adler had died for no reason other than to deliver a message from the Bear to me. Adler had just been a prop in his twisted performance. "This isn't the end of the game, which means he's going to kill again. How many more bodies before it's over?"

Jordan said, "I agree with you, he's not done. Each body has a message but not a clue. But collectively we've learned more about him. The Bear is clearly comfortable in the outdoors. He climbs trees and is likely an expert hiker."

"Perhaps he grew up in a forested area. Red Rose County or anywhere in the Pacific Northwest or areas with similar terrain."

Brady said, "If he's staying in Red Rose County he's probably holed up in an old hunting cabin or something similar. It's easy to stay hidden out here."

"That's a lot of area to search."

Jordan said, "Are there property records for all the cabins out here?"

Brady said, "Probably some, but not all."

I said, "It's a start, though."

Brady said, "I'll talk to Lucy and see what she can find."

Jordan was right, we weren't walking away without new information. We were beginning to zero in on his possible whereabouts. Unfortunately, it was vast terrain but it was better than nothing. And if anyone could help us, Lucy could. She was great with records searches.

My phone buzzed. A missed call from Sally and a text message.

Val. When you get a minute can you call me back? I need to talk.

What was that about? Before I could give it any further thought, Kieran approached. "What did I miss?"

Jordan filled him in on a possible search area for the Bear's location.

"Excellent, I'll call in additional resources for a search. It'll be dark soon. We can put together a team once we get a map of the homes in the area."

"Great. We should also alert the rangers and the public and tell them not to hike alone."

Brady said, "I'll talk to the sheriff and get the comms started."

Kieran nodded his approval, and Brady stepped away.

Kieran said, "There's not much more we can do tonight. We should get some rest. It's been a long day. We need to be rested for what's next."

"Agreed." It would be good to see Mom and Julie, and my adrenaline would only push me so far. I suddenly felt exhausted and could use a home-cooked meal. I'd call Sally back and then get some rest, so that we could find the Bear and end his reign of terror, once and for all.

TWENTY-TWO
SALLY

As I paced through my living room, the hardwood floor creaked beneath my feet, and I wondered if I was being ridiculous and shouldn't have sent that text to Val. I had no evidence or proof. All I had was a gnawing feeling deep inside telling me something wasn't right. I glanced at the clock again and saw it was almost 9:30 p.m. I should have been getting ready for bed and not worrying about the body they'd found, but I was supposed to be meeting with the FBI in the morning to discuss how I could help their medical examiner in the event more bodies surfaced. I couldn't turn off my mind. It was too much to digest.

I'd moved to Red Rose County thinking I was escaping the chaos of the big city. The image I had was of serene forests, trees, lakes, and hiking trails. But lately, every time I turned around, there was another murder victim.

I wanted to help, but I hadn't even been able to contribute to the cases over this past week. The only autopsies I had performed recently were on senior citizens who had passed peacefully at the retirement home. Their families wanted to know cause of death and I guessed I was giving answers, helping in my own way, but it didn't feel like it was enough.

There was a nervous energy inside me I couldn't shake. Every time I shut my eyes, I saw his face staring back at me threateningly, like he was hunting me. It was odd because I had no evidence or logic to think he was a threat. I was a scientist and I was supposed to make conclusions based on data, not gut feelings.

Maybe I was losing my mind.

If I wasn't so caught up in the case, or under constant surveillance by the sheriff's department, I'd go to a spa to have a day to myself. Or go for a run. I even contemplated opening a bottle of wine, but I knew that wouldn't be a good idea if I was meeting with FBI agents and their ME the next day.

My phone buzzed, and I hoped it was Val. It wasn't.

It was Dominic, again. He had called twice since dinner and I was beginning to think maybe he had sensed something was off.

Or maybe something *was* off with Dominic. I didn't have any real reason to think that, though. It could just be his odd way of speaking or how he was so matter-of-fact about death. It was as if death and murder didn't touch him.

My mind replayed our recent conversations, especially during the hike. He said he wouldn't "waste a beautiful view on a victim." Like that was supposed to be reassuring. Or was it a message?

But the part that really bothered me, the thing I couldn't shake, was how he knew about the body that had been found today. Only a handful of people in law enforcement knew about it. Brady had said they were keeping it under wraps. No press. No leaks. So how did Dominic know?

Maybe he had seen the police vehicles. Or heard it from a park ranger. He ran a hiking company, after all, and had lived in Red Rose County for six months. Maybe he was friends with the park rangers. I should have asked how he knew, but I was too stunned by his question and too shaken by the possibility that he knew something he shouldn't.

My phone buzzed again. This time, relief flooded me. "Val?"

"Hey, Sally."

"Are you home?"

"Yeah. It's been quite a day, and we decided we needed to take a break."

"Was it bad?"

"It's pretty bad, Sally. But we can talk more about that tomorrow. I'm more concerned about you. What's going on? You said you wanted to talk. Is everything okay?"

"I don't know, Val. I could just be... I don't know. You know there's been three murders here in the last week? That's a lot. There's a killer running around Red Rose County."

"That's true, Sally. And you're acting perfectly normal. People who know what's going on should be on edge. Actually, Brady's going to have the sheriff's department issue a communication advising hikers not to go out alone. They're going to spin it so it doesn't outright say there's a serial killer out there, but not to go hiking alone, okay?"

"It's strange, right? Two different murders on hard-to-access trails. This is an experienced hiker who's doing the killing."

"That's what we've deduced as well. We actually have a plan in place. We think we might be able to find him."

My thoughts drifted back to Dominic. "That's good."

"Are you sure you're okay? Has something happened?"

"I feel silly even saying this, Val. But I, uh, I just have this feeling. And I know how that sounds—it's not data, not a graph. Not facts." Was I mumbling?

"Sally, it's your intuition. What's it saying? Tell me."

"You're not going to laugh?"

"Of course not. If your instincts are telling you something's wrong, if you've got a feeling, I want to hear it."

"Okay," I said, swallowing hard. "It's just a feeling. Nothing's happened. But I'm starting to feel uncomfortable with Dominic. Does that make sense?"

"What did he do?"

"He didn't do anything. He's been very attentive. He came over for dinner. We went on a hike. He used to put me at ease, but now a few things he's said just keep replaying in my mind, like a bad movie."

"What kind of things?"

"On the hike, he asked a lot of questions about my job. About the dead. I told him he was freaking me out and that he sounded like a serial killer. Just joking, you know? And he looked out at the hills and said, 'I wouldn't waste a view like this on a victim.'"

"That's unsettling."

"I thought so too. I tried to change the subject. He said he was kidding, of course. But then, during dinner tonight, he asked me about the body that was found today. And I—I don't know how he would know about that. Maybe he knows a ranger. I don't know. It's probably nothing. I'm probably just being paranoid."

"Sally, there's something I need to do, but then I'm going to come over. Okay? We can talk when I come over."

"You don't have to do that. I'm just... I don't know. I'm driving myself crazy because I haven't been able to help with any of the cases. I should just go to sleep, but I can't relax."

"I'll come by after I finish up. We'll talk. Sit tight—we've got it covered."

"Are you sure? It's late. You've had a long day."

"It has been, but honestly, it'd be great to catch up and maybe have a glass of wine."

"What time will you get here? It's almost ten."

"I'm home now—just checking in with Mom and Julie. Then I need to run a quick errand. Will you still be up?"

"I will. Thanks, Val. It's probably just my imagination going into overdrive."

"Things have been strange lately. I'll see you in about half an hour. An hour tops."

"I look forward to it."

"It'll be okay, Sally."

"Thanks, Val."

As the call ended, I felt a little calmer. Talking to Val helped. But I could tell she was worried about me. She was a good friend. Maybe I'd got it all wrong about Dominic. Maybe he was just a bit odd.

But the more I thought about it, the more he started to fit the profile. It was probably just a coincidence, but it felt good to finally say it out loud. And now that I had, I realized just how ridiculous it all sounded. Everything would be fine, just like Val said.

TWENTY-THREE
VAL

When I hung up, I was more worried than ever about Sally. I could hear the fear in her voice. She sensed something was off with Dominic, and she might be right. Could he be the Bear? It seemed outrageous that she happened to be dating the man we'd been looking for. The man who had been hunting me and terrorizing the rest of Red Rose County. But the Bear wasn't the only serial killer out there, and certainly not the only creep.

Sally's instincts were telling her Dominic wasn't who he claimed to be. Maybe he wasn't the Bear, but that didn't mean he wasn't dangerous. She was smart and analytical. She knew how to piece together data, and if she had a hunch I wanted to look into it. Not only that, but I could tell she needed a friend. In a place like Red Rose County, if you didn't have friends or family, you could feel isolated pretty fast, and Sally didn't have any family nearby. The sheriff's department had become her family, with Lucy and I like sisters. Even though we hadn't known each other that long, there was a kinship between us.

I walked into the living room to find Mom curled up on the couch with Julie, both of them watching yet another episode of *The Great British Baking Show*.

"Hi, ladies," I said, grabbing my keys. "I'm just going to run out for a bit. I have to run an errand and then I'm heading over to Sally's place. Sounds like she needs someone to talk to."

"At this time of night?" Mom asked, raising an eyebrow.

"It's not even ten o'clock. I won't be out too late. I'll try to be home by midnight. I just want to make sure Sally's okay."

"Well, maybe you should bring Brady with you. Or someone from the sheriff's department. It's not safe out there, Val," she added.

"I can take care of myself. I'm on my guard. He won't get me a second time, I promise you that."

"If you're sure, Val..."

"I've got my phone on me. If I'm not home in two hours, you can call in the cavalry."

"Okay, well, just let the deputy outside know where you're going. That way they don't have to call it in or track your cell phone or whatever it is they'll do to try to find you."

"Thanks, Mom. Don't wait up for me."

"All right, Val."

With a wave, I grabbed my bag and headed out. It wasn't like I was going to be able to sleep anyway, and although I'd promised Kieran I would rest, just like everyone else from the FBI was doing back at the hotel, prepping for tomorrow's search across Red Rose County, I had one more thing to do before I could sleep.

I'd almost forgotten about the PO box. *Almost.* It wasn't a big deal to go on my own. I'd wear gloves and bag any evidence I found. Anything Thomas had left was likely meant for me anyway. It would take only few minutes considering the post office was barely five minutes from my house. That's when it struck me. Thomas had been five minutes from my house. He'd opened a PO box in my hometown and didn't even stop by to say hello. *Strange.* Maybe he didn't want to alert me he was working a case so that I couldn't tell the FBI he was working a case solo. It was dangerous, reckless, and could mess with their ongoing investigation. It was so very Thomas. And the more I thought about it, the more I had to think he was looking into the Bear. Why else leave a note for *me* and open a PO box in *my* hometown?

As I locked the front door behind me, I thought, *what a week. What a day.* As exhausted as I was, I couldn't just sit still. The fresh air would do more for me than tossing and turning in bed or worse, having another nightmare of being chained up in that barn.

In three days, we'd discovered four of the Bear's victims. Three in Red Rose County, one in Washington, although that one likely happened a few weeks ago. Still, that was a lot of death. No wonder Sally was rattled. I shook off the thoughts. I needed to focus on the task at hand. Check the PO box and talk to Sally.

I walked up to the deputy's car stationed near the curb and waved. He rolled down the window.

"Hey, Baker."

"Hey, Val. What's going on?"

"I'm just running an errand and heading over to Sally's house for a bit. Nothing to worry about. I've got my phone on me. Mom and Julie are safe inside."

A car pulled up, catching both our attention. I recognized the SUV immediately. It was Brady.

"Were you expecting him?" I asked.

"Yeah, he's taking the next shift. I'm just about to take off."

He was supposed to be off duty, like the rest of the team. Brady parked and climbed out of his car and approached us. "Is everything okay?"

It was good to see him. "I was just letting Baker know I'm running an errand, then heading to Sally's."

"By yourself?"

"I'm just going to the post office. Then to Sally's."

"By yourself?" he repeated, raising a brow.

Saying "post office" sounded benign enough, but he knew why I was going and what I might find. Technically, Jordan and I had agreed to go together, but I couldn't sleep without knowing what Thomas had sent me.

"I can stay longer if you need," Baker offered from the car.

Brady looked at me. "Do you mind if I go with you?"

It had been a while since Brady and I were alone. A little company could be nice. "How about you come with me to the PO box, and then I'll head over to Sally's?"

"Deal," he said.

"Thanks, Baker," I called as I walked toward my car.

"You don't want to take my car?" Brady asked.

"No, I'm going to Sally's after."

"What if I drop you there and wait while you're inside?"

I stopped and stared at him. "You'd really sit outside and wait with the other deputy?"

"I was going to be sitting outside your house anyway."

"If you'd told me you were coming, I would've had you come inside."

Ignoring my diversion, he said, "Let me drive you."

"How about I drive and you ride passenger? We can catch up."

"You never stop, do you, Val?"

"Not when it's something this important."

As we drove toward the post office, Brady asked, "Does your team know you're going off on your own to check the evidence Thomas left behind?"

"No. But it was a long day. Two bodies in one day, in two different states. They need the break."

"And you don't?"

"You know I wasn't going to sleep anyway, Brady. He's too close. I can't just switch off."

"And if there's anything I can do to help, I want to. I can't rest if you don't."

"I appreciate that. I'm really looking forward to this being over."

"It would be nice for things to get back to normal, or maybe better than normal," he said with a small smile.

I knew what he was referring to. *Us.* With a silly grin, I said, "I would like that. *A lot.*"

"Good. So, are you doing okay? I mean, you knew Thomas. You worked with him for a long time."

It had been such a whirlwind of a day I'd barely had a moment to process my feelings. "It's tough seeing him taken out like that. To know I'll never speak to him again. He held a special place in my life. But looking at the other victims, the people killed just to send me a message, it's almost worse. Linda Castillo was just trying to make a living, starting over in Red Rose County. The other two were just out for a hike, just trying to live a peaceful life and he murdered them to tell me he's thinking of me. That he wants to play a game. That he's digging into my past. They were completely innocent. Thomas knew what he was getting into."

Brady didn't say anything. The rage inside of me began to surface again. "I'm also really angry. This guy. This one human being is trying to terrorize me and my friends and family. My community. For Pete's sake, he climbed a tree in my backyard and took photos of me while I was having dinner with my girl-friends! It's maddening. I can't sleep. I can't stop until I stop him."

I felt Brady's hand on my shoulder. "I understand, Val. Like I said—anything you need. I'm here."

We pulled into the post office lot and I parked. I turned to look at him. "Thank you. I'm glad you're here."

"Me too. Do you want me to photograph everything?"

"Yeah, photograph while I'm opening it. That'd be a help."

It felt good to have him by my side. Maybe he knew intuitively, I was about to do something I shouldn't do alone. Maybe if Brady had been on my team back when I was in the FBI none of this would have happened. He would've known better than to think I'd sleep when I was so close to finding the Bear. But the fact I'd gone off on my own was nobody's fault but mine and as much as I regretted that decision when he'd captured me, I regretted it ten times more now. It was because of that moment that the Bear decided to play this sick game with me. It set everything in motion, all this death and destruction.

Who was the Bear? How did he become this twisted sociopath? And why me? Why fixate on me? He could've killed me in that barn, but he didn't. He must have been planning this far longer than I thought. The notes. The crime scenes. They weren't random. He was plotting. All building toward something I could feel in my gut was coming.

Brady opened the post office door—left unlocked for those with PO boxes. The automatic lights clicked on. I walked over to Box 6-2-4 and took a breath. Brady snapped a photo.

"Here goes," I whispered.

I turned the key and opened the box. There was a single envelope inside. I pulled on rubber gloves and removed it and walked over to the table near the garbage can.

There was no writing on the outside. It was just a plain white envelope. Brady continued snapping photos, then said, "I'm going to switch to video mode."

I nodded.

Upon opening the flap, I tilted it down. A flash drive and a folded handwritten note slid out.

Val, Three of his aliases. I lost track after the last one. It's him. I'd bet my life on it.

—Thomas.

Below that were three names. As I read, my body stiffened and I let out a gasp.

TWENTY-FOUR

HIM

What were they doing at the post office? It was nearly ten o'clock at night. The streets were silent, wrapped in darkness. A weak breeze stirred the trees, and the occasional buzz of a flickering streetlamp was the only sound for blocks.

I parked my vehicle a little way down the street and killed the lights. I stepped out slowly, shutting the door without a sound. The cool night air kissed my skin. It was quiet. *Perfect.* I crept along the sidewalk, sticking to the shadows, moving like a shadow myself. Then I peered through the glass. And there she was. *Valerie.*

It had been too long since I'd been this close to her. I watched her with a hunger I'd nearly forgotten I possessed. She was a beautiful specimen. She was strong, tenacious, and still standing after everything I'd put her through. And yet she looked tired. *Worn.* There were dark circles under her eyes, her skin pale under the humming fluorescent lights. I knew her better than anyone. Knew what haunted her. Knew what it would take to break her completely.

And *him.* Of course he was there. *Brady.* He was always there, hovering. He probably thought of himself as her protector. The loyal dog by her side. Maybe he thought he was keeping the big bad wolf away.

What a fool. That's not how this works. I didn't need to snatch her from the shadows. I didn't need to pounce. No, I enjoyed the long game and I'd already spun the web. She would come to me. That was the beauty of it. She wouldn't even realize it until it was too late. She belonged to me. Curiosity took over my thoughts, as Valerie's expression changed.

What's this now? She looked excited. Too excited. Her face lit up as she pulled out her phone and began talking quickly to Brady, her movements sharp and commanding.

What was it?

She'd found something. It was written all over her face. Whatever it was, was significant. My pulse ticked loudly in my ears. I didn't like surprises, especially not ones I had no control over.

She had something in her hand. An envelope. A small item... A key, maybe? No. It was hard to determine from this distance. Maybe a flash drive? A piece of paper? I shifted slightly for a better angle, my heart thudding now—not from fear, but fury. Unease clawed at the back of my throat. Could it be? Had Thomas left something behind?

No. No, he couldn't have. I had been thorough. I'd taken everything. His boards, his files, his box of notes, his pathetic little shrine to me. I'd dismantled his retirement project.

But what if... What if the old bastard had seen me coming? What if, in a final flash of insight, he'd mailed something and sent it to a PO box for Valerie to find? If he'd given her anything tied to me, that meant he'd been closer than I thought and I'd underestimated him. That also meant this wasn't going to plan and I really hated when things didn't go to plan.

The night suddenly felt colder. I clenched my fists, watching her hold that envelope like it was a key to salvation.

Maybe it was. And maybe that key unlocked something I didn't want anyone to find.

My timeline was tight. I was in control. Everything had been precisely calibrated—her descent into fear, the notes, the triggers, the pacing. And now this?

No, no, no. This wouldn't do. I had to revise the game. The timeline.

She wasn't supposed to be this far along. She wasn't supposed to find anything. But if she had—if she had even a shred of the information Thomas Ingram had uncovered, I'd have to act quickly.

I wouldn't lose her. I couldn't. I'd waited too long and had been so patient. I'd prepared for this moment. And it was here, sooner than expected. *Fine. So be it. But I would have her again.*

I shifted back, slipping into the dark, and circled the corner. My car waited like a silent beast, and I slid inside, keeping the lights off until I was well out of sight. Then I turned the headlights on and drove, heading back toward my home. I had to recalculate and shift the timeline. *It was going to be a long night.*

TWENTY-FIVE

VAL

"What is it? What does it say, Val?"

I showed the note to Brady. He read it slowly, brow furrowed. Then he looked up, his eyes wide. "This is great. He's narrowed down the suspect, the Bear, to three different people. That's incredible."

I shook my head, heart racing. "No, that's not it, Brady. It's... it's bigger than that. Don't you see? The three names—Daniel Stone, Derek Simmons, Dean Saunders. Don't you get it?"

He looked confused.

"The Bear's initials are D.S.," I said, voice trembling. "All three initials match."

Brady's expression shifted from confusion to something darker. "We should go to the station and have Lucy meet us there. We can research all three of these names and find out what's on that flash drive."

"Yes. I agree." I hesitated. He still didn't see it. "But there's something else."

He looked at me, expectantly.

"The guy Sally's dating, his name is Dominic Savage. His initials are D.S."

Brady blinked, processing the information.

"He's a hiking guide," I continued, my breath coming faster now. "An expert hiker who knows the woods inside and out. He showed up in Red Rose County six months ago, right after I returned. It has to be him, Brady. It *has* to be."

Even under the harsh fluorescent lights, I saw the color drain from Brady's face.

"You really think so?"

"It totally fits. Sally said he grew up in Washington State. What were we talking about just today? That whoever the Bear is, he must've grown up in terrain like Red Rose County—forests, trails, hills. The kind of place where someone could climb a tree and take photos of my backyard without anyone noticing." I was pacing now, unable to stand still. "And I didn't tell you earlier," I continued, "but Sally said something tonight, something that's been eating away at me. She said she had a weird feeling about Dominic. She couldn't explain it exactly, but there were some offhand comments he'd made that unnerved her. She'd tried to laugh it off like she was being paranoid because of all the killings, but I think it's more than that." I paused and shook my head. "It's her intuition, Brady. And she said he has bright blue eyes." I looked up at Brady, body trembling. "So does the Bear." My stomach twisted. "God, I can't believe I didn't see it. I was suspicious, but I didn't see it. I should've insisted on meeting him. But he just, he popped out of nowhere. Bright blue eyes. Hiking guide. Getting close to Sally... to get to me. That's how he knew about the backyard party."

Brady stepped forward, calm but serious. "Okay. You're right. We need to check on Sally. We need to call Lucy. We need to dig into all three of these names. And into Dominic Savage." He paused. "It might not even be his real name."

"Exactly," I said. "It's not uncommon for criminals to change names but keep the same initials. Like in witness protection. It's a continuity thing, easier to remember. Maybe his name is Dominic, but with a different last name. We need to know everything about those three names Thomas gave us, and everything about Dominic Savage." I grabbed the envelope and the contents from the counter, shoving them into my bag. "I don't care what the initial report said. No red flags? No criminal history? That could be because Dominic Savage is a fictional person. He could've stolen someone's identity. We don't know who this guy really is."

Brady nodded. "Okay. Let's stay calm and think this through. Let's check on Sally, then get to the station and call everyone in. This is important, Val. This is big."

"Sleep be damned," I muttered. "I'll call Kieran and Jordan on the way. Can you drive my car?"

Brady took the keys. "Yeah."

I looked at Brady, my voice barely a whisper. "Oh my... what if he's already gotten to her?" I didn't wait for an answer. "Come on," I said, breaking into a run. "Let's go."

TWENTY-SIX

VAL

On the way to Sally's, I called Jordan.

"Hey, Val. Couldn't sleep?"

"No, I couldn't. Look, I'm sorry, I went to the PO box. And we found something."

I explained to him what I'd discovered, the note, the flash drive, and my growing suspicion about Dominic Savage. That we were headed to her house immediately. I had to make sure she was okay. If she wasn't...

I couldn't even think that way. The idea that he'd gone after someone close to me, right under my nose, it drove me insane. How could I have missed it?

Jordan said, "All right. I'll notify Kieran and the team. We'll get everyone down at the station. It'll be all hands on deck. I'll pick up coffee and snacks on the way."

"I'm going to call Lucy. She's our researcher."

"We've got our team too."

"Yeah, but she works for the sheriff. She's already tapped in. We need maps of the county, especially for the homes hidden in the hills. The ones that aren't obvious. We need to check

Dominic Savage's address and find out everything we can about him. I just hope we're not too late."

"We're going to get him. Don't worry."

"Thanks, Jordan. I'll see you soon."

As soon as I ended the call with Jordan, I called Sally. My heart raced as the phone rang and rang until I her voicemail kicked in. I didn't like that one bit. I glanced at Brady, who was driving fast but cautiously, well above the speed limit, but it was warranted. "I just tried Sally. No answer." If anything had happened to her, I didn't think I could ever forgive myself.

Brady gave me a quick look. "We'll be there in seconds."

After what seemed like minutes, we pulled up in front of her house.

Brady said, "I'll talk to patrol, ask if they've seen anything out of the ordinary."

I nodded and ran to the front door, pounding on it. As I stood there, heart racing, practically in tears, fearing the worst, I tried to calm myself. There was no answer so I knocked again.

Footsteps sounded, quick and heavy and then a brief hesitation before the door opened.

Sally stood there, confused but unharmed.

"You're okay," I breathed, relief flooding me.

"Of course I'm okay. What's going on?"

"Are you alone?"

"Yes... Why? Come in."

My body still shaking, I said, "You didn't answer when I called."

"Sorry. I was just in the bathroom."

My body relaxed. I waved Brady over.

"Brady's here too. There's been a development," I said as we stepped inside.

We explained what we'd found and our growing concern about Dominic Savage. Sally locked the door behind her, her expression tense.

"Do you think he could actually be the Bear?"

I nodded. "Tell me about him. How tall is he? What does he weigh? You said he has blue eyes and he's a hiking guide, and that he grew up in Washington?"

"Yes, all of that's true," she said. "He's about six-two, lean, sandy hair. Grew up in Washington. Said his family were different. Off-the-grid types. I'm not sure how much schooling he had. He said they let him run free as a kid. He said he could hunt and fish before he could even read."

I nodded. "Does he have siblings? Are his parents still alive?"

"He's talked about his parents. I think he has a sister. You really think he could be the Bear? I mean, yeah, he gave me a weird vibe earlier, but... the body was found today. He was at my house for dinner. Could he really have killed someone and then come over like nothing had happened?"

With someone like him, anything was possible. If the body had been dead for 12 to 24 hours, he could've easily cleaned up and shown up for dinner.

"We're doing a full background check tonight on him and three other names. It's possible he's not the one, but I've got a bad feeling about him," I said. "Sally, I think we should move you."

"Move me? Move me where?"

Brady stepped in. "We could put you in a safe house." He turned to me. "Does the FBI have one here in Red Rose County?"

"Not an official one," I said, "but we can find somewhere he doesn't know about."

Sally said, "Like where? I mean, there's already patrol outside. I've got a security system. I know I freaked out earlier, but I don't think he'd hurt me."

"But you don't really know him, do you? When did you meet?"

"About two weeks ago."

"Exactly. Everything he told you could be a lie."

With a frown, she said, "You're right. I just don't know if I'd feel comfortable staying somewhere else. It might freak me out more. Can't we just add more security?"

"I don't know," I said, and thought that the Bear probably didn't know we'd got the tip or that we were starting to connect the dots. If he was watching, he might notice if we suddenly moved Sally and he could disappear and we'd lose him forever.

Despite the worry that crept across her face, Sally said, "I have a deputy outside. I've got a security system. I think I'll be okay."

"You could stay at my house," I offered.

"Are you going to be there?"

"No. I'm going to the office. This is a no-sleep situation. We've got to catch him. Do you know where he lives?"

Sally said, "I've never been to his house."

Brady said, "But they have his address, that was part of the initial background check when they first went hiking together."

"Okay. Let me call Jordan," I said, stepping away to make the call.

He answered immediately. I explained my concerns and Jordan said, "If he took everything from Thomas Ingram's cabin, he probably thinks there's nothing left. She's probably safe for tonight. Let's put our heads together, learn everything we can. No breaks until we figure this out. Then we hit him in the morning, in daylight. No call. No warning. We just show up at his house."

"But we don't have probable cause. All we have is that his initials match, and that a retired FBI agent doing an off-the-books investigation suspected someone with the same initials. We need to check that flash drive. We need real evidence."

"You're right," he said. "And if we move Sally, it might tip him off."

Exactly what I was thinking. "But if we don't..."

"It's a tough call," he said. "But I think we're better off keeping things as normal as possible. We'll add more security to her house."

"Okay."

I ended the call and returned to Sally. "Jordan's adding extra security outside. No one will get to you."

"Thank you. Honestly, I feel safer here than I would somewhere unfamiliar."

"Good," I said. "Plus, if we move you, we might tip him off that we're onto him."

Brady nodded. "It's a good point."

Sally added, "And if for some reason he does come for me, I'd rather you catch him in the act and stop him from doing this to anyone else. Plus, I can take care of myself."

I had thought that too until he'd captured me. "Are you sure you're okay?"

"Don't worry about me. Whether it's him or someone else, you need to find him, Val. You need to put a stop to this."

"You're right," I said. "I'll see you at work in the morning."

"Bright and early."

Brady and I said our goodbyes and drove to the station. We had work to do. We needed to learn everything we could about Dominic Savage and about the three other names on that list. The answers could be on that flash drive. And, I feared, we were running out of time.

TWENTY-SEVEN

VAL

Clutching a cup of coffee, I stood with the team in silence as the projector flickered to life. Lucy sat at the head of the table, the encrypted laptop ready. She held the flash drive in her hand, Thomas Ingram's final message to us, and then slipped it into the port.

Everyone in the room had already been debriefed on the last twenty-four hours. What I'd found in the PO box, the disturbing files, and my growing suspicion that Dominic Savage, if that was even his real name, was the Bear.

From Thomas' notes, it was clear he had identified at least three aliases for the Bear. Not including Dominic. But I couldn't work out how he had found those names. How had he connected the dots? I was hoping the flash drive would give us the answers we were looking for.

The screen blinked. A single folder appeared. "We're in," Lucy said. "No password."

That made sense. This wasn't a trap. It was a gift to me, to the Bureau, and to anyone still hunting the Bear. She clicked open the root folder. A tree of subfolders expanded across the screen, each neatly categorized and numbered:

- DNA Profiles—Field Samples—Private Lab Results
- Alias Analysis
- DMV Record Comparisons—Visual Overlap
- Employment Histories by Region
- Unsolved Case Correlation Charts
- Timeline Reconstruction
- Phase IV—Current Region (Likely: Red Rose County)

Nobody said a word.

My heart pounding, I said, "Let's start with the DNA." It was what had intrigued me the most. We hadn't collected usable DNA from any of the Bear's crime scenes, so how had Thomas?

Lucy opened the first folder. Two reports appeared, each from separate private forensic labs. Their file names were simple and precise:

- Field Sample A—2010—Washington—Delaney crime scene—men's sock found at scene
- Field Sample B—2012—Oregon—Cornell crime scene—rope fragment found at scene

I recognized the victim's names. "These were from the earliest confirmed kills," I said. "Before the task force was formed. Back when law enforcement thought these were isolated cases."

Jordan said, "How on earth did Thomas get access to these?"

"Is it possible he requested the samples from the Oregon and Washington crime labs before he retired? And then paid to have them tested at private labs?"

Kieran nodded slowly. "It's possible. We'll need to follow up. But let's see what else he found."

Why had he kept it a secret until now? And why hadn't the FBI requested it before? They weren't the type of samples one would expect to contain a suspect's DNA, but we should have looked. We should have tested everything. "This is huge. Why didn't he share the information with the FBI? He could've saved lives."

"Maybe he was trying to be the hero," Jordan said. "Solve the case the Bureau couldn't."

"One last big case," I murmured, before refocusing. "Let's keep going. If needed, we can go back and try to do genetic genealogy or see if we can build a profile based on his genetic material."

Lucy nodded, clicked out of the folder and into the next: Alias Analysis.

It was a massive spreadsheet—color-coded, precisely structured, and dense enough to make my eyes ache. I immediately recognized the formatting. It was exactly how Thomas used to build his profile boards back at the Bureau.

- D.S.—?—Washington (Before 2012)
- Daniel Stone—Forestry contractor—Oregon (2012–2016)
- Derek Simmons—Wilderness guide—Idaho (2016–2020)
- Dean Saunders—Survival instructor—Nevada (2020–2024)
- D.S.—?—California (2024–present)

Each alias came with employment history, job site addresses, timecards, tax filings, and social security numbers. "He must've dug through thousands of public records," I said, marveling at the results. "Employment registries, county clerk filings, public records..."

Lucy nodded. "It would've taken months to cross-reference all this. These D.S. identities appear pretty flimsy. Designed to last just long enough."

"To kill four people," I said quietly, "and then move on."

"Exactly," Lucy said.

"Let's go to the DMV comparison folder," I said.

Lucy opened the next folder: DMV Record Comparisons—Visual Overlap.

A row of images filled the screen. DMV photo IDs. Hunting permit headshots. Job application photos. Different lighting. Different haircuts. Beards, no beards. Some photos aged several years apart. *The eyes.* I knew those eyes. I pointed at the screen. "It's him. He shifted his part, grew facial hair, and his weight fluctuated, but the eyes are the same."

"And the same scar above the right eyebrow," Lucy said. "Thomas even labeled each image with match confidence. Ninety-four to ninety-seven percent. Manually verified—T. Ingram."

"He built his own facial recognition model?" Jordan said, stunned.

Lucy nodded. "He annotated ear structure, jaw angles, eye spacing, everything. Pixel by pixel."

"It's incredible," I said, gazing at the screen in awe. "Let's look at the timeline reconstruction next."

Lucy opened the next folder. The killings were mapped year by year, state by state.

- Washington—2010 to 2012—4 kills
- Oregon—2012 to 2016—4 kills
- Idaho—2016 to 2020—4 kills
- Nevada—2020 to 2024—3 kills (Val captured)
- California (Red Rose County)—Present

"What we don't have," I said, "are confirmed names for Washington—his first kills—and California, where he is now."

"If we assume Dominic Savage is his current alias," Jordan said, "then the only mystery left is the name used in Washington. It's probably his true identity."

"Which tracks," I said. "Dominic told Sally he grew up in Washington. That would make it his origin point. Every other name? Just an alias. He moves into a state, creates a new identity, blends into the wilderness industry, and kills."

"But didn't Sally say he told her he'd worked at a lab?" Lucy asked.

I said, "He was probably lying. He likely studied forensics online, along with other serial killers or by watching Dateline. The information is out there if you know where to look."

"Or maybe Dominic isn't him," Brady countered. "We still don't have definitive proof."

"The sheriff's department looked him up already. We can pull up Dominic's DMV photo."

Lucy said, "We sure can!"

Lucy tapped away while the rest of us remained silent. We were moments away from knowing if Sally's boyfriend was the serial killer we were looking for.

Lucy said, "Here it is."

I gasped, my heart pounding so hard it drowned out everything else. "It's him! We need to pick him up now!"

Jordan shook his head. "We can't. We have no probable cause."

"We have DNA. We have records. We have him in the vicinity of all the kills."

Kieran said, "It's all circumstantial. The DNA isn't actually tied to the D.S. identities. Not to mention the fact that all this information from Thomas was likely obtained illegally. If we picked him up he could walk on a technicality. Too risky. We can try and get all this legally—starting with the DNA. That would likely be the fastest way to nail him, assuming we can get a sample. We need to be smart about this. When we get him, we need to make sure he never gets away."

"I think we can get his DNA..." I said, with more confidence than I felt.

"What are you thinking?" Kieran asked.

"Maybe he left something at Sally's house. He was over at her place earlier for dinner. It's possible she has a dirty fork or glass he used. Or maybe she could invite him over again. She'll be in the office in a few hours, we can ask her."

"That could be dangerous," Lucy said, her voice low.

"We could have teams set up. We could wire Sally. We'll monitor the entire situation."

Jordan said, "That could work, but let's work through everything Thomas found first, put together a plan to corroborate it, legally, and come up with a solid plan to arrest him."

We were so close I could feel it. "Agreed."

After hours of going through data, multiple coffees, bags of fast food, and pages of notes, Lucy opened the final file.

A simple note, typed by Thomas.

The pattern is real. The identities are false. The face is constant. I don't have the current name he's using, but I know what he looks like. And now so do you. Be careful. I think he knows I found him.

A chill crept over me.

"He's right," I said. "Somehow, the Bear knew Thomas was closing in. That's why he killed him. That's why he took all his files."

"He probably doesn't know about the flash drive," Kieran said quietly. "And that is how we're going to catch him."

I said, "And now it's up to us to finish what Thomas started."

Despite the fact that it was nearing 6 a.m., my adrenaline hadn't dropped an inch. We were close. Closer than we'd ever been. I believed this nightmare would end soon, and that he'd never see us coming.

TWENTY-EIGHT

VAL

The war room smelled like burned coffee, adrenaline, and exhaustion. We'd worked through the night, with no breaks or sleep for anyone. Notes littered the table. Maps were tacked to the walls. People were making calls, requesting records, and coordinating surveillance. Screens glowed with DMV photos, timelines, and employment histories. All of it pointed to one terrifying truth: Dominic Savage, Sally's new boyfriend, was almost certainly the Bear.

The serial killer who had held me captive and the man responsible for nineteen murders, including Thomas Ingram, who, after death, had handed us the key to catching him. Thanks to Thomas' flash drive, we now had a plan.

All we needed was Sally's help to get Dominic's DNA. The Feds were confident it would be enough to make an arrest because if the samples from Oregon and Washington matched, we could tie him to those early murders. That should be sufficient to hold him while we built the rest of the case.

It was all mapped out, we just needed Sally's agreement. The plan was for Sally to invite Dominic over for dinner. She'd act causal and apologize for acting funny the night before by blaming the stress from the killings in Red Rose County. She would offer him a drink, make sure she secured the glass, and then we would swoop in and collect his DNA.

We would have teams surrounding the house. She'd wear a wire. Her surveillance cameras would be monitored in real time. If something went wrong, we'd be on her in seconds. Her backyard backed into the woods, leading to a trail and a small parking lot. We would have eyes there, too. There'd be nowhere for him to run.

Every inch of Sally's home had been mapped out over the last six hours. I couldn't even describe what I was feeling, mostly hope, anxiety, and overwhelming relief that the end might finally be in sight. I quietly thanked Thomas as I sat at the edge of the table. *We were so close.*

Kieran went over the final details one last time. "Are we sure she'll be okay with the plan?"

I nodded. "She wants him caught and I'm sure will help in any way she can. She's tough, and determined. She can pull it off." It was our best bet.

Kieran checked his watch. "What time is she supposed to be in?"

"She's usually in by eight," I said. I glanced at the clock on the wall. "It's 8:07."

Lucy said, "Should we go over to the ME's building and talk to her?"

"Or we could just call," Jordan said.

"What if he's monitoring her phone?" Lucy said. "Anything's possible. If he's this careful and methodical, he might be tracking her."

"Lucy and I can go," I said. "We're friends with Sally. It'll be easier to hear coming from us."

Jordan and Kieran exchanged a look, then nodded.

As Lucy and I headed down the hall, she whispered, "This is all so crazy, Val. I'm so glad it's almost over. This is why I left

New York. The constant body count... the sadness... I wanted peace."

"I know. I thought coming back to Red Rose County would be boring."

Lucy smirked. "Guess that's what we get for living in a town with an ex-FBI agent."

"I resent that."

She laughed. "I'm teasing. I'm glad you're here. We're going to catch him and make sure he never hurts you, me, or anyone else again. That's what we do, right?"

"Right. And Sally's part of that. She wants him stopped as much as we do."

When we arrived at her office, something was off. The lights were out. "Maybe she's just running late," Lucy said. "Remember when she showed up late to the Castillo scene because Dominic was over?"

The thought made me recoil. She'd slept with him. A serial killer. And if he had come over again last night...

"She would've told us if he was coming over," I said, trying to steady my voice.

"Right," Lucy agreed. "Maybe she just overslept."

But as I stared at the dark, cramped little office, I knew she hadn't overslept. "I don't like this," I said. "She wouldn't be late. Not today."

"Let's not panic. Not yet," Lucy said. "We'll call her. Keep it casual. Just ask if she wants to grab a coffee. If he's monitoring her phone, we don't want to tip him off."

"Good idea."

I pulled out my phone and dialed Sally's number. It rang and rang—then went to voicemail. I tried again. Same result. "She's not answering," I whispered.

"I'll try," Lucy said. She dialed. Once. Twice. The third time, she hung up and looked at me, her face pale.

"We have to tell the team."

We jogged back to the conference room.

"She's not answering," I said. "We've both called her five times."

Brady stood. "I'll call the patrol unit at her house. If anything had happened, they would've seen it."

Brady pulled out his phone and spoke with the deputy. "You're outside Sally's home? Everything's been quiet? No movement?" He nodded. "Her car's in the driveway? Okay, do me a favor—knock on the door."

We waited in silence, for what felt like an eternity.

Brady hung up and turned to us. "She's not answering."

Jordan said, "Maybe she's in the shower."

"I don't like this. I'm going to her house."

"I'll drive," Lucy said.

"You're not an officer," Brady protested.

Lucy said, "No, but I'm one of her best friends and I'm hoping that this is just a big misunderstanding, and when she opens the door confused, we'll all laugh about how we got excited over nothing. I want to be the first to give her a hug." Despite her positivity, I could tell Lucy was as frightened as I was.

"You can come with me, but I'm driving," I said.

With a nod, we rushed out of the station.

TWENTY-NINE
VAL

We drove in silence, each of us lost in private bargaining with the universe. *Please let her be okay. Please.* Outside, the sun was bright and the streets were quiet. Thoughts of everything we'd learned in the last few hours played in my mind, and the fear of being too late crept in. Shaking it off, I pulled up in front of her house. The patrol car was parked across the street, exactly where it should've been.

Everything looked normal. That's what made it worse.

Parked, I jumped out of the car and marched toward the cruiser. The deputy inside looked up as I approached, and he rolled down the window.

"Anything happen since Brady called?" I asked.

He shook his head. "Nothing. Lights went out around eleven. No one's come or gone since."

"She didn't leave this morning?" Lucy asked from behind me, her arms crossed over her chest like she was bracing herself for impact.

"No, ma'am," the deputy said. "Her car is still in the driveway."

I turned and sprinted to Sally's front door, the soles of my boots slapping hard against the pavement. I banged on the door with the side of my fist. "Sally! It's Val! Open up!"

Nothing.

I hit it again, harder this time. "Sally! If you can hear me, say something!"

Still no answer.

Lucy moved up beside me, her skin gray under the early morning light. Her voice was thin. "We're wasting time."

"I'll check the perimeter," I said, already running around the side of the house.

The grass was damp underfoot. I peered into the windows —each one covered, every blind drawn. No movement. No sound.

When I reached the backyard, I skidded to a stop and peered over the fence. I scanned the yard. All looked normal except for the sliding glass door which was open as far as it would go. Enough space for someone to go in and out with no resistance. My stomach plummeted.

Lucy said, "What do you see?"

I explained and then the two of us ran back around to the front of the house. To Brady and the others, I said, "The back slider, it's open. We have to get inside. She could be hurt."

Brady didn't hesitate. "Back up."

He moved past me, raised one leg, and with a single hard kick, the front door cracked open and slammed against the inside wall.

We entered, guns drawn, moving fast.

The air inside was stale, undisturbed. No music, no television, no murmuring signs of life.

The house was still. *Too still.*

The living room looked almost staged. A wine glass sat on the coffee table, half full. Sally's cream sweater was draped over the arm of the couch.

"Sally!" I called out, my voice echoing slightly in the silence. "Are you here?"

No answer. I moved down the hallway as the others spread out behind me. We checked the bathroom. Empty. The guest room. Nothing. Then the bedroom.

The covers were tangled. The pillow slightly indented. She'd been there, but now she wasn't. He must have taken her. My mind shifted to the image of a bloodied and chained Sally. I shuddered at the thought. If he had taken her, he would keep her until whatever he was planning next. Sally might have a day or an hour or a few days. If anything happened to her, it would be my fault. I should've never let her stay home alone. I should have insisted she come in with us.

"He took Sally. He came in through the slider," I said, swallowing hard. "Probably injected her with ketamine—just like with Linda Castillo—and then carried her out the back."

Brady cursed. "And we know from the sting we had planned, there was a trail just behind Sally's house that leads to a small parking lot. If he parked there and came in the back, the patrol car wouldn't have seen a thing."

I clenched my jaw, fury rising in my chest. "We should've been more careful. Why did he take her now? Did he know about the flash drive? Or was this always part of the plan?"

Jordan's voice was flat. "We'll check the trail's parking lot. Look for anything—tire marks, footprints, trash—anything he may have left behind."

I nodded, then turned to Lucy.

She stood frozen in the entryway, her hand pressed to her mouth, eyes rimmed red and brimming with tears.

"He got her," she whispered. "Val, we can't lose Sally."

I stepped forward and pulled her into a hug, holding her tight. "We're not going to lose her. We're going to bring her home."

I pulled back and looked her in the eye. "Can you access her security system? Break into the software if you have to?"

She wiped at her eyes and nodded. "Yes. I can do it."

"Then we do it now. We pull footage. Figure out how he got in, when, how long he was here. We follow that electronic trail while Kieran and Jordan follow the others."

Lucy nodded again, this time with fire in her expression. "We can't lose her."

"We won't," I said. But even as the words left my mouth, the pit in my stomach grew deeper. I knew there would be another message from the Bear. The Bear's messages always came with bodies. We had to find Sally before it was too late.

THIRTY

SALLY

Something was wrong. That was my first thought as I drifted toward consciousness. I was thick-headed, heavy-limbed, and dry-mouthed. My body felt like it had been dropped into molasses. My arms ached and my legs tingled.

I tried to move. Metal clinked. My right wrist was shackled. My ankles too. A short chain clattered softly against the wood behind me as I shifted. Panic flared. Where was I? I forced my eyes open. *Darkness.*

The air was damp. It smelled of stale wood, mildew, and rust. I swallowed hard, trying not to gag.

I reached out with my free hand and found rough wood walls on either side. The last thing I remembered before that moment was going to bed. I'd brushed my teeth. Locked the doors. Maybe I'd lit a candle? No, I'd blown it out. I'd turned off the light. I was texting Val, joking about how tired I was.

There'd been no sound. No footsteps. No break-in. I would've heard something. Wouldn't I?

Had I been drugged? My stomach turned. Had he been in the house with me while I'd been sleeping? Had he been watching? How did he even get in? The doors were locked. The alarm was on. Patrol had been outside. How did no one notice?

I shifted again, testing the limits of the chains. They rattled loudly now, echoing in the confined space. The more I moved, the more real it became.

This wasn't a nightmare. I was chained in a dark room that had a faint draft whisper down from somewhere above. There were no windows that I could see. And then came the sound.

A low, mechanical click. The whir of a switch, and then there was light. A single bulb above me flickered to life, casting a yellowish glow over the room. I blinked hard, my eyes watering. The room looked even smaller in the light. There was no furniture. The walls were made of wood where the thick metal rings anchored my chains. On the floor next to me was a tray with a plastic water bottle and granola bar set on top. I stared at it for a long moment. The items hadn't been thrown in. They'd been placed there. Arranged.

My stomach dropped. I looked at the walls again. No clock. No sounds from outside. Nothing that gave away where I was. Was this Dominic?

I tried to picture his face. His voice. The way he smiled. The way he touched the small of my back. It couldn't be him. Could it?

He was charming. He was normal. He brought wine. He had a sister. He kissed me goodnight.

He made me feel safe. Until he didn't. Or maybe that was the point.

I didn't hear the door open. I heard his voice. "Hello, Sally."

I turned so fast it made my head spin.

He was standing just inside the room. *Dominic.*

He was calm in a way that made my skin crawl. He wore a dark jacket and hiking boots. His hair was slicked back, his face freshly shaved. He looked like he was about to sit down for a casual coffee, not face the woman he'd kidnapped.

"Why?" I croaked.

He tilted his head ever so slightly. "You'll understand soon enough."

My heart pounded so loud I could barely hear him. "What do you want?"

"I just want time," he said. "Time to talk. To explain. You deserve that much."

"People will be looking for me," I said, my voice stronger now. "They'll find you."

He smiled softly. "I know they're looking. They always look. But no one ever finds me."

He stepped closer, just enough for the light to catch the scar above his right eyebrow. I hadn't noticed it before. It was barely noticeable even now.

"I trusted you."

His expression didn't change. "I didn't lie to you."

I stared at him, willing my voice not to shake. "You drugged me. You chained me to a wall. Do you call this honesty?"

"I call this necessary. Be sure to hydrate and have a snack. You'll need your strength."

Then he turned, stepping back into the shadows. The door closed behind him with a soft click.

And I was alone in the nightmare.

THIRTY-ONE
VAL

After doing another full sweep of Sally's house and following the trail to the empty parking lot, Lucy and I made our way back to the station so we could try to access Sally's surveillance system. We hadn't spoken for several minutes when Lucy finally broke the silence.

"I think she's still alive. She'll be okay, Val."

"I know. We just have to find her."

"And we could be wrong. He might not have taken her. Maybe she went on a hike and didn't want to bring her keys. Or maybe I'm just grasping at straws."

"Anything is possible. We don't have any evidence, just that Sally wasn't in her bed and she's not answering her phone. Come to think of it," I glanced over at Lucy, "we didn't find her phone inside her house."

Lucy's eyes widened. "You're right. Oh my gosh. We can find her!"

"We need to get to the station, see if we can pull her records. Get a location."

"Let's hope the cell phone company doesn't give us any grief."

"She's a missing person, and they'll be getting a call from the FBI." A burst of hope surged through me. If we could get a warrant for her phone records, we could track the last tower it pinged. Maybe she *was* on a hike. *Highly unlikely.* Most likely, he'd taken her. But maybe she had her phone on her, or he'd taken it with him. If that were true, he knew better than to keep it on. But maybe, just maybe, he'd forgotten to turn it off or she had it hidden on her and he didn't know about it.

We arrived at the station and rushed inside, heading straight for the war room. A few people were milling about, already updated on the situation.

Lucy spoke quickly. "We just realized Sally's cell phone wasn't in her house. We need to find out where it is."

Troy, one of the FBI analysts, turned toward us. "I'll call it in. Do you have her phone number?"

Lucy dashed over and gave it to him.

"I'll get right on it," he said.

Lucy hurried back over and pulled out her laptop. "I'll get into the surveillance footage."

I sat beside her silently as she began typing. She smirked. "The system's not very secure, Val. I'm in already."

She sounded confident, but she was still pale. Her lips pressed into a tight line, her jaw clenched. She was worried and so was I. I couldn't let him hurt Sally. She was our best friend.

"Okay, how far should I go back? Where should I start?"

"Brady and I left her house around 10:30 p.m. Maybe start there."

She nodded, and pressed play. We sat quietly as we saw nothing of note. The front yard was quiet. The porch light glowed.

"Switch to the back cameras," I said. "Chances are, he came in that way. I think he wants us to know he took her."

She nodded and fast-forwarded to 2 a.m. There it was at 2:03 a.m.

A dark figure emerged from the woods behind Sally's house, barely visible on the edge of the camera's reach. He was wearing a hood and gloves. He moved confidently, fluid, no panic, and no hesitation. He was skilled at breaking into people's homes. When the intruder reached her back fence, he extended his hand over, unlatched the lock, and pushed the gate open. We watched as he pulled out a lock-pick set and slid open the back door.

"Why didn't the alarm sound?"

Lucy shrugged. "I don't know. Maybe he cut it earlier. Or she doesn't have a loud alarm, or it's set to a low level or it's off."

"But would Sally turn down the sound on the alarm?"

"Most security systems have options for different sound levels. Maybe he changed hers when he was at her house for dinner."

True. We watched, heart pounding, waiting for any sign of Sally.

Exactly four minutes later, he emerged, with Sally flung over his shoulder like a rag doll. He exited the same way he'd come in, closing the gate behind him, but not the slider.

He wanted me to know he'd taken her.

"He knew exactly what he was doing," Lucy whispered.

My stomach dropped. Lucy's hand flew to her mouth, her eyes welling with tears—but she didn't stop. She clicked to the backyard feed, watching the Bear glide back into the shadows, taking our friend with him.

Disappearing into the woods. 2:07 a.m.

Lucy and I sat back, stunned.

"How long had he planned this?" I thought aloud.

"No idea," she said.

I shook my head. "If he parked in the lot in the back, there wouldn't be any cameras. But the closest gas station might have surveillance. It could tell us which direction he went. Can you pull it up?"

"They won't like me hacking into their system, but if we run over to the gas station they'll probably let us take a look."

I turned to Troy. "Did you get a location on her cell yet?"

"Not yet."

"Lucy and I are heading to the gas station closest to Sally's house to see if they caught any vehicles around 2:07 a.m., when we think he left with her."

As we got up to leave, Kieran and Jordan walked in.

"Where are you two going?" Kieran asked.

"Gas station," we replied.

Twenty minutes later, we were back in the conference room updating the team.

Disappointed, I reported, "The gas station didn't catch anybody between 2:05 and 2:20 a.m. He didn't go west."

"That's not nothing," Kieran said. "That means he drove east. That narrows it down a little."

I nodded. "He knew which direction was safest. He knew where not to be seen. He planned every last detail."

Lucy's voice cracked. "He took her right out from under us, Val. She was supposed to be safe... but she wasn't, was she?"

I reached out and placed a hand on her shoulder. "We're going to get her back."

Kieran stepped forward. "We need to move fast. We can find him and Sally."

"What about her cell phone?" I called over to Troy.

"Still working on it," he said. "But we should have it any minute. They're usually pretty speedy in a missing person case."

"Okay," I said. "Do you have a plan, Kieran?"

"Lucy, can you pull up the topographical maps? Cabins, outbuildings and anything east of Sally's house," Kieran said.

I said, "Didn't you pull those earlier?"

"I did," she said, already typing.

I said, "Let's start with a ten-mile radius. We'll expand if we need to." My mind drifted back to the image of Dominic, the Bear, or whatever his real name was, disappearing down the trail with Sally over his shoulder. He'd known we were closing in. But how? Had he been watching me? Had he seen see us at the post office, and then Sally's? Had he been watching the sheriff's station and seen the swarm of Feds return late last night. Had we tipped him off?

"If he has her in a structure, I'll find it." Lucy stopped typing. "Wait. Would he bring her back to his house? We have the address."

I glanced over at Jordan.

He said, "Lucy, you continue mapping out our search. It's not likely he brought her to his house, but we have to check."

To Jordan, I said, "Let's go."

THIRTY-TWO

VAL

Jordan and I pulled up to Dominic Savage's small home about fifteen minutes east of Sally's house, along with backup in two separate vehicles. We were ready for anything.

We had to check his house, but I knew better than to think Dominic would bring her back there. It was too obvious. Too easy. But we couldn't not check.

Jordan and I got out of the SUV. He said, "We'll knock. See if he's home. If he's not, we'll leave."

"Okay, let's go." I walked up to the door and banged three times. Silence. I banged again. "Dominic Savage. FBI. Open up!" *Nothing.*

I glanced at the driveway. There was no car. We knew he had a jeep, but it could have been in the garage.

"I'm gonna take a look around. Maybe I'll be able to see something through the windows."

"All right."

With that, I hurried to the side of the garage and peered through the door's small window. There it was. The jeep. The same one the patrol had run the plates for. Did he have another vehicle? Could he be inside? Maybe he had headphones on or was in the shower and couldn't hear us.

I continued down the side of the house until I came to the fence. I really wanted to hop over and see what I could find, but that would be trespassing. As much as I didn't like it, I agreed with Jordan we couldn't give Dominic any technicality to slip through. Still, I got the sense he wasn't there and nor was Sally. Unless he had built one of those creepy, sound-proofed hostage rooms serial killers tended to be so fond of.

It wouldn't be the first time I'd found out a killer had kept victims in secret rooms, or rather, a bunker, in Red Rose County. Growing up here, I had never imagined there could be so much crime. Was it because I was in law enforcement? No place was truly safe, but Red Rose County was quieter than most. Especially compared to the big cities I had left behind. There were fewer people, and more space. Nature usually brings peace. But peace doesn't preclude violence.

I jogged back toward the front. "The jeep is inside the garage. He must have another vehicle."

"I'll knock again," Jordan said.

I moved to the other side of the house, trying to see through the windows. Nothing interesting to be seen. I circled back and tried to peer over the fence, but it was too high for me to see. I heard footsteps crunch behind me, and I turned to find Jordan.

"Want a leg up?"

As I nodded, he clasped his hands together, and I stepped into his grip. I was lifted up just enough to see over the fence. Native plants, gravel paths, and trees backing up to the forest, like most of the homes in the area. There were no signs of life. "I don't think he's here," I said, dropping back down. "What do we do now?"

"I could call his cell, but maybe you should do it. He'd be more likely to answer if it's you. You're the one he's been chasing."

As much as I hated it, it was true. I pulled out my phone. "Read the number to me."

Jordan read it aloud as I tapped it in and pressed send. It rang three times before I was met with a generic voicemail message. "Hi Dominic. This is Valerie Costa. I'm with the FBI and the sheriff's department. Sally didn't show up for work today. I'm just wondering if you've seen her or heard from her. Please give me a call back on this number. Thanks. Bye."

Jordan watched me, his expression unreadable. "Now we wait."

Just then, my phone buzzed. My heart skipped. Was it Dominic? I checked the screen. It was Lucy. "Hey, Lucy. What's up?"

"We just got Sally's cell phone records. We have her last known location."

THIRTY-THREE

VAL

With my phone pressed to my ear, I hoped for a miracle.

Lucy's voice cracked through. "The last ping was at her house, at 2:06 a.m. to be exact. That was it. After that there is nothing. He either yanked the SIM card, which isn't exactly easy to do with an iPhone, or he dropped it in a Faraday bag. Maybe even wrapped it in foil. Either way, no signal. It's dead."

Dang it. A Faraday bag. I'd seen enough of them over the years. It was sleek, black, and unassuming. From the outside, it looked like any padded tech pouch, but inside, it was something else entirely. Lined with layers of metallic mesh, usually copper or nickel, it blocked everything including cell signals, Wi-Fi, GPS, and Bluetooth. Once a device went in and the bag was sealed, it was like it vanished off the face of the earth. No tracking. No remote access. No last known pings. It was the kind of thing law enforcement used to preserve evidence. The kind of thing a killer used when he didn't want to be found. I stared out at Dominic Savage's quiet little house. Neat lawn. Wind chimes swaying gently. Deceptively peaceful.

Sally's phone was a dead end. "Okay," I said, barely keeping the frustration from my voice. "We didn't find anything here. We'll head back."

Lucy said, "Copy that. See you soon."

I hung up and turned to Jordan. "He killed the phone. We can't track her that way."

Jordan's jaw clenched. "We'll regroup back at the station and put together a search team. We can start combing the woods for them."

I glanced at the time, it was almost 10 a.m. "He took her around 2:07. That's nearly eight hours ago, Jordan. He could be in another state by now. Oregon. Nevada. Heck, he could be halfway to Canada."

"You think he ran?"

"No." I shook my head slowly. "He's not finished with me." What did that mean for Sally?

Jordan looked at me, waiting.

"That's what scares me," I said. "He didn't take her to disappear. He took her to send a message. And if I'm right, we're on a clock."

"You think she's still alive?"

"I have to." I met his eyes. "But I also think he's changing his plan. He saw something last night. Maybe he was following me and saw the activity near Sally's house and at the sheriff's station. He got spooked and took her. Or he wasn't watching me and had planned to take her all along."

"If he did get nervous, he could be unpredictable."

"And that makes him even more dangerous."

We stood in silence, both of us scanning the house again. Maybe we'd missed something. My phone buzzed in my hand again. I looked down, expecting Lucy's name. But it wasn't Lucy. It was a blocked number. A chill slid down my spine.

I exchanged a glance with Jordan, then answered.

"Val Costa."

There was a pause.

Then a deep, controlled voice came through the line. "If you want to see the lovely Dr. Sally Edison alive again, stop looking for me and wait for my instructions."

The line went dead.

THIRTY-FOUR

HIM

I flicked on the light in the little room. The light buzzed, casting a yellow glow over the small, windowless space. "Hello, Sally. How are you? Did you miss me?"

She squinted against the sudden brightness. "How am I? Let me out of here, now!"

"Are you saying that you didn't miss me?" I tilted my head, smiling. "I missed you. Ever since I've gotten to know you, I truly think you're spectacular. And I hate to say this, I hope this doesn't make you feel bad, but if I hadn't met Valerie first, I think you could've been my destiny." I chuckled softly. "I probably shouldn't have said that."

"Let me go."

"Oh, Sally, I think you know I'm not going to do that. Not unless our friend Valerie cooperates. You see, I just spoke with her. And now that she and her friends at the FBI and the sheriff's department are going to run around in circles trying to trace the phone call I made to her, that gives us a little more time together."

I studied Sally's once-creamy complexion. It had dulled since I'd brought her here. She looked hopeful by this information. She thought I might have slipped up. She thought I'd made a mistake by calling Valerie, and that law enforcement would be able to trace the location of the call and find her. And yes, they'd be able to trace where I made the call from, even though I used a burner. But that location wouldn't lead them to Sally.

I was not an idiot and I truly believed Valerie knew that. Of course, not all members of law enforcement were quite as brilliant as my Valerie. Valerie would understand tracking the cell phone wouldn't lead them to me, but she'd do it anyway. She had to, and I counted on it. And she'd realize that I'd wanted to send her to that location, and I believed that when she arrived she'd be relieved to not have found Sally, at least for the moment. Gazing at Sally, I said, "I'm sorry, my dear. I didn't mean to get your hopes up. They aren't going to find you. Not because of the phone call. You must know by now that I'm no fool."

"What are you planning?" Sally asked, her voice low and steady.

Sally had spunk. I had to give her that. She hadn't cried or screamed when she realized she'd been taken and chained to a wall. Nor had she seemed surprised when I'd walked in to check on her. She'd known exactly what had happened. That's what I liked about her so much. And I meant what I said. If I hadn't met Valerie first, Sally and I could have had something really special.

We had had a nice couple of weeks, though. It even made me wonder if I could have had a normal life. *Be normal.* To have had a woman like Sally or Valerie by my side. I mean, it was too late for Valerie and me. But Sally... When I'd met her, she'd captivated me. I didn't know her like I did Valerie, but I was beginning to. I would have liked to learn more. I would like to understand what it would take to break her. She wasn't near that point, that much I could tell. She believed in Valerie. She believed Valerie and all her friends at the FBI would save her.

With a grin, I said, "Don't worry about that. In time, all will be clear."

"So what is all this? You got close to me, just to torture me for your own twisted fantasy? I know monsters like you!" *She was a pistol.*

"No, Sally, my dear. That wasn't my intention. I'm not sure if I should tell you this..."

She sat there, stony-faced. Chained, yet defiant. "Okay, I'll tell you. I wasn't going to because I don't want to hurt your feelings, but I admit that meeting you at the restaurant, casually bumping into you, getting to know you, it was all so I could get to Valerie."

"She won't fall for it!"

"No, Valerie won't fall for anything. She's far too clever."

Sally shook her head as if she couldn't believe this was happening. *Poor Sally.*

I said, "Don't worry. Everything's going to turn out exactly as it should. Soon, I'll have Valerie right here with us. And you love Valerie, don't you?"

"You'll never beat her."

I snorted. "Oh, Sally. Valerie is so lucky to have such a wonderful friend like you. Smart. Determined. Fierce. But I'm afraid everyone has weaknesses. And Valerie... well, she has a few. One, and you can give me your feedback on this, I'd appreciate it, really. But I don't think Valerie will let anything happen to you, if she has a choice. Do you?"

Sally's face grew long. She knew exactly what I was intending to do. "I won't let her."

My dear Sally. She didn't understand that she had no choice in the matter. I was going to miss Sally. My only consolation was that I would have Valerie right where I wanted her. It was going to be glorious.

THIRTY-FIVE

VAL

Staring at the screen on my phone, I was stunned into silence. The Bear, Dominic, had just called me. His voice still echoed in my head. Calm. Cold. Confident.

Jordan stepped beside me, sensing the shift instantly. "What was that about?"

I swallowed. My mouth had gone dry. "It was him," I said quietly. "He has Sally."

Jordan's eyes hardened. "What did he say?"

"He said... if I want to see her again, I have to stop looking for him and wait for further instructions."

The morning air felt suddenly heavier. Damp. Drenched in dread.

Jordan's jaw clenched. "This is part of his game. He won't stop until you play along. I don't like this one bit, Val."

"I don't either, but what choice do we have? He'll kill her."

"He could kill you and a number of other people. We have to find him and stop him."

Shaking my head, I said, "I'm not going to argue about this. Sally's one of my best friends and I'll do whatever it takes to get her back."

"Calling off the search feels like walking right into a trap. What number did he call from?"

"It said blocked."

Jordan frowned.

I said, "But both of us know we can still trace it. Phone company logs, tower triangulation, we'll find where it came from."

"Let's do it," he said. "We'll find him today."

"He won't be there."

"I know, but we still have to check it. He could've left something behind."

As the words left his mouth, the reality of it settled in my bones. Jordan was right. Everything the Bear had done had been meticulously planned. The call wasn't just a threat; it was an invitation. A breadcrumb. He knew we'd trace it. He wanted us to so we would know where he was. But then why tell me to stop looking for him? Maybe he knew we'd ignore that part. Maybe he didn't care. Maybe he wanted to see how far I'd go. Or maybe the place itself meant something to him. My stomach twisted at the thought.

Jordan said, "Let's get back to the station. We'll start tracing the call."

"Okay. I'll call Lucy on the way and let her know I need to know the location of the last call made to my cell phone."

As we drove through the forest-lined road, sunlight dappled across the windshield, but it did nothing to lift the darkness pressing down on my chest. My mind raced, trying to make sense of his motives, trying to find a way to get ahead of whatever was coming next.

"We'll need a plan for when he contacts you again," Jordan said.

I nodded, eyes on the road. "All right."

He looked at me sideways. "We can't afford to lose you."

I didn't answer. The idea that my life was somehow more important than Sally's was stupid. Sally had her whole life ahead of her. She hadn't signed up for this. She didn't deserve it. She mattered. And the Bear knew I'd do anything to get her back.

By the time we arrived at the sheriff's station, my nerves were frayed. Lucy, Brady, and Troy were already inside, huddled around the tech station. As I walked in, they looked up, three faces etched with tension.

Lucy's eyes met mine and she stepped forward. "Who called you?"

"It was him. Dominic. The Bear. He has her. He told me to wait for instructions."

Brady let out a slow breath. Troy immediately turned to his screen.

Lucy gasped. She blinked rapidly, her face pale. "Is she... did he say if she was okay?"

"He said if I want to see her again. So, I think she's alive. For now."

Troy cleared his throat, drawing our attention. "We already got a hit on the call. One ping. Burner phone. Location's about an hour south—Coyote Ridge area."

"What's the exact location?" I asked.

"I just dropped the coordinates to your phone."

Jordan whistled. "That was fast."

Thank goodness. Out loud, I said, "Let's go."

Lucy looked at me, tears just behind her eyes. "Do you think Sally's there?"

"I doubt it," I said honestly. At least, I hoped not.

She closed her eyes for a moment, steadying herself. "If she is..."

"She's alive," I said, gripping her shoulder gently. "And we're going to bring her home."

Jordan was already moving. "We'll call the local sheriff to get the scene secured before we arrive."

"Smart," Brady added, pulling up the map. "That area's remote. You'll need to move fast if you want to search it in daylight."

One hour later, we pulled off the road into a clearing flanked by thick woods. Three sheriff's department vehicles were already parked in the dirt turnout. A yellow band of crime scene tape fluttered across the trees, cutting through the quiet wilderness. I frowned. That felt like overkill. We were just here to follow up on a phone ping. Jordan gave me a puzzled look as we climbed out of the vehicle. Something was off.

We jogged toward a group of deputies standing near the tree line. The air smelled of pine and morning dew, but there was something else riding the breeze, something metallic, faint, and wrong.

Jordan showed his badge. "Special Agent Jordan Wexler, FBI. Why did you cordon off the area?"

A young deputy stepped forward, face pale, eyes hollow. He pointed toward the woods. "They found a body."

My heart sank.

Please... don't let it be her. *It can't be her.*

THIRTY-SIX

VAL

I ducked under the tape and rushed toward the body. Two deputies stepped forward, lifting their hands to stop us.

"I'm Val Costa," I said, breathless. "This is FBI Special Agent Jordan Wexler. We're the ones who called this in. We need to see the body."

From my pocket, I slipped on a pair of gloves. The deputies exchanged a glance, then stepped aside.

The smell hit me first, of earth, decay, and blood. I crouched beside the deceased, my heart pounding. A flood of relief washed over me. It wasn't Sally. Just some other poor soul. A man, it looked like a hiker. Mid-thirties, maybe. Backpack beside him, boots muddy. He'd probably been dead overnight. It wasn't fresh.

"We'll need the ME to confirm," I muttered, more to myself than anyone else, "but I've seen enough crime scenes to know he's been here a while."

I was reluctant to touch him, but something caught my eye, something tucked under the collar of his hiking shirt. A white envelope. Crisp. Blood-smeared. It was the victim's blood.

I knelt down to get a better look. Every instinct told me to rip it open, but I paused, forcing myself to breathe, to document everything properly. I stood up, took out my phone, and photographed the scene from multiple angles.

Jordan stepped beside me. "I'll call the ME. We need them out here now."

"All right." My eyes stayed fixed on the envelope. "There's something else. I'm going to take a look."

He nodded.

With a gloved hand, I carefully slid the envelope from beneath the man's tan hiking shirt. My momentary relief curdled into rage. Typed neatly across the front: VALERIE COSTA.

Like the previous notes, it hadn't been written in haste. This was deliberate, thought out, and orchestrated. The Bear was always two dang steps ahead, and I hated him for it. I opened the envelope and pulled out two things: a folded 8x10 sheet of white paper and a small white notecard. I unfolded the paper first. My breath caught as I took in the contents. It was a photocopy of a newspaper article. The headline read, *Mass Casualty in FBI Fumble.*

The story was burned into my memory. A failed operation. One I had been a part of. There had been a credible threat. We had received intel suggesting women and children were being held hostage. We'd gone in, believing we were rescuing innocents. But we'd found no hostages. Just people defending their land. Survivors had claimed we were the aggressors, and the fallout had been national news. They compared it to Waco. It was the biggest failure of my entire career, even worse than being captured by the Bear. I shut my eyes, the shame washed over me all over again. That day had never really left me.

Swallowing hard, I looked at the notecard. I didn't need to flip it over to know what it would say. But I did.

You couldn't save them. You can save Sally. Wait for my instructions.

Jordan returned, his voice tense. "What is it? What's the message this time?"

I handed him the notecard and the photocopied article.

His eyes scanned the text, then met mine. "We have to stop him."

"No kidding," I snapped. "But we can't just storm the woods. We need to call off the grid search we had planned. It would be like looking for a needle in a haystack anyway. We need to wait for him to contact me again." I stared down at the hiker's body, my chest tight. "I don't want to see any more bodies, Jordan. Do you understand?"

He looked at me. "We need to talk about this."

"Nobody else is going to die because of me," I said, my voice cracking. "I won't have it. I don't care what it takes. Do you understand me?"

Just then, Brady came running through the trees. "We heard on the way over."

"It's not her," I said quickly.

His shoulders sagged. "Is there a message?"

I nodded and explained, watching his face darken as I spoke.

"So what do we do?" he asked. He glanced between Jordan and me.

"We stand down," I said. "We wait for his next message. I'm not risking Sally's life."

"That's not FBI protocol, Val," Jordan argued. "You know that. We don't negotiate with terrorists. He's terrorizing this entire region, maybe others. He's killing random people who happen to cross his path. We don't even know who this latest victim is or how long he's been here."

"No, we don't know, and we need to find out. We need to

tell his family. We need justice for him and all the others the Bear has killed." My voice rose. "And we need to find Sally. We need to stop this man. And if that means playing his game then that's what I'll do."

"That's not up to you, Val."

I turned sharply at the voice from behind me. Kieran stood there, his deep brown eyes steady and unreadable. "If you don't want to be part of our investigation," Kieran continued, "that's up to you. We want you here. But we can't have you going rogue again. That's what got us into this mess in the first place."

I took a step back, as if the words themselves had hit me in the chest. The words stung. Not because they were cruel, but because they were true. It was my fault these people had died. "If we continue with the search, he'll kill her."

"We'll work out a plan to assure we have the highest chance of getting her back."

"Like what?" I spat, incredulous.

"I don't know. We make it look like we're not searching. We'll put our heads together and come up with a solution, Val."

They could do whatever they wanted. I was going to wait for the Bear to call or for the next piece of the puzzle. I would not let another person die at his hands. I was going to stop him, even if it meant killing him myself. Even if it meant dying in the process.

THIRTY-SEVEN

SALLY

Sitting on the new mattress he'd brought for me, I tried to be grateful. It was much better than the hard, wooden floor. Dominic had said he wanted me to be comfortable. It would have been more believable if he hadn't kept me chained to the wall. That, and the fact that I knew he was planning something terrible. I suspected he was going to lure Valerie to him, but I couldn't let him go through with it. I had to think of something. I couldn't let him hurt her. I had to figure out a way to get Dominic to let me go, or find a way to warn Val. Something. *Anything.*

We'd talked a lot over the last two weeks and I'd got to know him a little. I thought maybe I could use what I learned during that time against him. *Ugh.* I couldn't believe I'd been so stupid. I'd slept with him on the first date and had him spend the night in my house. He had been in my bed, sleeping next to me. I had made him coffee and dinner. I'd thought he was special. In some ways, he was. *But not in a good way.*

How had I not seen how sick and twisted he was? It was too late when I'd started to feel something was off. The weird comments. The whole "why waste a view on a victim?" And now I know. He's had so many victims. Nobody got a view. He liked to chain them up and then torture them. Carving a letter "S" into their chests just like he did to Val.

But I knew I couldn't just sit here beating myself up. I had to figure out what to do. Because he was right—Val wouldn't let him hurt me if she could help it. That's what scared me, but that's also what I needed to prepare for.

The door opened, and Dominic turned on the light. I winced as my eyes readjusted once again.

"Good evening, Sally. How are you feeling? Are you more comfortable now?"

"I'd feel a lot more comfortable if I wasn't chained to a wall, Dominic. If that's even your real name. Is that your real name?"

A sneer spread across his face. He was loving this. My thoughts flashed back to Val's description about him. The Bear. He enjoyed suffering. Pain. Screaming. Begging. Well, I wouldn't give him any of that. I'd had some time to think, and I needed to be smart. I knew Val would come. And I'd have to help her. I knew every way to kill a human being and I knew all the ways the human body was vulnerable. Maybe I could kill him before she arrived.

"Well, I can't quite do that, Sally, I'm afraid. You've eaten the granola bar and you've drunk some water, but you must be hungry. I don't want you to be uncomfortable or starving. That's not my plan, you see. So I was thinking... how would you like a sandwich? Or maybe some pasta?"

Was he seriously taking my dinner order? Pretending like this was one of our dates? Would there be wine?

My stomach turned at the memory of our last encounter, when I'd let him put his hands on me, and his lips on mine. I'd thought he was wonderful and a good presence in my life. Now I understood it was all an act. A psychopath masquerading as a human. He knew how to behave, how to say all the right things, just to manipulate me. I should've known better.

"I wouldn't mind some pasta. Or a sandwich. I am very hungry," I said, keeping my tone calm. Would it make him happy for me to be compliant? Or would it annoy him that I wasn't more hysterical?

He moved toward me, and I instinctively drew back.

"It's me, Sally. Don't worry." He sat down on the mattress next to me. "See? This is pretty comfortable. It could be like one of our dates. I did enjoy having dinner with you, and the lunch. That hike was great, wasn't it? Maybe we should have wine. Do you feel like wine?"

For someone usually so calm and collected, he was acting kind of deranged. Maybe he was trying to scare me. Maybe this was all a trick. "Sounds great," I said.

"You know, I've been on dates before. You're not the first person I've dated. But you're the first one I've chained up. Isn't that funny? You're my first confined date. We should celebrate," he said with a smile.

I tried not to let the horror show on my face, but it was difficult. I couldn't believe this was the same man I had dated. I mean, I hadn't known him long, but to see two completely different sides to him was frightening.

"Well, lucky me, huh?" I said, adjusting my position and sitting up straighter, trying to act confident. The worst he could do was kill me. Well, he could torture me, then kill me. But if he killed me, he'd lose his leverage with Val.

So maybe I had more leverage than I thought. I inched a little closer to him and the chains clinked softly. Leaning toward him, I said, "You know what sounds great? Why don't we have one last night just the two of us? Like old times."

He ran his fingers through my hair. I did everything I could not to recoil. "You are truly something, Dr. Sally Edison. Oh, how I wish things were different."

He yanked my hair back suddenly. My head jerked and his

lips went to my neck. He kissed my skin, mumbling in my ear, "You taste so good. I'm going to miss you so much, Sally."

He released me, and my head fell forward.

"Shall we do red wine? That pairs best with a red sauce, right?"

"Yes," I said, my voice tight.

"Wonderful."

Staring straight into his evil eyes, I said, "And by the way, I know what you like. And I'm not going to give it to you."

"You say that now." Then he laughed like it was the funniest thing he'd ever heard. "Oh, Sally..." He shook his head, almost affectionately, and then left the cabin.

I was relieved he was gone and that he had left the light on. But a new fear crept over me. What was he going to do to me?

Maybe he would hurt me. Maybe he'd give me the same brand he gave Val and all his other victims. Maybe worse. Just because he wouldn't kill me before Val got here didn't mean I wouldn't wish I was dead. Which is why, the first chance I got, I had to kill him.

THIRTY-EIGHT

VAL

We'd learned at 9 a.m. that Sally had been abducted. Since then we'd received a message from the Bear and found one of his victims. And now we'd been strategizing for hours, and I hadn't received any new calls or messages from the Bear. I was taking his threat seriously, and refused to do anything that would jeopardize Sally's safety. The team knew me well enough to know I was planning to do whatever I needed to get Sally back. Sure, they could go on and on about covert operations and backup, but the Bear wasn't like other killers we had tracked, and I knew he'd sense law enforcement was near.

Until I received a message, I would go along with what they were saying because I needed to be apprised of all their plans. Besides, there were things we could be doing that didn't involve physically searching for Sally and him—we needed to know everything about the Bear.

We already knew that whoever he was, he was calling himself Dominic Savage. Using the information Sally had given me, we also knew he hadn't gone to school when he was young, and that he had a prepper-type background. That was where we had started digging. If we combined that information with

Washington State as his supposed hometown, we might actually be able to figure out who he really was and maybe even why
he did what he did.

It could be important because I had a feeling he wouldn't
tell us the truth if we caught him. Or who knows, maybe I was
wrong and he would. Some serial killers loved the spotlight.
They wanted to boast about their gruesome crimes. Others liked
to cry on an investigator's shoulder, spinning sob stories about
the terrible childhood that had made them into monsters.

From what I could tell, Dominic deserved zero sympathy. If
he'd had a tragic childhood, he wasn't that child anymore. He
was an adult and made his own decisions. Anxious to find out if
the team had made any progress, I called out, "Troy and Lucy,
have you found anything yet?"

Lucy looked up with wide eyes, and said, "I might have
found him. Let me show you."

She hooked her laptop to the projector, and everyone in the
room turned to look, including Kieran, Jordan, Troy, and Brady.

"Okay," Lucy began, "based on what Sally told us about
Dominic, he's from Washington State, he's a hiking guide, he
grew up hunting and fishing, and he didn't go to school, at
least in his early years. I used that information to search
within Washington for areas where fringe communities exist."
She clicked to the next slide, a regional map with an area
highlighted in red. "I've narrowed it down to these regions
that are known for off-the-grid, anti-government, and sometimes deeply religious groups. Washington has a number of
those."

I leaned forward, glued to the screen.

"From there," Lucy continued, "I looked for unsolved
murders, with the thought that he may have started young, but
hadn't been caught for those. The search included unsolved
homicides dating back twenty to twenty-five years, in regions
close to where these communities existed." She paused, then

clicked again. "Three unsolved murders came up that might be of interest."

Kieran raised a brow. "So what you're saying is, you're basically looking for an unknown killer in Washington State, and hoping he's the Bear?"

I glanced over at Kieran, trying to gauge whether he was being critical or just skeptical. Either way, Lucy didn't flinch. She swallowed and nodded. "Exactly. It's a way of narrowing down his identity, because if we find someone who could be the guy and he still has family in the area, we might be able to find him. Maybe he talks to them. Maybe they can help us catch him."

"Good for you, Lucy," I said quickly, stepping in before anyone else could weigh in. "I think it's a great lead to follow." I wasn't just defending one of my best friends; I was defending one of the best researchers I'd ever worked with in all my years in the FBI, and at the sheriff's department. "Please continue, Lucy," I said, giving Kieran a pointed look. He just shrugged.

Nobody had slept in almost two days and our nerves were on edge. Maybe we should've taken a break and waited until he actually sent that next message, the one that would help us find Sally. Maybe we should've called it a night, but we hadn't.

Lucy said, "Like I mentioned, in the three different areas I've highlighted, there were three unsolved murders. The first was a young girl, thirteen-year-old Hannah Coffey. She was found in the woods. She'd been hiking with her parents and got lost. They found her a few hours later, at the bottom of a ravine." She hesitated. "I looked at the crime scene photos. I can show you or I can spare you." She looked at me.

"Spare us, for now," I said. "We've seen enough death and destruction in the last five days."

"At first glance," Lucy went on, "it looked like a fall. Maybe she slipped. But when they did the autopsy, she had been manually strangled."

"Within a few hours of being lost from her family?" I asked.

Lucy nodded. "Her family was visiting from California."

Kieran leaned forward. "Were there any suspects?"

"There were no official suspects, but there's a note in the case file. About ten years later, when a new cold case division reopened it, they canvassed the area again. One man, Randy Truckee, said he didn't know who killed Hannah, but he remembered a kid who lived a few properties down. Said the boy was a real psycho and that he liked to torture animals and show them off. All the other neighborhood kids were horrified. He thought it was funny."

I exchanged a glance with Jordan and Kieran. I didn't say it aloud, but we were all thinking the same thing. Lucy may have found him.

Lucy continued. "They asked Randy for the name. The kid's name was Damien Stokes. D.S."

In near disbelief, I crossed my arms and stared at the screen. "Okay. And the other murders?"

She nodded. "Yes. A few miles away, a child... this one's tough and you're definitely not going to want to see the photos. A six-year-old boy, Cody Devers, was found in the woods. He'd been stabbed, cut, and strangled to death."

Jordan looked over at her. "Did they have any suspects?"

"Nope. But again, the same cold case squad asked around and the same name came up. Damien Stokes. The neighborhood psychopath."

Troy let out a low whistle. "Two cases. Same name."

Lucy nodded again. "I could bore you with the details of the third and fourth murders, but they all happened within two years of each other. It would've been when Damien was fifteen to seventeen years old."

I stood there, stunned. His first pattern of four, four victims we knew nothing about. Although, we had attributed four other victims in Washington State, making his total in the state eight.

It was possible the four deaths between states wasn't significant after all. "Were there any more unsolved cases in the area?" I asked.

"Not until 2010 to 2012. That's when we picked up four murders by an unknown suspect attributed to the Bear."

We had him. Damien Stokes.

"The third and fourth murders, I don't need all the gruesome details," I said, "but what can you tell me about the injuries and the evidence collected at the crime scenes?"

Lucy nodded and clicked the button on her laptop. A new table appeared on the screen. I couldn't believe she had done all this with no sleep.

"As you can see," she said, pointing to the screen, "the method of murder became more sophisticated with each victim. The first was manual strangulation, likely his first human kill. He would've been fifteen years old. The second victim, he used a knife, but then finished the job with his hands. The third, no manual strangulation, all knife work. The fourth was similar." She paused. "Now I'm going to show you this next thing, and then we can discuss." She clicked again. On the screen appeared an image of a body with an "S" carved across the chest.

"At nineteen years old," she said softly, "the Bear had found his signature."

The room was silent.

"What do we know about Damien Stokes?" I asked. "His family, hometown?"

"There aren't a ton of records," Lucy said, "but like he told Sally—which now seems to be the truth, he grew up in a fringe community. Didn't go to school until he was ten years old and he didn't graduate high school and dropped out when he was a senior. Notes indicated that he hated class. He has a mother, sister and a brother that are still alive. His father is deceased. The family still lives in Washington State."

"You found him," Jordan said. "Nice job, Lucy."

"What else do you know? Can you dig deeper?" I asked.

"It'll take some time."

"It could be useful. We could use his history against him. It could throw him off guard. He's taken great steps to hide who he is. We need to know everything we can about Damien Stokes. Every alias. Every fact. The more we know, the more we can use."

Jordan nodded. "I agree with Val. We should also reach out to the police department that handled those four earlier murders. Maybe they collected evidence we can test now, it could make the case stronger when we catch him."

"Agreed," said Troy.

Heads nodded around the room.

I looked around. Everyone was tired. Bone-tired. We needed answers, but we also needed rest. Our team had to be ready for when he contacted me again. Because he would be ready and I would have to be too.

"Great work, everyone. We've made real progress. We've been at it for almost forty-eight hours straight. I'm going to suggest we take a break. Let's bring in a fresh team to keep the research going."

I turned to Lucy, who looked exhausted but still focused. "Not because I don't think you're capable. Just that we could all use the rest. We need to be sharp when we take him down."

And I needed to be alone. Because if the Bear made demands, whatever they might be, I had to be ready to face them. If I knew him like I thought I did, he'd want me to come for Sally by myself. And I would, because nobody else was going to die on my watch.

THIRTY-NINE

VAL

Standing on the doorstep to Mom's house, I looked into Brady's eyes. There was so much I wanted to say, like how I wished things were different and I wanted to be with him, but I had to prioritize this case over everything else.

"Val, do you want me to stay over?" he asked gently.

"No, I'm fine. We're fine," I said. "We've got patrol outside. Our security system makes an ear-shattering noise. I'll double-check everything before I go to bed."

"Will you be able to sleep?"

"Honestly? I have no idea. But my body needs to rest. I'll shut my eyes, do some breathing exercises, maybe a guided meditation, something to calm my nerves. I have to be at the top of my game. Resting is the only way I can do that."

"You're right." He placed his hand on mine, giving it a gentle squeeze. "If you change your mind, just let me know and I'll be right over."

A small smile formed on my face for the first time in... probably since he and I had kissed. "Thank you, Brady. You have a good night."

I reached out, placed my hand on his cheek, and gave him

a soft kiss on the lips. We stared at each other for a long moment before I reluctantly pulled away from him and stepped inside.

"Good night, Brady."

"Good night, Val."

I shut the door behind me. My body relaxed. It was good to be home.

I could hear the low hum of the television coming from the living room. Mom was still up. I figured I owed her a bit of an update, I'd been texting throughout the day, her and Harrison both. The message had been the same each time: "Everybody is A-OK."

I kicked off my shoes, hung up my bag, and walked into the living room.

Mom looked up from the TV. "You're home."

"I am. Time for the team to take a break."

"Are you okay?" Julia asked.

"Exhausted." I stepped closer, sitting on the sofa and curling up my feet beneath me. "So, what are you watching?"

Julie paused the TV. "Just baking shows. How are you doing, hon?"

"He took Sally."

Mom gasped.

"But we're learning more about him. And we're gonna get him. Soon. I can feel it."

"I'm surprised you're not all out searching for him. That poor girl—" Mom looked at Julie, who shook her head. "Sorry, Sally is not a girl," she corrected gently. "She's a medical examiner. Dr. Sally Edison."

"Sally's tough. I think she'll hang in there." I had to believe that.

Mom said, "I think so too. She's got a fire in her. I saw it the first time I met her."

"She's pretty special."

Julie stood. "You want lasagna? I made it just today. It's your mom's recipe."

I nodded.

"Perfect." She smiled. "Let me heat it up," she said as she headed into the kitchen to fix me a plate.

"How are you doing, Mom?" I asked.

"Worried about my daughter."

"Other than that?"

"I'm doing pretty good. I was showing Julie my recipe. Helped a little."

"That's great, Mom. I can tell you're getting closer to being the old you. Before you know it, I think you'll be baking *ziti* and popping bottles of wine."

"I look forward to that. So... was that Brady outside? You were on the porch a while."

"It was. He offered to stay over, but I told him to go. We all need to get some rest."

"Exactly. You're going to need all your energy to get through this. I can feel it."

Julie called from the kitchen, "Your lasagna's ready!"

"All right," I said, rising. "I'm gonna have something to eat, then take a shower and settle in."

"Okay, dear. Mind if I keep you company in the kitchen?"

"Of course. I'd love that."

I helped my mom up from the couch, and she used her cane to make her way to the kitchen. It was strange after such an exhausting few days, there was still hope. Still things to look forward to. But I knew there was only one way I could keep that hope alive. I had to stop the Bear. Lucy had discovered his true identity, and I couldn't wait to face him again and put him in his rightful place, behind bars or six feet under.

. . .

With freshly shampooed hair and a belly full of lasagna and red wine, I slipped into my pajamas, soft cotton that felt like heaven, climbed into bed, and sat up, about to open the guided meditation app my therapist had recommended for moments like this. That's when my phone buzzed. A message. From Sally. I clicked on the video, and my hand flew to my mouth.

Sally sat on a mattress, chained to a wooden wall. She spoke. "Hi, Val. I'm doing fine, as you can see. Now, he wants to talk to you."

The camera panned to a man in a black ski mask with piercing blue eyes. *He doesn't know we know what he looks like. That we know his name—his real name and where he came from and what he's done.*

"Hello, Valerie. As I promised, I will give you further instructions. I've held up my end of the bargain. Sally is still alive and well. We just enjoyed a lovely dinner. She's been fed. She's been treated quite nicely. I know the chains look a little uncomfortable, but I needed to keep her in place. I have a feeling she'd run." He grinned. It was chilling.

He continued, "But I'll cut to the chase. I know you're probably anxious to hear what your next move is going to be. And thank you, for playing along." He paused before delivering his terms. "Sally will remain alive as long as you do as I ask. If you come to me, I'll let Sally go. But I'll only do that on one condition and it's nonnegotiable. You can't tell the FBI or the sheriff's department or *anyone* that we've been in contact and that you're coming to me. This is between you and me, Valerie. No one else."

My breath caught.

"I have a little test for you. I'm going to give you twenty-four hours to complete a task. One that nobody can know about. Not your mother. Not Brady. Not any of your friends in law enforcement. Are you ready for the task?" He paused. "Good. Here goes. I need you to go to Sally's house and tie a ribbon on her front door. That's it. You have twenty-four hours. I'll be in touch." The video ended.

My shoulders dropped and I exhaled. *She's alive.*

And now, I had to figure out how to go to Sally's house, no explanation, just to tie a ribbon around her doorknob without detection. It was strange, yes. But it was clearly a test to prove I wouldn't go to the authorities when I exchanged myself for Sally. I had to prove I would play by his rules. I checked the time on my phone. I had until 9 p.m. tomorrow. And I would do it because I was going to get Sally back. But I had to think this through. If he let Sally go and it came down to just him and me, only one of us would get out alive. I had to make sure it was me.

FORTY

VAL

To my surprise, I only woke up twice during the night. And the next morning, I woke up with a plan, clear and simple. Sally was depending on me. Every other potential victim of the Bear was depending on me too. I would stop him, once and for all.

After getting dressed, I headed downstairs and found my mother and Julie in the kitchen. Julie had decided to move into Mom's old bedroom while Mom kept the downstairs suite. It was nice having them both here, comforting, in a way I hadn't realized I needed.

"Good morning, Val."

"Good morning, Mom. Good morning, Julie," I said.

Julie smiled. "You look rested. You look fantastic, actually."

"Thanks. I didn't sleep too bad last night. Woke up twice, but that's pretty good for me."

Julie said, "Well, let's get you some coffee to get you going."

"You're up early," Mom said.

"Yep. I'm ready to go. Ready to end this. We're going to get Sally back."

"That's great, Val. Everyone will be happy when it's over."

"Me too. Can I get the coffee to go?"

"Oh, sure," Julie said. She pulled a travel mug from the cupboard and filled it with coffee, adding a splash of milk.

"How about a banana or something to put in your stomach other than caffeine?" Mom said.

"Sure."

"I can make you some toast too," Julie offered.

"I can get it. You don't have to—"

"Oh, nonsense, Val. You have bigger things to do like save the world. The least I can do is make you some toast."

Quitting the fight, I relented. "So how are you two this morning?" I asked.

Julie and Mom exchanged a look. "Well," Mom said, "Julie and I were just talking. We wanted to discuss something with you. We don't have to decide now, but we're thinking about having Julie move in permanently. Even when I'm fully back on my feet."

Julie added, "It's been so nice, and I'm all alone at my house. It just makes sense."

"I think it's a great idea. Absolutely."

"I won't cramp your style?" Julie asked.

"Are you kidding me? You two have a more active social life than I do."

They laughed, and I smiled. I envied what they had, their ease, their humor, and their companionship. Between Diane and the two of them, they were like their own little *Golden Girls* group. I scarfed down my toast and banana, thanked them both, and headed out.

It only took five minutes to get to Sally's house. There was no longer a patrol stationed there, so it should be simple. I pulled into the driveway, glanced around, and then took the ribbon I'd found in Mom's sewing bin and tied it around the front doorknob. Quick. Clean. I hurried back to my car and sped toward the station. But my mind raced.

If the Bear was watching Sally's house, then he had to be nearby. Unless he had somehow hacked her system and was watching through her own security cameras. Maybe that was the point of the test. To see if I'd bring law enforcement with me. But honestly, the test was flawed. I could easily not tell law enforcement about it and still let them know he had contacted me. It was almost too easy. Still, I had to wait for his next message to understand what came next. Maybe he already knew I wouldn't risk Sally's life. Maybe this was just one more twisted move in his game. He was toying with me. But I felt good and ready for the final showdown. I would end his life, if needed, and I wouldn't feel a hint of remorse.

I walked into the station and headed straight for the war room. Lucy was already there, along with Brady, Jordan, Kieran, and Troy. I guessed they were all rested and ready to conquer the day too.

Jordan explained that we had received the autopsy report for the fourth Red Rose County victim. And in that moment it hit me, the Bear had his four California victims, but he also had Sally. It didn't fit the pattern. I was beginning to think there wasn't a pattern after all.

"What did the ME say?"

"You were right, he'd been dead for twelve hours. The call to you was likely to tell you where to find it."

And to give me the message, or rather a reminder of the biggest mistake of my career. On second thoughts, was it a reminder or was it a message that I was about to make my second biggest mistake? I nodded. "What about the victim? What do we know?"

"He's been identified as Walt Smythe, aged sixty-three. Married with two grown children. Mr. Smythe worked at Mountain Savings & Loan as a mortgage broker."

An innocent victim and a family torn apart. "Have you talked to the family yet?"

"Yes, they came in earlier to report him missing. They thought they had to wait twenty-four hours."

That was a common misconception. If a person was missing and thought to have met with foul play they could be reported missing immediately. "When was the last time they spoke to him?"

"Before he left for his hike around 9 a.m. yesterday. He was expected back by noon, but when he didn't turn up his wife assumed he'd gone to the office. When he didn't come home after work, that's when she became concerned and started calling around. He didn't show up this morning, which convinced her there was something really wrong, and she had some neighbors help look for him, but couldn't find him. Her description matched the deceased. She IDed the body."

That was tough. "What did the ME say?"

"Cause of death, exsanguination. Bled out from the cut to the carotid artery. He died quick after that."

Small mercies? "I'm guessing there was no trace evidence found on the body?"

"The lab is testing samples pulled from his clothing and the soil around the body in case the killer cut himself during the act or got sloppy."

I doubt it. "Anything else on Mr. Smythe?"

"Not until we get the lab reports back. In the meantime, I think we should finalize our strategy for finding Sally."

"Let's do it."

And with that, Jordan launched into our strategy. Like how we could move forward with locating the Bear and Sally, what to do if I received another message, how to provide cover and backup in the event he wanted me to go alone.

But I knew how that would go. The Bear would somehow

know if I brought others and he'd kill Sally without hesitation.

A few hours later, I turned to Lucy. "Wanna get some coffee?"

"Absolutely."

As we walked down the hall, I asked, "So, how's Jonathan?"

"He's doing well." Lucy smiled.

"How's the new house?"

"It's great. Getting cozy. More homely. I've been hanging pictures on the walls."

"That sounds wonderful."

At the coffee machine, I turned to her and said, "There's something I have to tell you."

She blinked. "Oh?"

"Act normal," I said. "Don't react. Just listen."

She nodded slowly, her face carefully composed.

"He contacted me last night," I whispered. "Says he'll swap Sally for me but only if I don't tell anyone in law enforcement. He had me do a test to prove it. He told me to tie a ribbon around Sally's front door knob."

Lucy kept her voice level as she pulled a mug from the cupboard. "Did he tell you where she is?"

"No. Not yet. I think he's waiting to confirm that I passed the test. That I didn't tell anyone. You can't tell anyone. What I'm telling you now is just in case something goes wrong."

Lucy placed her cup under the machine and nodded.

"You can't tell a soul, not even Jonathan."

Lucy nodded again.

"I know it's hard to pretend like we didn't have this conversation, but you must understand how important this is. Only one person is walking away from this, and it's not going to be him."

"Understood. Let me know if you need anything. This stays between us. This is for Sally."

I nodded. As we headed back to the conference room, I said

casually, "So, are you going to be painting the new place? Any other decorating plans?"

She smiled. "Yeah. We're looking at paint chips now. Thinking maybe sage green or a soft off-white. Something cozy."

We continued the chitchat as we returned to the table and slipped back into work. Lucy didn't miss a beat. She was pulling it off perfectly. We would get the Bear. Sally, Lucy, and me. He didn't stand a chance.

FORTY-ONE

SALLY

Sleep was fitful, though hardly surprising given I was chained to a wall in God knows where. But I've had a lot of time to think. Maybe if I could get him close, or somehow convince him to let me go, I could do some real damage. Or maybe I was just being delusional. I was chained up, after all. Or should I wait until Val got here? Or the FBI? Or whoever else might be looking for me. I had to believe someone would find me.

The door creaked open, and light flooded the small space as he flicked on the switch.

"Good morning, Sally. How did you sleep?"

He was such a creep. "I've slept better, you know. Like when I was in my own bed," I said with a sickly-sweet smile.

"Don't worry," he said, almost gleeful. "Valerie will be here soon. We just need to make her another video, an invitation, if you will."

He was still clinging to the narrative that Val would be here soon. What else had he said in that video? I'd thought of trying to give her a clue when he was filming me, something she could use. But what could I tell her? I didn't know where I was or where he planned to take me. The only thing I had was that I knew his identity. Unless she'd already figured it out. Thank goodness I called her the other night and told her I was worried. Hopefully, she'd put together that it was him. That it was Dominic who took me. He was the Bear.

"Is that right?" I said.

"It is. We need to invite her to join us, but we have to give her a clue as to our location. She's been such a fantastic player so far and has followed all of my instructions and passed with flying colors. So, soon, Dr. Sally Edison, you'll be back to life as it was before."

He said it in a tone that made my skin crawl. To be honest, I didn't believe him for one second. "So, really, just like that, you're gonna let me walk out of here when Val shows up? I know who you are. Won't that kind of mess with your whole serial killer thing?"

He chuckled. "You are clever."

"That's right, I know exactly who you are. You're the serial killer they call the Bear. I know you've been stalking Val. I know you have no mercy for your victims, and that you're a deranged psychopath obsessed with my best friend."

"Oh, Sally. You don't know the half of it."

"Really? Why don't you enlighten me, Dominic? Is that even your real name? You seem pretty evasive on that front. Come on, who else are you going to talk to?"

He smiled. "Well, I've already told you a lot about myself, Sally. Remember when we were lovers?"

I shut my eyes, trying to block out the image of us together.

"Yes, Sally, you were quite smitten with me. And I wasn't pretending, I was smitten with you. You're lovely. Smart. Got a fire in you. And I must admit, I'd like to see that fire extinguished. But you're right. I can't just let you go around telling everybody who I am. Although really, what would you tell them? You wouldn't be a credible witness. You were drugged, placed in a shack, chained up, swearing it was the guy you dated."

"No. But I know what you look like."

"You'd do, what? A composite sketch? Tons of guys look like me."

"They ran your background when you picked me up for that hike. They have your name, your driver's license photo. Everyone knows what you look like. And that whole mask routine for Val? I'd bet my life she knows exactly who you are. I think you've underestimated her. Yes, she'll come for me, because that's who she is. But if you think you have the upper hand..." I shook my head slowly. "Think again. She's a lot smarter than you."

His face flushed red. *He didn't like that.* That's right, he was a narcissist. He thought he was the smartest, the best looking, the most cunning. But he wasn't. Because I believed with all my heart that Val would figure out exactly who he was.

"Oh, Sally, if you're trying to make me angry, you're wasting your time. What you're saying is nonsense. I will outsmart Val. As wonderful as she is, let's not pretend she's superior to me."

"She's so far above you, you can't even see it. And if you didn't know it yet, you're not walking away from Red Rose County alive. If I know anything about Val, you'll be dead within twenty-four hours of seeing her again."

"You're awfully confident, Sally, *for someone chained to a wall.*"

I laughed. "You don't scare me. What are you going to do— cut me up? Carve your little 'S' into my chest like the others? Strangle me?"

His eyes narrowed. "You're not afraid of being tortured and killed? Is that what you're trying to tell me?"

"Do I want to be tortured and killed? No. But do I fear it? Not really. I'm already chained up." I looked down at my wrists and pulled, the chains clinking. "I guess I've just accepted it. I don't think you'll follow through with your promise to Val. I don't think you'll let me go. So mentally, I'm preparing for the inevitable. I'm a bit of a realist."

"Oh? So if it's inevitable, you're just going to sit there? Give up? Not even fight?"

I sighed. I wanted to goad him. Because if I did, he might lose control. He might slip and hurt me and that could be the end of his power over Val. That was the best I could do to help her stop this madman. Val would find him, I knew she would, and I did think she already had his photo. He didn't stand a chance.

"No, Dominic. I won't fight you. Because I've read your profile. That's exactly what you want."

"You know, I can enjoy it even if you don't scream. That skin... my knife... the color of fresh blood against—"

"Go for it. Less talk and more action. I'm getting bored."

He shut his eyes, and sucked his teeth. "Oh, Sally. You are very smart, but I know what you're trying to do, and I'm not going to let it happen. We have another video to make and then we can work on that boredom of yours."

Did I fear what he'd do to me? *Yes.* But I couldn't sit there and do *nothing.* "What if I don't want to be in the video? What if I don't cooperate?"

"Now you're starting to try my patience, Sally. I can make things happen she won't be able to see in the video. So, I think you'd regret that. You only need to be alive long enough to film the message."

I shrugged. "My torture and death will be worth it, knowing yours is coming soon."

"Valerie won't outsmart me."

"She will. She's going to kill you. And you know what? I think she's going to enjoy it. Because deep down, you're just a weak, sad, pathetic excuse for a man. And you know what?

When we were lovers?" I leaned in and smiled coldly. "I faked it."

He rushed at me, grabbing my throat, squeezing until my vision blurred. His face turned scarlet, rage blazing in his eyes. Then suddenly, he let go.

I collapsed, coughing.

"Just remember," he hissed, "it could be over that fast, Sally. Now sit up. We have a message to record. And you *will* do it. Or I'll make you wish you were never born."

FORTY-TWO

VAL

I paced the conference room as everyone worked diligently, putting together a complete profile of Damien Stokes. It had been over twenty-four hours since I placed that ribbon on Sally's front door. And I hadn't received any new messages or further instructions from the Bear.

It was getting increasingly difficult to tell Kieran and Jordan to stand down. Not to send in the dogs. Not to deploy helicopters to utilize thermal imaging to detect human heat signatures in the woods. I loved Sally, and in any other circumstances, I would say to spare no expense, to put every resource we had into this, but I knew that wouldn't help. He'd hear helicopters a mile away, literally. And who knew where he had her, or what kind of traps he'd set up? We could spook him, force him to kill her quickly, without hesitation, and vanish again without a trace. We needed to stop him, not provoke him.

This was a completely different situation to anything I'd been involved in before. But I'd been studying him for so long and I knew he was unpredictable but also that he was highly intelligent and tech-savvy, despite his humble beginnings. He knew exactly how to avoid detection, until now.

Getting close to Sally would be his undoing. If he hadn't gotten that close, and if he hadn't been a total creep setting off her intuition, we likely wouldn't be able to catch him. When I saw Sally, I was going to tell her it was because of her that we were able to end his reign of terror.

I worried about what she was going through. He'd had her for two days. I knew the fear she must be feeling. That helplessness. That complete loss of control. But Sally knew him too. She understood his profile. She'd dated him, however briefly, I hoped she could use that knowledge to her advantage. Maybe she could get him to slip up and she could free herself.

Lucy came over. I stopped pacing. "What's up?"

"Nothing. You?"

"Just pulling records," she said, holding a stack of printouts. "Compiling the criminal background for Damien Stokes. We found some little stuff, and some bigger stuff. Some violent, some petty theft, burglaries. He has warrants for his arrest. It's probably what prompted him to change his name in the first place. Despite his long rap sheet, he was never actually questioned in any of the murders we believe he was responsible for."

I nodded. That tracked. He took whatever he wanted by any means necessary. He didn't care who he hurt to get it.

"Maybe we should grab some lunch," Lucy said.

"You're right. Want to go to Drake's?"

"I could go for a burger and fries."

"Me too."

Brady must've heard the words burger and fries, because he suddenly appeared next to us. "You guys thinking about going to lunch?"

I said, "Yes. Do you want to join us?"

"Sure."

Lucy shot me a quick look, one I knew well. She didn't want him to come. She wanted to talk more. About Sally. About the plan. About what came next.

"Let me grab my keys," Brady said.

But before he could head out the door, Lucy cut in. "I was going to drive. I have an errand to run. Val, you want to drive with me?"

"Sure." I thought, *Very smooth, Lucy.* To Brady, I said, "We'll meet you there."

Once we were in her car, she looked over and said, "So you got my drift, huh?"

"I did."

"So—nothing? Nothing from the Bear? No videos, no messages, nothing?"

"Nothing yet. It's driving me crazy. Is there any way to tell if anyone's hacked into Sally's surveillance system to know if he saw that I placed the ribbon on the door knob?"

"I can check the security logs and see if there were any logins other than mine."

"I keep trying to think of ways he could see that I actually did what he asked without telling anyone."

"Maybe he can't and just wants to put some time between the task and the next video. Making sure there's nobody waiting in the wings."

"True."

"Where do you think he has her?" Lucy asked, glancing at me as she made a right turn.

"My guess is somewhere in the woods. I just don't know where."

"Well, if you get a message, will you let me know? In case I don't hear from you for, I don't know, a certain amount of time. Then I'll know to send in a search team."

As much as I knew I had to go in alone, I also knew that at a certain point backup might be necessary. "Let's think of a phrase." I gave it some thought. "If you're there when I get the message, I'll pretend the message is from Harrison and I'll say he passed his first final."

Lucy nodded. "Perfect... Are you getting nervous?"

"Nervous. Apprehensive. Excited. I just can't wait for this to end. One way or another."

"Me too. You're going to get through this. And so is Sally. He's not going to take the two of you from me."

"Agreed."

At Drake's, we were all seated in a booth. My thoughts drifted back to the moment Sally had told us she'd met someone right here, in this very restaurant. Of course, none of us had realized it at the time, but she'd been talking about him. The Bear. A serial killer. The man who would later take her. I wished I'd known. But I couldn't beat myself up about that. I had to stay focused. As soon as I got a message, I would be ready.

I sat next to Brady, across from Lucy. He turned to me.

"Everything okay?" he asked gently.

"As okay as things can be. How are you holding up? Did you get much sleep?"

"Some. How about you?"

"So-so, but I'm getting some rest, which is good."

"Yeah... it's kind of been a little quiet," he said. "Maybe too quiet."

"That's what we were just talking about," I said, nodding toward Lucy.

The waitress arrived with our orders, giving us a much-needed distraction. Over lunch, we didn't talk serial killers or strategy or about any of the darkness hovering over us. We stuck to small talk, the weather, summer plans, and Harrison. All the good things in life. It was a nice break from the storm waiting just outside the door.

. . .

Back at the station, we regrouped and discussed the next steps, like what to do if I didn't hear from the Bear soon. They still believed I'd tell them if he contacted me. But I had no intention of doing that.

"We're still updating his profile," Jordan said, looking over a document. "Soon enough we'll have everything we need on this guy. Then we can start interviews in his hometown. If we can't find him, we start questioning friends, neighbors, and anyone who ever knew him. This is big. This is real progress."

"You're right," I said, nodding. "It is. And I'm confident we're going to get him soon."

After calling it a day, I headed toward the parking lot. About to approach my car, I saw Lucy and gave her a quick wave just as my phone buzzed in my hand. I froze, glanced down. A message from Sally. Another video.

I pressed play.

The footage opened in the woods with towering redwoods, then a cabin, and then another smaller cabin. A door. A gloved hand reached for it and pushed it open to a darkened room. A light flicked on, and there she was. Sally was sitting on a mattress, her vibrant red hair still bright, her skin pale, her eyes steely with determination. *She hadn't given up.*

"Say hi, Sally," a voice said.

"Hi, Val," she said, and gave a small wave. The camera showed the chains on her wrists.

I paused the video. Was she trying to tell me something? I replayed it and watched her eyes.

She gave the slightest shake of her head. Subtle. Barely perceptible. But it was there. Then the video continued. The camera backed out. The door shut. The screen went black for a second. And then he appeared. The Bear, wearing the black ski mask with his bright blue eyes staring straight into the lens.

"Hello, Valerie. I hope you're well. Here is the deal. I'll let Sally go if you take her place. The rules are as follows: You can't alert any of your friends in law enforcement or anyone else about this. You can't bring any weapons or a cell phone. You follow these rules and Sally lives. I've shown you where we are. We're both looking forward to seeing you again."

I stood still, heart racing. What did he mean, he'd showed me where they were?

All he'd shown me was some cabins in the woods. That wasn't a location. That wasn't a map. It wasn't nearly enough.

Lucy stepped closer, her voice low. "Did you get a message?"

"It was Harrison," I said calmly. "He passed his first final."

Lucy stiffened. "Cool. When's his next one?"

"I'm not sure yet."

I thought back to the video. Two cabins. Log-style. Small. Rustic. Almost like...

"I know where he is," I muttered under my breath.

I looked at Lucy. Our eyes locked.

I said, "Give me eight hours."

FORTY-THREE

HIM

Sally sat up when I entered the room. She'd been sleeping like an angel.

"Good news, Sally. Valerie will be joining us very shortly."

"Well," she said, her voice flat. "Sounds like you have very little time left on earth, then."

Sally's disdain for me was obvious, but what was she angling at? She wasn't going to walk out of this alive. Did she know that? I think she did. She said she'd come to terms with it. Maybe she wanted to get a few digs in before the end. It didn't matter. It just showed me she was scared. She'd tried so hard not to appear full of fear, but this told me she was. She thought she was going to die. She wanted to push me, provoke me. She wanted me to kill her so I couldn't have my Valerie.

Well, that was not going to happen. "Truth be told," I said, stepping closer, "you probably won't live much longer either. How do you feel about that, Sally?"

"You're not gonna get what you want, Dominic."

"I'm already getting what I want, Sally. And now that I have the video I need, I don't need you anymore, or your smart mouth."

"She won't trade places with me if I'm dead, will she?"

I took a step back, watching her carefully. Despite her negativity and hostility toward me, which I suppose I understood, given the situation I had put her in, she should treat me with a little more respect. "That may be, Sally. But that doesn't mean I can't have a little fun with you. You did say you were bored, right?"

"This whole creepy guy persona? It's not very interesting. You're pretty, I don't know... basic."

I chuckled. *She was a spitfire.* "I know you're just saying this because you're scared. And I don't blame you. Honestly, it would be nice if things were different between us, Sally. Maybe I could actually trust you. Maybe I could let you go so you could carry on living your life, your days filled with the dead, and determining how they died. But you're right. That's not how this is going to end." I gazed down, meeting her eyes. "But Valerie won't know that until it's too late."

Sally shook her head. "You don't think she trusts you, do you? You're ridiculous. Totally delusional. Has anybody ever told you that before, that you're delusional?"

I was tiring of her attitude. "You know, you should try being a little nicer to me. I've been very kind since you've been here."

"Chaining me to a wall and making me sleep on the floor is not kind," she snapped.

She dared to raise her voice at me. "It could be a lot worse. *Much worse.*"

"Fine, then I won't say anything at all. Would you prefer that?"

I rubbed my chin, considering. Would I rather have a nice conversation while we waited for Valerie, or should I give her my signature? A stunning "S" across her beautiful chest. Lately, I'd conducted that part while they were sedated, so I could get it just right, but I had a feeling that despite her words, Sally would fight like the Dickens.

I pulled my knife from its sheath. "Sally," I said softly, "do you want to play with me now? Or do you want to continue to disrespect me?"

Her face was like stone.

"You know, I'm guessing Valerie will be here sooner rather than later. I can make it so your body looks fresh. It'll be too late for her to run away. That could be interesting. What do you think about that?" She turned away from me. "Of course, you wouldn't get to see her again because you'd be dead, and I know you want to see her, don't you? I'd hate to take that from you, but it would be kind of fun to trick her like that, wouldn't it? The big bad FBI agent coming to save her friend, only to see she was too late." I knelt down and leaned into her. "You know, Sally, I want to tell you a little story. You were asking about me earlier, and there is something I didn't tell you about my past. One of my hobbies. Pastimes, really. I studied all the serial killers before me. Ed Gein. Ted Bundy. BTK. H.H. Holmes. And I took a little bit from each one of them. It's how I've outsmarted all of law enforcement." She smirked. "You disagree?"

She said, "I'd bet you that knife, Val knows exactly who you are."

That made me smile. "Deal!" That didn't get a response, I thought she'd be happier that I'd play along with her own delusion. I continued, "One of my favorites was Ted Bundy. He charmed his victims and when they had no idea he was a killer, he'd pounce. You see how I did that with you, right? You never even suspected me. But here we are. This was a very Ted Bundy-type situation, wasn't it?"

She remained silent.

"Are you familiar with Ted Bundy?"

"I've heard of him."

"When he was arrested, all the people could say was, 'He was so handsome.' You said I was handsome too, didn't you?"

"I did but you're rotten on the inside. So your outside looks different to me now. It's like your inner self is shining through, like fire from the depths of hell. It's quite hideous."

"Interesting."

She eyed me, that false confidence returning. "So who hurt you, Dominic?" she asked. "Why do you feel the need to take other people's power? To cut them up. To break them. Who hurt you?"

"Nobody hurt me. *Nobody* can hurt me."

"What about your mother?"

She was searching for a reason, but she was barking up the wrong tree. Not all sociopaths have a sad origin story. "My mother was a fine woman."

"And your father?"

"My father wasn't the nicest man. But he got what was coming to him."

Sally tipped her head. "You killed him? Was he your first?"

"Sally, I can't give too much away all at once. Where's the fun in that?"

"You might as well tell someone your story, considering it's about to end."

"Oh, Sally..." I shook my head. "This is likely our very last night together. Ever. Can't we enjoy it? Like we used to?"

She frowned.

"Come on. I'll bring you some wine. We can have one last romantic interlude."

She wrinkled her nose, and said, "As if."

"Sally, Sally, Sally." I scooted next to her on the mattress and I pressed my knife against her cheek. "If you don't want tender love there is another way that I like to show how I feel about a person."

With a tip of the blade, I applied a bit of pressure and cut into her cheek. Crimson dripped down her face. She didn't scream. She squirmed, tried to pull away, but she didn't scream.

I held her tight and whispered in her ear, "They say the first cut is always the deepest. But that's not true, Sally. You'll see. I'm only getting started and it's going to be a night to remember. I believe you *will* remember it forever."

FORTY-FOUR

VAL

After a day of strategizing with the team, and receiving the message with Sally's location, I had to mentally and physically prepare for the challenge ahead. The Bear had held Sally for two days. What shape was she in? Had he hurt her after the film had been made? I couldn't help but wonder how this would play out. I couldn't bring a weapon or a cell phone. How was I going to overpower him? How would I save Sally? I'd have to be resourceful.

I was going into the woods, to an old summer camp I'd attended when I was seven years old. It had been shut down for years. I wondered if he knew I had once gone there, although I wasn't sure how he possibly could. There probably weren't any photos and there definitely weren't electronic records back then. Maybe he'd just assumed or stumbled across it during one of his hikes. I didn't think I would've ever remembered it myself. But he had shown me, and he knew I'd know the location. How did he know so much about me?

He'd been in Red Rose County for six months, and I hadn't known where he was. He'd been watching. Studying. Infiltrating. Planning. Plotting. Waiting for the perfect moment to strike.

Death after death after death, all to lead me back to him.

I had to be creative. Prepared. Everyday items could be considered weapons. I assumed he'd meant no knives or guns, but there were other things I could use, things he wouldn't detect. I wasn't naïve. I knew I'd have to fight him to the death and I knew it wouldn't be easy.

With my bag slung over my shoulder, I jetted down the stairs.

"Looks like you're going somewhere," my mother said.

"Yeah, I'm just going to run out to the store and meet up with Lucy for a drink. It's been a long day."

"At this hour?" Julie asked, eyebrows raised.

"Yeah. I think it's all this extra energy. Waiting for something to happen, you know? There are some things she wants to talk about."

"Wouldn't it be better if you brought her over here? Safer, I mean," my mother said.

All logical suggestions. "I think going out could do us some good. Plus, I think there are a couple of relationship issues she wants to talk about and she doesn't need an audience."

Mom narrowed her eyes. "Didn't she just move in with Jonathan? I thought they were really happy."

One of the setbacks of having a mother who was a former sheriff was that it made lying and getting away with it pretty tricky. "They are. I think she just wants to talk about a few things."

My mother wasn't convinced. "Are you telling us the truth?"

Dang it. *Be cool.* "Mother, you worry too much." I leaned in to kiss her cheek. "I'll see you in a bit. Don't wait up."

I headed out the door and walked up to the patrol car. Deputy Baker again.

He rolled down his window. "Headed out?"

"Yep. I'm just going to the grocery store and then meeting a friend for some girl talk."

"All right. Have a good time. Got your cell phone with you?"

"I do." And I did. The Bear had said I couldn't bring it to the location, but I could leave it in my car. I waved and walked nonchalantly over to my car, climbed inside, and pulled onto the highway. It had been two hours since I'd received the Bear's message, and Sally was still alive. I hoped she was alive when I got there.

FORTY-FIVE
VAL

I pulled off the highway and turned into a gravel turnout near the path that led to the old summer camp. The trees surrounded both the turnout and the narrow trail, their limbs arching over-head like a tunnel. The sun was long gone, and the darkness had descended. I cut the engine, and silence ensued.

I sat for a moment, gripping the steering wheel, my heart pounding with anticipation—not fear exactly, but that quiet pressure that builds before something big. A defining moment. I pulled my phone from my bag and slid it underneath the passenger seat and set the bag on the floorboard. Then I reached back into the bag for my flashlight. It could easily be used in defense, or an attack, if handled correctly. Next, I took two protein bars from the bag and slipped them into my back pocket. I stepped out of the car and left it unlocked behind me. The air was cold, crisp, and sharp. I flicked on the flashlight and a pale beam sliced through the trees and lit up the trail ahead.

With a deep breath, I stepped toward the trail. The air smelled of pine needles and damp earth. Gravel crunched under my boots as I slowly made my way down the path. I recalled from my teenage years, we used to come out here to do dumb kids' stuff like drinking stolen wine coolers and making out with random boys, though I didn't do that too much.

Despite the camp no longer being in operation, the trail was surprisingly well maintained. As I walked, memories surfaced. Me at seven years old, excited for my first sleep-away camp. It had been my only year attending, but I remembered having fun. At least, that's what Mom told me. It was almost forty years ago. It's strange how some memories stick, even when you think they shouldn't.

The flashlight bobbed as I walked. A few flickers of movement, lizards or small creatures, skittered away from my steps. Every sound felt amplified, yet the stillness between them was even more unnerving. But I kept going. It took nearly ten minutes to reach the crest of the hill. That's when I saw it—the sign to the summer camp: Camp Wrenwood. The paint had almost completely faded away, making the lettering barely visible. No one had repainted it, and no one had bothered to take it down.

The wooden arch still stood, but looked like it could collapse at any moment. The slats were warped, covered in dirt and moss, but the ground beneath had been cleared recently.

Near the base of the sign was a small wooden plank with a white card nailed to it. I stepped closer to read it, my flashlight beam narrowing in.

Welcome back.

My light slid lower, and that's when I saw it.
A large hunting knife with a black handle and a gleaming steel blade.
My stomach twisted.
There was another note beneath the knife, folded neatly

and tucked beneath the tip of the blade. I crouched and picked it up with shaking fingers.

Valerie, a party favor.

—S.

I stared at the note. Then at the knife in my hand. Was this a trap? He'd told me no weapons. So why give me one now?

Did he want a fair fight? Or did he plan to disarm me and use it against me, to finish what he'd started? He had to know that I wasn't there to talk; I was there to stop him.

Some might call that murder. But it wouldn't be. There was no chance he wouldn't try to kill me. It would be self-defense. Plain and simple. I gripped the knife, and a chill rippled through me. It wasn't from the air, but from the unmistakable feeling that I was being watched.

Gripping the knife tightly, I slowly inched toward the first cabin. I remembered it from the video. Sally wasn't in there. Nor was she in the one on the right. There was another small wooden structure just ahead. I paused and listened, sweeping my flashlight across the area. Everything was still. Too still.

Memories flashed, being seven years old and eating sticky popsicles on the bunk beds, and then being fifteen, drinking wine coolers with Brady under the stars. *Brady.* Would he be mad I didn't tell him about the messages? That I went after Sally on my own. Would he forgive me? My thoughts shot back to the more recent memories, Sally's voice on the phone, shaky and scared. Her telling me something was off about Dominic.

Two videos sent. Proof of life. Chained to a wall. Where were they? Why wasn't he stopping me?

The silence stretched, pressing in on all sides. My boots crunched softly as I moved forward, flashlight raised, scanning. And then from a distance, I heard a voice. Calm. Familiar.

"Hello, Valerie."

I stopped dead in my tracks. My breath caught in my throat and my heart was hammering. I turned in a sharp circle, shining the beam into the trees. Nothing.

But I knew that voice. I'd heard it in all my nightmares. In video footage. In memories I'd tried to erase. *He's here.* Watching. And now? *It was go time.*

FORTY-SIX

BRADY

As I approached Val's house, the weight of the night settled over me like a damp blanket. The sky had darkened, and the street was mostly quiet except for the faint chirp of crickets and the low hum of a distant car. I considered calling her. I was there to take over patrol for the night—everyone was pulling double shifts, but more than anything, I felt better being close to her. Something about her had seemed a little off at the station earlier. I hadn't pushed it. It wasn't the place, not with the ever-present eyes and ears of our FBI colleagues, always looming like shadows in the corners of the room.

I parked and walked over to the patrol car already stationed in front of Val's house and knocked on the window. Baker rolled it down with a soft whir.

"Hey, Baker. How's it going?"

"Pretty good. All quiet here."

I glanced toward the dark driveway, then to the illuminated front porch. "Where's Val's car?"

"Oh, she went to the grocery store and then out with the girls."

Tonight? "With Lucy?"

"She didn't say."

"All right. Thanks, Baker. You have a good night."

It was past nine on a Thursday night. After the week we'd all had, she deserved a break. Maybe she just needed a distraction or a way to keep moving. Val had the kind of restless energy that didn't let her sit on the couch with her mom and Julie watching baking shows. Still, something didn't feel right.

I headed up the steps and knocked on the door. A moment passed. I heard footsteps, the scuff of slippers on wood floors, and then the door creaked open.

"Hi, Brady! Good to see you," Julie said, smiling warmly, her hair tied back and a faint scent of vanilla trailing from the open doorway.

"Good to see you too, Julie. How are you doing?"

"I'm all right, thanks."

"No Diane tonight?"

Julie shook her head. "She has family in town. What can I help you with?"

From the living room came Elizabeth's familiar voice. "Is that Brady? Come on in!"

I stepped inside. The house smelled of fresh-baked cookies and brewed coffee, comforting and homey. Elizabeth was on the sofa, a blanket across her lap.

"Good to see you, Brady. How's it going?"

"Doing all right. It's been a busy week."

"I heard. You and Val have so much energy. Can you believe she went out with Lucy tonight? She's like the Energizer Bunny."

"What time did she leave?" I asked.

"About eight o'clock, I believe."

"Did she say what time she'd be back?"

"She didn't. Said she had her phone."

"Brady, can I get you a cup of coffee?" Julie asked. "You

want to wait inside instead of sitting out front all alone? We've got cameras."

"I should stay outside," I said. "But I'll take that coffee."

"I made some chocolate chip cookies too. Want a few?"

"Yes, please."

"I'll pack some up for you. You can nibble on them while you watch over us. Our knight in shining armor," Julie added with a wink.

I smiled. "Thank you."

"Brady," Elizabeth called again as I stepped back toward the door. "I just want to say, this whole thing, it's been terrifying. But I feel safer with you here. Knowing you're looking out for Val, it means a lot."

"I'm glad to be here. Hopefully it'll all be over soon."

"Any progress? Have you figured out where they took Sally?"

"Val told you?"

"She didn't give us any details. But we know Sally's missing. We're afraid he took her. Val is too. I've only met Sally a few times, but she's such a lovely woman."

"She is. We're doing everything we can. We've made good progress this week."

Elizabeth hesitated, her voice softening. "You know, Brady, maybe I'm just getting old. But something about tonight, it just feels off. Like Val's hiding something."

It felt off to me too. "Oh?"

"She's my daughter. And I trust her. But maybe just call her. Make sure she's okay."

"I will."

Julie returned with a paper bag full of still-warm cookies and a steaming travel mug. The smell of chocolate and caffeine rose in the air as she handed them over.

"Thank you, Julie. Good night, to the both of you. Now, I'd

better get back to the car. If anything happened to you two, Val would have my head."

Julie laughed and tapped my arm. "You're too sweet."

After letting myself out, I glanced around before heading back to the patrol car. I took a sip of the coffee then pulled out my phone and called Val.

No answer.

I told myself she and Lucy were probably deep in conversation, but my gut twisted. I called Lucy's patrol.

"Deputy Whitehorse."

"Hey, it's Brady Tanner. You're outside Lucy's house?"

"Yes, sir."

"Is Lucy home?"

"Yep. Been home since about six o'clock."

"Any visitors?"

"No."

"You sure she didn't leave?"

"I'm pretty sure. No one's come in or out."

It was almost 10 p.m. Val's mom said she'd left around 8 p.m. Where was she? The pit in my stomach hardened and I called Lucy.

"Hello?"

"Hey, Lucy. It's Brady."

"What's up?"

"Is Val with you?"

"No..."

"Have you talked to her in the last two hours?"

"No. Why?"

My heart pounded. "She told her mom she was going out with you. That was two hours ago." After hearing silence for too long, I said, "Lucy?"

"I don't know where she is."

"Do you know where she went?"

"I'm supposed to give her some time."

My mind immediately flew to the worst-case scenario. "Time for what, Lucy?"

"I shouldn't say over the phone."

Heart pounding, I thought, *Val, no.* "I'm coming over."

I called Baker and had him return. As soon as he arrived, I took off toward Lucy's place. I banged on the front door. It opened almost immediately. Lucy stood there in pajama pants and a hoodie, her blonde hair pulled back in a ponytail. Her face was pale.

"Come in."

"What's going on?" I asked, hoping her answer would be better than what I was thinking.

Jonathan walked into the kitchen. "Hey, Brady."

After a quick wave, I said, "Lucy. Tell me."

She let out a shaky breath and led me toward the living room. "I'm not supposed to tell anyone. But Val got a message from the Bear. He has Sally. He offered to exchange her for Val. She recognized the place in the video he sent. That's all I know."

I froze. "She went to meet the Bear? Alone? To trade herself for Sally?"

Lucy nodded quickly, her eyes shining.

"And you didn't tell anyone?"

"She said it was the only way. I'm sorry, Brady. We have to get Sally back."

"You have no idea where she went?"

Lucy shook her head.

"We need to get to the station. We need to trace her phone. Now."

"Okay. I'll grab my stuff."

My heart pounded so hard I could hear it in my ears. I couldn't bear the thought of Val, out there alone, walking straight into danger, into the arms of the man who had once chained her up in the dark and marked her for life. It was the bravest, and stupidest, thing she had ever done and I had never been more terrified. We had to find her before it was too late.

On the drive back to the station, Lucy sat in the passenger seat, phone to her ear as she called to alert everyone. First the sheriff and then Jordan and Kieran.

"This is worst-case scenario, isn't it?" Lucy said with a shaky voice.

I couldn't believe Val had gone off on her own, but then again, I could. "We'll find her," I said, gripping the wheel tighter.

"She didn't say where she was going?"

"No. She just kind of mumbled that she knew where it was. Made me think he'd sent her another video, one she didn't show me."

In my mind, every terrible situation swirled like a storm. I thought back to the first time Val was caught, how she'd barely made it out. We hadn't spoken in years, but since she told me what had happened, I'd always feared it would happen again. Just when I finally had her back in my life. We'd only shared one kiss, but for us, it was so much more. I knew she was it—the person I was meant to be with. The one who would stand by me, support me, and love me. And I'd do the same for her. I couldn't lose her. *I just couldn't.*

Dread washed over me as we pulled up to the station. I put the car in park and turned to Lucy. "Go ahead inside," I said. "I need to make a call."

She nodded and headed up the steps.

I dialed Elizabeth's number. After a few rings, she answered.

"Hello?"

"Hi, Elizabeth. It's Brady."

"Brady, how's it going? Is something wrong?"

"I'm afraid so. I just got confirmation that Val is... She's missing."

"Missing?" Her voice caught.

"I don't have a lot of time to explain. I'm back at the station with Lucy. Val didn't have plans with Lucy tonight."

"She went after him, didn't she? I knew she wasn't telling me the truth. I could hear it in her voice."

"You didn't believe her?"

"I know my daughter. I knew something was off when she left. The look in her eye, the deliberateness of her actions. She lied to me, Brady."

"She lied to all of us. Well, except Lucy."

"And Lucy didn't say anything until now?"

"She was sworn to secrecy. She's convinced that if we went after Val, the Bear would kill Sally. Maybe Val too."

"That man cannot be trusted, Brady. You and I both know that."

"Val doesn't necessarily trust him. But in her mind, if there's any chance she can save Sally, she's going to take it."

"She's too stubborn for her own good. Oh, Brady, you have to find her. Wait, who's watching the house?"

"Baker came back. I switched places with him. He's there

now. But if you hear from Val, or if anything seems off, call me immediately."

"I will. Find our girl, Brady."

"That's exactly what I intend to do."

I ended the call and walked into the station. The place was eerily quiet, with just a skeleton crew on duty. I made my way to the conference room where Kieran, Jordan, and Lucy sat, their faces grim.

"I talked to Val's mom," I said. "Told her what's going on. She's going to call me if she hears anything."

Kieran let out a long sigh. "I knew she was hiding something. I knew she wouldn't tell us if he contacted her."

"Maybe so," I said. "But we've got a serial killer out there, and Val and Sally are both in danger. We can deal with the lectures later. Right now, we need to find them."

"We've already contacted the cell phone company," Jordan said. "We're waiting on a ping. Should have her last known location any minute."

Lucy looked down. "I'm sorry. I should've told you. But she begged me not to. I figured, at least I knew."

Kieran's temper snapped. "And how is that helpful if she's already dead? Or who knows what else? Last time she did this she was held captive for almost two days. That decision set off a spiral, a serial killer coming to this town, killing four people, not to mention an ex-FBI agent in Washington. This is why you follow the rules!"

His anger crackled like electricity in the air, and I understood it. "Look, I get it," I said. "None of us want this situation. But we can yell at Val when she's back home safe. Until then, we concentrate on finding them."

Kieran looked at me and nodded. Jordan cocked his head and peered down at his laptop. "I got it. We have the location of her cell phone. The coordinates just came in." He rattled off the numbers.

"Do we know what's there?" Kieran asked.

"Nope. Lucy?"

She was already typing. "I've got maps. Aerial view looks like some old buildings. A cluster of them. Maybe twenty minutes from here."

I sat next to her, looking at the screen. My heart thudded. "I know where she is."

"Where?" Kieran asked.

"The old summer camp. We used to go there as kids."

"Let's go," Kieran said. "We'll put together a tactical team. We'll move out in five."

"I'm going now," I said, already halfway out the door.

"I'm coming too," Lucy added. "I'll bring my laptop."

"Fine," I said, as I rushed out of the station. I was not going to let Val die out there.

FORTY-EIGHT

VAL

I spun around, trying to pinpoint where the voice had come from. It wasn't right beside me, rather I'd guess it was ten, maybe twenty yards out. He was watching me. I was sure of it.

Did he have cameras set up? *Out here?* That didn't make sense. We were in the middle of nowhere. There was no way a cell phone would even work out here, let alone enough electricity for some high-tech security system.

Knife gripped tight in my hand, I moved toward the row of crumbling cabins. That had to be where he was keeping Sally. My heart hammered as I stepped forward.

I screamed her name. "Sally!" Again, louder. "Sally!" A third time, desperate now. "Sally!"

Nothing. Not a sound.

Maybe she wasn't there. Maybe he'd moved her, or he'd tricked me and lured me here after killing her. I knew it was a possibility and I could be in real danger, but I had to keep going.

Besides, I hadn't just gone there to rescue Sally. I'd gone there to end him and his killing spree. I didn't usually believe in murder, but this didn't feel like murder. This felt like spraying pesticide to kill the parasites ravaging your crops, the crops that fed your family and kept your community alive. That's what he was. He was a parasite that needed to be eliminated.

The FBI wouldn't see it that way. They'd say it wasn't my call. But I was certain, absolutely certain, he would try to kill me. If I had to kill him in self-defense, so be it. And if he happened to bleed out? I wouldn't be scrambling for a first aid kit. Especially not if he had killed Sally.

The cabins loomed ahead, weathered and half collapsed. Their wooden planks warped from years of storms and sun, the windows broken and dirty. I crept around to the first cabin and yanked the door open. It creaked loudly and I winced. *So much for trying to be stealthy.* But he already knew I was there, so it didn't matter too much.

He could come from any direction, just like that night in the barn, when I was searching for him and he'd grabbed me in one swift, brutal motion. That memory struck hard, just as I turned back to the open door and swung my flashlight inside. Empty. I moved to the next. And the next. One by one, I checked each cabin with their dark interiors, and a few broken beds. Then I heard it again. That voice.

"Getting cold, Valerie."

The voice was closer now. I screamed into the night, "Where is she?! We had a deal!"

A maniacal laugh answered me. It was shrill and echoing until it faded away. Was he trying to lure me away from the camp? Away from Sally? I scanned the remaining buildings. There was one left. It was smaller than the others, possibly a utility closet or maintenance shack. I approached it cautiously, heart pounding in my ears. Just as I reached for the handle, I heard footsteps behind me. They were fast and closing in. I spun around, knife raised, flashlight beam slicing through the dark, and there he was. After all these months of hiding his identity, he stood before me with no mask. Part of me couldn't believe it. It was Damien Stokes, the serial killer known as the Bear. The source of my deepest pain. And it was, finally, time to end this game, once and for all.

FORTY-NINE

HIM

I held the flashlight under my chin, casting a long, warped shadow over my face as I smiled at Valerie. The clearing was barely lit with only her flashlight and mine flickering through the dense trees, but I'd recognize her anywhere.

"Valerie," I said, savoring the name. "You're just as fearless as I remembered."

She stepped forward, clutching the knife I'd left her.

"Where is she?" she demanded.

Valerie always thought about others and always thought she was in control, but we both knew this time she wasn't.

"We had a deal," she continued. "You said Sally would be alive and that if I came here alone, you would let her go. I have fulfilled my end of the bargain. I'm on my own with no weapon other than this lovely gift you gave me."

I nodded. "Yes. I thought it only fair. When I first met you, Valerie, I didn't know who you were. But then I realized that you were different. FBI agent or not, you had something special. I could see it in your eyes. As if I'd finally met an equal, a worthy opponent. I thought, what better way to level the playing field?"

I held up my own knife. "I have one too. I have the utmost respect for you, so I wanted to show you we're equals."

She stared at me, her expression unreadable. A flicker of confusion, perhaps.

"You want me to fight you?"

"If you must," I replied calmly. "But I've never liked guns. Too impersonal. A knife, however, that's something intimate. I thought you should feel what I feel. Besides, there are other things we could do with it later." I gave a smile. "But I won't ruin all the surprises."

Her jaw clenched. "Is that why you've been watching me since I came back to Red Rose County after my team rescued me from that barn?"

I laughed lightly. "Rescued? Valerie, do you really believe that? I gave you back to them. If I'd wanted to kill you, I could've done it then. But I didn't. I let you go. Because I wanted you back, on my terms."

She didn't move a muscle.

"You were special. Of all the friends I've had, and I've had many, you were the only one who never begged. Never cried. You would've fought me to the death. I have no doubt about that, and it impressed me. I didn't want our relationship to end that night."

"So you started planning how to bring us back together," she said flatly.

"Exactly. I knew you'd understand."

"Why are you so sure I'm not just going to lunge at you and kill you right now?"

I smiled. "Because that's not who you are. You came here for Sally. But I think maybe you came here for me too. Sally was just an extra incentive."

"Where is Sally? Is she alive? You told me she would be."

"Sally..." I trailed off, sighing softly. "She's fascinating, isn't she? She has the same fire inside her as you. She's incredible.

Sally hasn't screamed or cried once. I really thought she would. I tested her, but she didn't break."

Val stared at me, unmoving.

I continued, "If I hadn't met you first, I think she and I could've had something real."

Val cocked her head slightly, puzzled. "You're telling me that you like Sally and that's why you held her captive and chained her to a wall?"

"No. I mean, I was always planning to take her, but when I created the plan I didn't realize just how remarkable she was until we spent some time together. During our brief romance I felt how connected we were. We are two sides of the same coin."

She didn't respond, so I went on.

"Her life is death. Every day she goes to work to speak for the dead. And I bring her the bodies. I study death too. I'm fascinated by what creatures, large and small, do when they know the end is near. And now I've found two women who never cower or cry. You and Sally. Fascinating."

"Is that why you've kept her alive?" Valerie asked tightly.

I tilted my head, amused by her focus. "Is that all you really care about? If Sally's still breathing?"

She didn't flinch. I let out a small chuckle. "So selfless of you, Valerie. Coming here alone. Risking everything. For her. But why?"

"I already told you," she said, stepping forward slightly. "Because she's my friend. She's a good person. A wonderful person. And she doesn't deserve to die at the hands of someone like you."

"But don't you think you deserve the same consideration? You're risking everything by coming here. The last time you came for me, I got the upper hand, remember? I chained you up in a barn. I cut you. I hit you." I paused. "If I'd known how spectacular you were then, I wouldn't have bruised you. I'd still have cut and carved, though. It's very soothing."

Her eyes never left mine.

"You didn't just come here for Sally," I said. "You came for me too."

A faint smile crossed her lips. "I've been waiting for this day."

"Just as I suspected."

She straightened. "But first things first. You promised you wouldn't hurt Sally."

I raised a finger. "I said I wouldn't *kill* Sally."

"You said, if I came here alone, you wouldn't kill her. Well, here I am. Alone. We both have a knife. We're equals. I've done my part, now you need to do yours. Where is Sally?"

I hesitated for a moment, relishing the drama. "You know, my original plan was to give you Sally and then, of course, kill her. You know how I work. But I couldn't do it. I just couldn't. Just like I couldn't end it with you back then. I didn't want to let her go."

"She's still alive?"

"Of course she is," I said, smiling. "I made you a promise, Valerie. And if I make a promise, I keep it."

She nodded slowly. "I appreciate that. Now take me to her."

"Of course," I said, turning toward the path. "Follow me."

FIFTY

VAL

Everything felt surreal as I followed the Bear deeper into the abandoned summer camp. He didn't speak at first, and I stayed close, trying to quiet the thousand thoughts racing through my head. Why had he killed four and then stopped? Or maybe he hadn't. In Washington, we'd only attributed four kills to him, but we had uncovered more. I had been wrong about the four kills being significant. I'd been wrong about a lot of things.

"So, Valerie," he said suddenly, his voice casual like we were just two old friends out for a walk. "How's your mother doing?"

The question made me freeze for half a beat. His light tone unnerved me, but I chose to match his energy. "She's doing well. Thanks for asking."

"She does seem to be healing quite nicely. Is she walking around without assistance yet?"

I didn't like him knowing about my mother's condition, but I couldn't be surprised. I knew he'd been watching our house. "She has a cane, and she can get around pretty well now."

"I could tell she means a lot to you. You're a wonderful daughter, Valerie. I don't think I've ever met anyone quite like you."

He stopped walking and turned to face me. "I mean it. I know you probably think I'm some kind of psychopath, or whatever your profile says about me, but I see you. You're different. You quit the FBI to take care of your mother, right after surviving an ordeal yourself. That's really something."

He turned and continued walking again, and I followed, unsettled. Did he think we were friends? Had he created some fantasy in his head about us? It reminded me of the early notes that were congratulatory and admiring. Never once had they been threatening toward me. He even helped me solve one of the cases, indirectly. The fire. The messages. Did he really think we'd be friends?

He glanced over his shoulder. "Almost there."

Ahead, I saw it, the mess hall. The old building where we used to eat our meals back when we were campers. And as teenagers where groups would gather with cheap beer and wine coolers we'd stashed in backpacks. The late-night kisses in dark corners, the utility closet we used to sneak off to. My stomach clenched. *I knew exactly where she was.*

He walked up the creaky steps of the mess hall and stopped outside the door. "We're here," he said. "But before we go in, I want to have a conversation. I need you to understand what's about to happen."

Meeting his gaze, I said, "I'm listening."

"Sally's alive," he said, "but as much as I adore her, and I do, she's been pushing my buttons a bit. I had to make sure she knew who was in charge. She's going to need some medical attention, I'm guessing. But she'll probably make it."

"Probably isn't good enough."

He shrugged. "Well, we'll see how it goes."

He opened the door and stepped inside. I followed a few steps behind. He could've turned and slit my throat right then, but I didn't think he would. He trusted that I wouldn't do the same. And he was right, for now. I could stab him in the back, both literally and metaphorically. I could end it right now. But that wasn't who I was, was it? First, I had to get Sally to safety, and then the Bear could rot in hell.

I hesitated and he turned back to look me. "If she's injured, how is she supposed to get out of here? How is she going to survive?"

He shrugged. "She'll just have to try her hardest to make it down the trail. Maybe she'll flag down a car. If anyone can do it, it's Sally."

"And then what?"

He smiled. "Then it's just you and me."

"What does that mean? We talk? We fight? What happens next?"

"You don't like surprises, do you, Valerie?"

"No. I don't. And what should I even call you—Dominic?"

"Ah, I suspected you'd know it was me. Yes, you can call me Dominic. It's a good enough name."

"All right then, Dominic. What's your next move?"

"I'll give you a little hint," he said, playfully. "I'll let Sally go. Hopefully she makes it. She might not. I didn't make any promises about that. Then it's you and me. First, I'd like to have a conversation. I've read about you, and talked to Sally about you. I want to know more." He tilted his head. "You and I are opposites, but we're also similar, in a way. You try to save people. I study them, test them. It's fascinating. And just like your work as an FBI profiler, figuring out the minds of killers, I want to figure you out. What makes Valerie Costa tick? What drives you?"

He paused, then added, "If you're hungry, we've got food. It's late, but I have wine. Sally and I shared some earlier, back when she was being nicer. One thing I will not tolerate is disrespect." His tone darkened. "She was getting bitter toward the end. Mean. That's not the Sally I liked. I liked the sweet one."

I clenched my jaw. "Okay," I said. "And after the conversation?"

"We'll see where the night takes us," he said with a grin.

He headed for the back of the mess hall, toward the utility closet. I remembered it.

He placed his hand on the knob and turned to me. "Remember what I said," he warned. "She wasn't being very nice."

I swallowed down the rage boiling inside me, holding back the instinct to plunge the knife into his back. Not yet. Not until he made the first move. "I'm ready. You can open it now."

A slow grin spread across his face. "As you wish."

FIFTY-ONE

SALLY

Voices. I could hear voices. Muffled, at first, faint and echoing through the warped walls of the old building. My heart stuttered in my chest. Was it real? Was someone really here? It was her. *Val.* She actually came. I knew she would. Was Dominic with her? Or did she bring backup? No, she wouldn't. She wouldn't jeopardize my life. It had to be Dominic with her, so I didn't have time to waste. My fingers fumbled against the floor, closing around the screw I'd been working loose over the last day. I slipped it under the mattress just as I'd practiced. My only weapon. Crude, but maybe, just maybe, I could get it into his eye if I got the chance. It was the best I could do.

If I'd had more time and more strength, maybe I could've worked it between the cuffs and freed myself completely. But I didn't.

And then I heard her voice again, it was clearer this time. It was really her, and she had come alone just like he'd asked. I knew she would. *Of course she would.* But I'd prayed she wouldn't.

I wasn't in any shape to help her, to save myself, or to do anything but exist in the pain he'd left me in. He hadn't exactly appreciated my insults. Fragile ego, thin skin, no tolerance for mockery. I'd told him he was pathetic. Weak. The type of person who only felt power when someone else was powerless. He didn't like that one bit.

My ankle was throbbing. He had twisted it until I'd cried out, and something inside popped and burned. It was then I bit the inside of my cheek to keep from screaming again. That was his first prize. Then he went for my arm. I hadn't screamed that time. I'd bitten down and let the pain wash over me, refusing to give him what he wanted. My ankle and wrist raged with pain and my skin burned where he'd carved his mark into me. He'd told me I was his now. That I would always be with him. The doorknob turned with a soft metallic click.

Two sets of footsteps followed.

I squinted into the dark, heart hammering. Then the harsh light snapped on, flooding the room. I turned my head away, instinctively raising my arm to shield my eyes.

"Sally, we have a visitor."

I didn't answer as I was still blinking away the light. When I finally managed to open my eyes, I looked up and saw her. Val looked pale and drawn, but unharmed other than a knife in her hand. She looked like salvation. "I'm so happy to see you," I whispered, voice hoarse.

Val stepped forward like she might come to me, but Dominic raised his hand and stopped her with a quiet, "Not yet."

He shut the door behind him, sealing us into the tight, suffocating room. The air felt stale, thick with sweat, metal, and fear. We were all together. Me, Val, and the monster. What was he going to do?

FIFTY-TWO

BRADY

My truck skidded to a stop on the gravel shoulder of the narrow forest road, the tires crunching as I killed the engine. We were surrounded by towering pines and thick brush, the air dense with pine sap and distant mist. The only other vehicle in the lot was Val's SUV.

She was here. She had to be close. I jumped out of my car, my heart pounding so hard I could feel it in my throat. I scanned the tree line, eyes adjusting to the fading light.

"The hike to the summer camp isn't more than ten or fifteen minutes," I said to Lucy as she emerged from the passenger side. Her face was pale, eyes wide. She didn't say anything at first, instead she just stared at the car like it might disappear.

Then she said, "We should check her car. See if she left us any clues."

I hurried to the driver's side, tried the handle. It was unlocked. Of course it was. She wanted us to find it. Her bag sat in the footwell. I reached under the driver's seat, feeling around blindly. Then I opened the glove box. Nothing of note, it was just the registration, a car manual, and a hair tie. I bent over to the passenger side and reached beneath the seat. My fingers closed around something smooth and cold. I pulled it out and climbed out of the car. It was Val's cell phone. It was either powered off or dead. I pressed the power button and the screen lit up. No passcode. She usually had a passcode. "She took off the screen lock," I said aloud.

Lucy came closer and huddle around the phone "She did it on purpose. She wanted us to see whatever's on there, in case..."

I nodded, brows drawn as I opened the messages app. There were two messages from Sally, which meant it had to be the Bear using her phone. I tapped the first message.

Sally's face appeared on the screen. She sat on a mattress, chained to a wooden wall. She was likely in one of the old cabins. She said, "Hi Val. I'm doing fine, as you can see. Now... he wants to talk to you."

The camera panned to a man in a black ski mask with piercing blue eyes. He spoke. "Hello, Valerie. As I told you, I would give you further instructions..."

As I processed the message from the Bear giving Val a test to tie a ribbon around Sally's door, I couldn't believe Val hadn't told me or anyone. The only good news was that Sally was alive. When it ended, Lucy and I exchanged worried glances.

Lucy said, "She told me about this one. She did it. She tied the ribbon. Open the second message."

I swallowed hard. Lucy leaned in as I played the second message.

The footage opened in the woods, followed by a cabin and then another smaller cabin. A door. A gloved hand reached for it and pushed it open to a darkened room. A light turned on, and there she was. Sally sitting on a mattress.

"Say hi, Sally," a voice said.

"Hi, Val," she said, and gave a small wave.

The camera zoomed in on the chains on her wrists and then backed out. The door shut. The screen went black for a second. And then he appeared. The man in the ski mask, staring straight into the lens, telling Val he would trade Sally for her, but that she couldn't tell anyone.

My heart thudded. "She walked into a hostage situation with a serial killer, unarmed, without a phone," I said out loud in disbelief. Why would she do something so foolish? Did she have a plan? A weapon tucked away where he wouldn't find it? She must have. Otherwise it would be a suicide mission.

Lucy stared at me. "We need to get to her, fast, but we should call it in. Let Jordan know what we found."

I nodded, knowing we could be walking into a trap ourselves, and pulled out my phone. Jordan answered on the first ring.

"We're at the scene," I told him. "We found her car in the parking lot. She's not here, but we found her phone. She left it on purpose. There are videos that are communications from the Bear. She's gone in alone. No phone. No weapon. She's headed to the summer camp. I'd bet everything on it."

Jordan's tone sharpened. "Anything else?"

"Sally's alive. She's in the videos."

"We'll be there in five. Brady, you need to wait for us."

"I can't. She's unarmed and with a serial killer."

Jordan didn't hesitate. "That's exactly why you have to wait. This could turn out very badly for you. If he's holding Val and Sally, and you rush in, you're just making yourself hostage number three, not a hero."

I stared at the trail ahead. The forest swallowed the narrow path in shadows and silence. My stomach twisted. I knew this place. We all did. The summer camp from our teenage years where we'd sneak off with beer, and ironically play spin the bottle.

But now? The woman I loved was somewhere beyond those trees, and if she died tonight, a part of me would die too. But I had my kids to think about. I had to be smart.

"I'm going in," I said. "I'll head up the trail. But Lucy's staying behind."

"I'm not staying behind," Lucy cut in sharply.

I turned. "Lucy, you're not law enforcement. You're not trained for this. You're a researcher."

"Yeah," she said, lifting her chin, "and what if you need help? I can run back, let the team know what we found. There's not going to be reception up there."

Jordan was still on the line. "She shouldn't go. You shouldn't go. But she *really* shouldn't go."

"I'll tell her. See you soon." I ended the call and turned to Lucy. "Please. Wait here. You're her best friend, I get it. But if something goes wrong, someone needs to guide the FBI in. Tell them exactly where I went. That's the best way you can help."

Lucy hesitated, then nodded reluctantly. "Just don't do anything stupid."

"I'll bring her back."

I grabbed my flashlight and stepped onto the trail. Darkness wrapped around the narrow path. Branches scraped at my arms. My breath clouded in the chilled air. Sweat dripped down my temples, despite the cold. My pulse thundered. All I could think about was Val alone with a madman. Was she still alive?

I had to believe she was. Val was a fighter. Not only that, but I had to think that if the Bear had gone to all this trouble to lure Val here, he wouldn't kill her immediately. No, I think he wanted something more. A game. A performance. He had a plan for her, and the thought made my stomach churn. Every step I took felt heavier than the last, but I kept going, quickening my pace, because there was no time to waste. Every minute counted and I had to get to Val before it was too late.

FIFTY-THREE

VAL

The relief I felt from seeing Sally alive, although bruised and battered, quickly dissipated with the slam of the door. Dominic had us trapped in the small windowless room. The only light emitted within it was from a floor lamp operated by a small generator. There were two metal chairs and a mattress on the floor, where Sally was chained. All I could think was, *what is he planning?*

"All right, Dominic, we had a deal. I'm here. Now you let Sally go."

"I'd assumed you'd want to spend a few minutes together, catch up, before it's just you and me, Valerie. Who knows, maybe you'll never see one another again," he said in that creepy monotone voice.

Despite the chill in the air, a trickle of sweat ran down my back. "All right. If we're all going to get reacquainted, why don't we all take a seat?"

I wasn't exactly a hostage negotiator, but I could read Dominic's demeanor. He wanted me to play along, to pretend we had some kind of kinship. He was interested, too interested, in knowing more about me. All I wanted was to end this.

Dominic smiled and took a seat on the chair next to the lamp. He motioned to the other one positioned near the mattress where Sally sat.

I placed my hand gently on Sally's. Her eyes met mine. If she could read my mind, she'd know he wasn't going to kill me and he wasn't going to kill her. We would fight him to our last breath, if necessary.

Dominic sighed and lined up some sort of rehearsed sentiment. "So touching. Now, I was just explaining to Valerie that I really wanted to get to know her better. But before I do that, I'd like to say that you two are my utmost favorite women I've ever encountered, and to see your friendship, it's really something unique."

"I'm happy to share more about myself with you, Dominic," I said evenly. "But I would prefer Sally not to be chained to a wall. If we're all going to talk for a little while, it seems reasonable Sally is freed. No need to keep her chained. That seems fair, right, Sally?"

Sally gave me a small nod.

Dominic glanced between the two of us.

"Unless you don't want to follow through on your promise. In that case, all bets are off."

I tapped the knife against my leg, slow, and deliberate, letting him know exactly what would happen if he crossed me. I'd stab him and I wouldn't stop until he bled to death.

He stood, walked over to Sally and me. I shifted my chair, giving him space to move while also putting myself in a position to strike, if needed.

As he approached Sally, he said, "Now, no funny business. I'm freeing you."

She nodded, raising her uninjured arm for him to unlock the cuff. But just before that, I saw her tap the edge of the mattress that touched the floor. Had she hidden something there? Something she could use as a weapon?

As Dominic removed the cuff, Sally let out a soft breath in relief.

"There," he said, stepping back. "I've fulfilled my promise. And further shown I'm true to my word. If Sally would like to leave, she's welcome to. Or, if she'd like to stay and speak with us for a few more moments, I would personally appreciate it. But there is no obligation."

"I won't leave Val," Sally said quietly.

Dominic tilted his head, somewhere between disbelief and delight. "May I start the questioning? Or Valerie, if you have any questions, for Sally or for me, I'd be happy to hear anything you have to say."

I ignored him and turned to Sally, holding her good hand. The other one looked swollen, maybe even broken.

"Would you be more comfortable up here?" I asked.

She shook her head. "No. My ankle's swollen. If I had some-thing to prop it up, that'd probably help."

I nodded, stood and placed the chair in front of her, and scooted it close so she could elevate her foot. Her ankle was black and blue and swollen like a balloon. He'd crippled her. Even free, she wouldn't be able to run. There was only one way Sally was getting out of this alive. I had to kill the Bear.

"Is that better?" I asked.

She nodded.

I turned to the Bear and said, "Yes, Dominic, I do have a few questions. How long have you been in Red Rose County?"

"That's a great question, Valerie." He smiled, casually. "I arrived six months ago. It took me a little while to move my life here, but one thing about me, I'm quite tenacious when I want something. It wasn't difficult to find you, though. You were easy to track down. You still use your maiden name, which is connected to your mother, Elizabeth Costa. When I saw you weren't at your home in DC, I figured maybe you'd gone home to be with her. And I was right."

"How did you know how to find me?"

"The internet. You can find out anything about anyone on there. It didn't take long to learn you'd retired from the FBI to take care of her. That was when I decided to move here. You know, it's actually pretty easy to blend in. Wear some hiking clothes, and they assume you're an out-of-town visitor. It's helpful that people talk quite freely in Red Rose County. They discuss how Val Costa returned and retired and about the cases you worked with the sheriff's department. That's what they talk about at the diner, and the pizza restaurant. You're big news around here, Val."

He'd just been out there, sitting among everyone else. Blending in. It was disturbing. "The first note you left... you hired someone online? A kid?" I asked.

He nodded.

"And the second note, at the Nelsons. How did you know what he really was?"

"I watched him, of course. You know what they say, it takes one to know one. We can recognize each other. It was easy to find his secret. And yes, I set the fire."

My instincts had been screaming it was him the entire time. But everyone else had doubted me. They'd said I didn't have any evidence, that I had no proof, that it was far-fetched, that it was probably someone local, a fan, maybe even someone I'd grown up with. But I'd known it was him.

"And you've been watching me, Dominic?" I asked, voice cold.

"Yeah, I know it seems a little creepy," he said, almost sheepishly. "But really, you should be flattered. I usually watch my friends before they join me. But like with Sally, I wanted to take my time. I wanted to be able to have a true conversation. I've never really had that before."

"That's too bad. Human connection is one of the world's greatest gifts."

"I see that now," he said thoughtfully. "My connection with others, it's always been a little different. Watching you and Sally, friends who would risk their lives for each other, it has captured my attention." Then he cocked his head and studied me. "You chose to save people for a living. It's your life's work. Yet you gave it up to take care of your mother. So selfless, Valerie. It's truly inspiring." He paused, and said, "Do you have any other questions for me?"

"I do. When you met Sally, was it planned?"

He chuckled. "Not really. I mean, it was a bit of luck, honestly. I saw her sitting there by herself. Of course, I'd watched you, so I knew she was the medical examiner. So, I sat down to talk to her. I must admit, I was immediately mesmerized. I mean it, Sally. I really was."

Sally and I exchanged a glance. I could tell she was deeply creeped out, and understandably so.

"Okay," I said carefully. "And you never really left any forensics behind at your crime scenes."

He shrugged. "That's pretty simple, right? Between all the true crime podcasts and *Forensic Files* on TV, you'd have to be a fool to leave evidence behind nowadays."

"But it wasn't always like that, was it... *Damien?*"

His smile vanished and the jovial mask dropped. His body went rigid, his eyes dark. I'd poked the Bear—and he was *angry*.

FIFTY-FOUR

VAL

With a grin, I said, "That's right. I know who you really are—Damien Stokes. From Washington. Mother, father, brother, sister. Father deceased. Terrible accident. But I'm sure you know all about that."

I could tell by the look on his face that I'd struck a nerve. I paused, realizing, unsettlingly really, that I was actually enjoying this. But it was also a way to buy time. I still held onto hope that we'd get out of there alive. If I could stay one step ahead of him. He hadn't locked the door. Technically, we could leave. But the air inside the room was starting to feel suffocating. Too quiet. Too still.

"You must be surprised I know who you are. You look surprised. But I do. We know all about you. Thanks to Thomas. He sent me a flash drive with all the files you took from his cabin. He was a retired special agent with the FBI. You didn't think he had a backup?"

I watched his hand curl into a fist. His fingers tightened around the handle of his hunting knife.

"That is interesting, right? How did you know Thomas was on to you?"

Through gritted teeth, he said, "He contacted me. He didn't even realize it. He kept calling my previous aliases. But I never got rid of my phones. I had a burner in each location."

"Interesting. Did you know he sent us a flash drive and placed it in a PO box right here in Red Rose County? Plus, Sally told me she was starting to have concerns that maybe you weren't who you said you were. Between Thomas' information and Sally's instincts, we uncovered your entire pattern, or at least most of it. We think we've even identified your first four victims. You started young. The first one, when you were only fifteen, that must've been really something. The second one, well, that was before you knew much about forensics."

I watched his face carefully, waiting to see if he understood what I was implying. He was like a pot of water just about to boil. I was getting to him, but was it enough to provoke him into a fight?

I continued, "That's right. We have DNA from your first and second crime scenes. Then we found the third. And the fourth. And of course, we'd already linked you to four more in Washington. Plus Idaho, Oregon, Nevada... and now four more in California. Not to mention Thomas. And that's why it's interesting that you wanted to talk to me because I really wanted to talk to you too. Because, Damien, you're special too, aren't you?"

His jaw flexed. "Who else knows of this information?"

"The FBI. The sheriff's department. Pretty much everyone. We have your photo. And you know, I always knew we'd get you one day. Because people like you? You think no one's ever going to figure it out. You think you're too smart, too cunning. But you made a mistake—two mistakes actually. The first was killing Thomas. When you took the files, you left a void, a negative space. That told me there was something there the killer wanted. I knew it was you, because you left me a note at the scene."

I watched his face distort. He was about to bubble over.

"And then when Thomas gave me the flash drive, we probably could've found you with that information alone. But then you got close to my friend Sally. And that was your biggest mistake. You got too close. She suspected you. So with all of that, there's no way you are walking out of here a free man."

He stood and I braced myself for a fight.

"How does that make you feel, Damien?"

"You know, Valerie," he said, voice low, trembling with fury. "I don't like it one bit."

The sickly-sweet, creepy tone was gone, replaced by something colder and angrier. Something dangerous.

"Who made you like this, Damien?" I pushed. "Was it your mother? Your father? From what I understand, he wasn't a very nice guy. Is that why you killed him?"

He ignored me, turned, and marched to the door. He yanked it open. "We had a deal," he said. "This is between you and me. Sally leaves. Now."

I glanced down at her. "How are you doing?"

"I can probably limp along with a little help. But I don't want to leave you."

"It's okay. I've got this." I propped her up, keeping one eye on Damien the entire time. Using my body as her crutch, I said, "All right. I'm going to help Sally to the door. Sally, you can use the walls to lean on once you're out."

Damien/Dominic/the Bear watched as I began to lead Sally out of the room. Just as I stepped, out, he grabbed my arm and pulled me back. "Not so fast, Valerie. You for her, that was the deal. She can go. You can't."

Eyes on Sally, I said, "It's okay, Sally. Go."

She gave me a look, half fear and half hesitation, and I gave her another quick nod, letting her know it was okay. I had him right where I wanted him. She hobbled away and I was glad she was free. I yanked out of his grip and stepped back into the room.

His eyes grew dark, and in a low voice, he said, "Now, we play."

FIFTY-FIVE

HIM

Valerie thought she was so clever. And I thought she was so special. We had both been wrong. She was just like all the others. Just a stupid cop, thinking she knows everything about me. Who I was. Who I am. She actually believed she had all my kills, all my victims. She really thought she was smarter than me. Well, I was just going to have to teach her a lesson.

And poor little Sally, she wouldn't get very far on that ankle. Once I was done with Val, I'd go get Sally. Drag her back if I had to. She'd finally scream, but no one would hear her.

They were wrong about me. I *would* walk away a free man. Because I was smarter. More determined. More evolved.

Sally might make it to the trail eventually—it would take her a while hobbling like that—but it could happen. Which meant I didn't have much time to finish what I'd started nine months ago, when Valerie had stumbled into that barn.

"What are you going to do now, Damien?"

That name again. *Damien.* It had been a while since someone had called me that.

"Damien," she repeated, slower this time, like she was trying to get under my skin.

I smiled. "You know, I must admit, I'm a little disappointed in you, Valerie. I thought you were different. Special. But you're just like all the others. You tricked me. You came here with a plan. You probably have backup. But you see, that's not working in your favor, Valerie. And that's what's disappointing."

She took a step closer, the knife glinting slightly in the dim light.

"Because now I know I don't have a lot of time, when all I wanted was more time. If you had just upheld your end of the bargain, we could've been something special. But I see now that you're just like the rest."

"Oh, really?" she said, her voice sharp and steady. "Is that what you thought when you strangled fifteen-year-old Hannah?"

"You always remember your first," I said. "That was opportunity."

She took another step toward me, eyes blazing. "You left DNA at the scene. As soon as they catch you, and they will, you're going to prison. Federal prison. And it's not a pleasant place. Considering you killed a teenage girl and a little boy and so many others, prison's not going to be kind to you."

I watched her carefully. Her demeanor hadn't changed. She wasn't scared. She wasn't even pretending to be scared. I shouldn't have given her the knife. That was a mistake.

But she was wrong, I could get away a free man. All I had to do was change my identity again. It was easy. Cops were imbeciles.

She had figured me out, but she was sharper than the average member of law enforcement. Although, if I thought about it, it wasn't really her who'd figured me out, was it? It was Thomas Ingram. A bored old man with nothing better to do than obsess over an elusive serial killer. "The Bear." What a stupid nickname. I should kill her just for that. Why not something better? "The Northwest Slasher." Or "The Zorro Killer." Anything but *the Bear*.

"Valerie," I said, raising my knife. "That's where you're wrong. I'm not going to prison. But you? You're going to die."

She gave me a smirk. Calm. Controlled. "I don't think so."

Oh, Valerie. She would fight to the very end and I expected nothing less. Still, she was a disappointment. And once again, our time together would be cut short, but this time there would be a different ending.

FIFTY-SIX

VAL

My body was hot with adrenaline. I was ready for the fight and most definitely ready to end this. "It's not me who's going to die today, *Damien.*"

He flinched. *Good.* He hated that name, so I'd do nothing but call him Damien until he gave in to the rage. That's how the game really would start, the game that I hoped would end his reign of terror. But I wasn't foolish, I knew only one of us would win, and I couldn't let it be him.

He growled, then rushed at me.

I slashed with the knife and caught his arm. Blood spilled out, but it didn't even slow him down. His hands went to my throat, one gripping hard while the other still clutched his blade. He drove me backward, throwing me down onto the mattress. I kneed him in the groin.

He curled over with a sharp grunt, dropping the knife. I didn't hesitate. I kicked him in the ribs, then again in the side of the head as he tried to snatch it back.

"Still feeling confident, *Damien?*" I goaded.

"You. Will. Die," he spat, scrambling to his feet.

He grabbed for the knife, but I was faster. I lunged, tackling him on the mattress. My knee hit him square in the groin again. He landed on top of me, but I slashed at him, cutting deep across his midsection, then his thigh.

It only slowed him *a little*. Adrenaline and fear surged through me, electric and dizzying. I may have underestimated him. He was strong, but I had something he didn't. I had a reason to keep breathing. I had my son, my family, and my friends. He had nothing. He was just a sick monster who needed to be stopped.

He slammed his forearm against my throat, crushing my windpipe. I thrashed, trying to drive the knife into him again, but he knocked it from my hand. It clattered across the floor.

Now we were both unarmed. He pinned my arms above my head, his knee digging into my chest, heavy and suffocating.

"I knew you wouldn't go down without a fight, *Valerie*," he rasped "Unfortunately, we're not going to do this the way I'd hoped. But considering I've already given you my mark..."

With my remaining breath, I eeked out, "You mean, the 'S' for sicko. You're a sicko, *Damien*."

He struck me hard across the face and my cheek exploded in pain.

"Now let's get those chains on you, shall we?"

I struggled beneath him, twisting hard. I just needed to get one hand free. He'd have to loosen his grip to reach the chain, and then I'd take my chance.

He struck another open-handed smack across my face and my head snapped to the side. The world stopped for a moment, then came rushing back in a wash of stars.

"If you just calm down and let me get these on you, this won't be so tough," he said, his voice a manic purr. "We can be civilized about this, can't we, Valerie?"

Civilized. He was delusional.

I forced my body to go still. Limp. Defeated. So he would think I'd given up. "Okay," I whispered. "Fine. I won't fight."

He hesitated, eyes narrowing. "You don't have a weapon, Valerie. Fighting would be ill-advised. But then again, either way, I don't think this is going to be pleasant for you."

He removed his knee from my chest and straddled me as he shifted to reach for the chain.

That was his mistake. After recovering my breath, I writhed beneath him to mask the subtle movement of my hand. It slipped down between the mattress and the floor to search for… *There.* My fingers brushed cold metal. It was a screw. Sally had hidden it. *Well done.*

He leaned closer, breathing against my ear. "Have you had enough, Valerie? Or do you still have some fight left in you?"

He leaned over and reached for my left arm to fit the shackle. He was right where I wanted him. With every last shred of strength I had, I shoved the screw straight into his eye. He screamed. A raw, unearthly sound emanated from him as he reeled back, howling, with blood gushing down his cheek. He clawed at his eye, screaming curses and threats at me.

With a swift turn, I climbed onto my hands and knees and crawled across the floor to grab the knife. As I scurried, my ribs throbbed and my vision pulsed. But I found the knife. Just as I grabbed it, I looked up and saw he was coming for me.

Blood poured from his face, the screw still lodged in his eye, but he was coming. I didn't hesitate. On my feet, I turned and took aim. With every ounce of fury and love and survival in me, I struck.

FIFTY-SEVEN

VAL

Sweat ran down my back and temples as I released the knife and he crumpled to the floor.

Had I done it? Had I stopped him, once and for all? I'd aimed for his neck, trying to hit the carotid so he'd bleed out quick. So I could get away. So he'd die fast. That was the hope. He didn't deserve a jury or a trial. He deserved to be ended. No more innocent lives would be taken by this monster. This abomination. The world would be a safer place without him.

I was sore, my head pounding, but I could move. I could get out of there. I turned toward the door, ready to make my exit, when I heard a groan, and something grabbed my ankle.

I screamed as I hit the floor, landing hard on my wrist, and pain shot through my arm.

I kicked and clawed at the hand, twisting to look. Blood gushed from his chest, but I saw it immediately, I'd missed. Missed the artery. Missed my chance. *Dang it!*

He didn't speak. Just let out a low, guttural growl like a wounded animal. He was hurt, hurt bad, but like me, he would fight to the death.

And that's exactly what he intended to do.

I scrambled back, kicking at him. My fingernails tore at his skin as I jerked free. Back on my hands and knees, I tried to rise, tried to run, but I froze and watched in stunned horror as he reached for the knife. His fingers wrapped around the handle protruding from his chest, just below the collarbone, and he pulled it out.

A fresh gush of blood streamed from the wound, splattering onto the floor.

"No," I whispered. I hadn't hit anything vital. Not even close. He could live without an eye, and this wound wouldn't kill him either, not if he could stop the bleeding.

He looked like something out of a 1980s slasher movie, a one-eyed, blood-soaked monster that refused to die. I had to end this.

He was already trying to get to his feet, and I rushed to mine, desperate to beat him to it. But he was faster. His hand caught my arm. The knife was in his other. He slashed at my leg and I cried out, pain erupting like fire along my thigh.

"Yes," he hissed, slow and deliberate. "Give me more of that, Valerie."

I kicked, shoved, struggled to break free. His arm wrapped around my torso as he continued to slice at my skin. Burning. Piercing.

Did I still have a chance? I knew I couldn't give up. With all my strength, I drove my knee into his groin. He grunted, his grip loosening just enough for me to slip free. But he shoved me. *Hard.* My body landed with a thud on the mattress.

I thought, *No. Not here. This was not where I was going to die. It couldn't happen. Not like this.*

He came at me again. My knife was gone. I had nothing left. Just my body, and I wasn't done yet.

As he lunged, I lifted my legs and kicked as hard as I could. He stumbled backward, but didn't fall. And in a blink, he was on me again.

I grabbed at his leg, trying to take him down with me. He slipped, slightly, but fell on top of me in the process. His weight crushed my chest. His hands found my neck.

"No," I gasped, but the word barely escaped.

He punched me on the side of my face—hard. Then he straddled me and wrapped both hands around my throat. His fingers tightened. I could feel them digging into my skin, crushing my windpipe. I choked and struggled.

But it was no use. The awful realization hit me: *I'm going to die.*

FIFTY-EIGHT
BRADY

I pushed up the narrow forest path, my boots crunching against loose gravel and pine needles. Towering trees pressed in from both sides as if the pines and redwoods were leading the way, while thick underbrush crowded the edges, hiding who knew what. Creatures. People. Threats.

The air smelled of sap, moss, and damp earth. Normally I loved hiking, but this was different. There was a heaviness to the air, a sense of foreboding that clung to everything. Up ahead was the old summer camp.

I hoped we were right and that Val was there. That she was still alive.

I scanned the trees, flashlight beam sweeping across shadowed trunks and dense brush. The only sounds were rustling leaves, the distant hoot of an owl, and the quick skitter of something small in the undergrowth. Squirrels maybe. Or something worse.

I strained to hear more. A voice. A scream. Anything.

Was I too late? Was Val okay?

And Sally? She'd been taken two days ago and was probably hurt. Or worse.

I tried to force down the dark thoughts, but the pit in my stomach was growing. I didn't have time to spiral. I needed to be clear-headed. I needed to find them.

My grip tightened on the flashlight. My other hand hovered near my service weapon, fingers twitching. I wished Val hadn't gone off on her own. We could've come up with a plan. One the Bear wouldn't have detected. Why had she done this? I knew why. Because she would do anything to save Sally. Even if it meant sacrificing herself. She always put everyone else first and now she was out there, alone, with a killer.

I picked up my pace, heart thudding, breath coming fast and shallow. The path curved into the trees, tighter now. If anyone was watching, I was an easy target.

Beyond the beam of my flashlight, it was pitch-black.

I listened harder. Then—crunch. Not my footstep. I froze. An animal? A mountain lion? They were known sightings in the area. I called out, "Is there somebody out there? Val?"

No answer. Just silence. Then a whisper—ragged and weak. "Brady."

The voice was familiar, but it wasn't Val's. It had come from the thicket just off the trail.

I plunged into the underbrush, low branches whipping across my body. My flashlight flickered across roots, dead leaves, and then I saw her.

A slumped shape at the base of a tree. I swung the light to her feet, up to her face. "Sally!" I rushed forward.

She was leaning against the rough bark, half sitting, half collapsed. Her clothes were torn, smeared with blood and dirt. One eye was swollen shut. Her lip split. Dried blood streaked down from her temple. Her wrist bent at an unnatural angle. She blinked up at me.

"Sally, talk to me. Are you okay?" I asked, voice tight.

She gave a pained shake of her head. "He broke my ankle. My wrist too."

Her voice trembled. "I'm not in good shape, Brady, but I'll make it. Nothing life-threatening."

I crouched beside her, reaching out to steady her. My gaze swept over her injuries, and fury rose in my chest. The Bear had done this. He'd hurt her. Maybe left her to die. Or maybe... maybe she'd escaped. "How did you get here?" I asked.

"He let me go," she whispered. "He did what he promised. Val came. She said that was the deal: he'd release me if she went with him."

Sally grabbed my shirt with her good hand, her voice urgent. "You have to get to her. She's all alone with him. He's going to kill her, Brady."

My stomach twisted. "Do you know where she is?"

"It's at the summer camp. A big room. It's maybe a kitchen and a dining room. I don't know, maybe an auditorium. A big building, not one of the cabins." Her breath hitched. "It's all kind of a blur. But he has her, Brady."

I nodded. I wanted to run straight to Val, but what if something happened to Sally while I was gone? "The others are only a few minutes out," I said. "Backup is close."

"You need to go. He'll kill her. I know he will. I'll be fine. I'll make it. Trust me, I'm a doctor."

She could have internal injuries and not realize it. "Are you sure?"

She nodded again, her gaze clear despite everything. "Go."

I met her eyes, bloodshot, terrified, but steady.

"Help's on the way," I said. "When you hear boots, just call out. They're with us."

"Go."

I turned and ran. What I'd just seen, what he'd done to Sally, what he might've done to Val, it lit something inside me. Fear. Rage. Adrenaline burned through every single muscle as I charged toward the summer camp.

The place loomed ahead. The old wooden sign, weathered

and warped, swung slightly in the breeze. Dark silhouettes of the cabins stood to either side, empty and silent. I sprinted past them, my boots pounding against the packed earth, flashlight beam slicing through the blackness.

It looked just as I remembered it from high school. At the far end of the camp, a larger structure came into view. The mess hall. It had a wide double door. It had to be the place Sally had just described.

Back when we were kids, this was where we ate meals, gathered for plays, laughed through announcements. A place full of noise and life. Now it was a place of silence. Maybe death. *Val, please be alive.*

I bounded up the steps two at a time and grabbed the handle, throwing the door wide open, and pulling my weapon. The stench of rot and mildew hit me like a wall. It was pitch-black inside.

My flashlight beam swept across the room. Dust hung in the air like smoke. Broken tables. Abandoned chairs. The mess hall looked deserted but it didn't feel that way. There was a weight in the air. A heaviness. I raised my weapon in one hand, flashlight in the other, scanning the area slowly.

Then I saw it, a thin line of light glowing beneath a door at the back of the building.

I moved fast, my footsteps quiet, breath steadying as I approached. Every nerve in my body screamed to hurry, but I couldn't risk making a sound.

At the door, I raised my foot and kicked hard. The door slammed open with a crash. The scene inside was straight out of a nightmare. A bloodstained mattress lay on the floor. A man crouched over a limp figure, her arms sprawled out, unmoving. I couldn't see her face, but I knew it was Val.

"Freeze!" I roared.

The man turned his head slowly, as if he'd been expecting me. His face was a grotesque mask, with blood streaking down from his temple, one eye impaled and the other locked onto mine. His jaw was red with gore, blood dripping from the corner of his mouth.

"Let her go," I said, gun trained on him.

"Never," he rasped.

"I will shoot."

"You don't have it in you, *Brady*."

My grip tightened on the weapon. I took a step forward. Then I looked down.

It was Val. Her eyes were closed. Her body was still.

Was I too late?

FIFTY-NINE

VAL

Understanding there was no point anymore, I stopped struggling and let go. As I did, my life played behind my eyes in flickering snapshots. There I was on a trail with Mom and Dad as a little girl, my sister toddling behind. Hanging out in the woods during high school with Brady and our friends. Meeting Nathan, our wedding day, and then holding Harrison in my arms for the first time. Harrison's first smile and his first steps. The moment he babbled, "Mama." There were so many joyous memories. I had lived my life. It was a good one. My energy was fading fast and I couldn't hear anything. Unconsciousness loomed like a thick fog, and I welcomed the stillness. I'd made peace with the inevitable. I had lived. I had loved. I had regrets.

I was about to drift away when a gunshot rang out. The fingers around my neck loosened. I gasped for air, choking, wheezing, and then the weight on top of me shifted and was gone. I rolled over, my lungs screaming for breath, my body too weak to move fast. My vision blurred. Then there was another sound. The metallic clink of handcuffs. Relief and disbelief crashed into me all at once. *They'd found me.*

Still dazed from the lack of oxygen, I managed to open my

eyes. And there he was, *Brady*. Tears welled. The look on his face was one I would never forget. A mix of horror and relief, but above all else, love.

Damien lay bleeding on the floor. I didn't know where Brady had shot him, but he'd cuffed him, and that was good enough for me. Brady rushed to me and dropped to his knees, his hand gripping my arm gently. "Are you okay?"

I nodded faintly, voice raspy. "I am now." I paused for breath. "How did you find me?"

"I couldn't get a hold of you. Your mom said you went out with Lucy so I went round to see her. She told me everything. We traced your phone and then found it in your car."

I smiled through the tears, but then dread filled my thoughts. He hadn't mentioned Sally. "Did you find Sally?"

"Yes. She's going to be okay. She was hiding along the trail. She looks pretty banged up."

"But she's okay?"

"Yes. You're going to be okay too. He might not."

I sniffled and wrapped my arms around Brady, clinging to him as he lifted me gently to my feet. "Thank you so much."

He leaned in close. "I'll never let anyone hurt you ever again."

We stood there for a moment, just holding each other. Then I pulled back, shaky but steady. "We have to get to Sally."

"We need to stay put and keep an eye on him. Jordan, Kieran, and a tactical team were only a few minutes behind me, they'll find her." He paused, and then said, "They told me to stay back, but I couldn't wait."

Part of me wanted to lecture him for going into an extremely dangerous situation, *alone*, but with all things considered, I refrained. "I wouldn't have waited either, if the situation was reversed."

"I have no doubt."

I looked down at Damien. He wasn't moving. Brady had

shot him, but from the way the blood poured from his side, it might not be fatal, the combination of eye and chest wounds, maybe. It wasn't a guarantee.

"Did you check for a pulse?"

"No. I cuffed him and ran straight to you."

I hoped he bled out, if he wasn't already dead. But I knew that likely wasn't how Brady thought. "Can you call for help?" I asked.

"No reception. We'll have to wait until the team gets here."

We stood side-by-side in silence. Then Brady said quietly, "We've got a few minutes. Can you promise me something?"

"What is it?"

"Please never do this again. Please let me in. Why didn't you trust me the way you trusted Lucy?"

I swallowed hard. "I didn't think you'd let me do it."

"You're right, but we could've come up with a plan. You could've given me a heads-up, something, anything. You scared me, Val, really scared me."

"I'm sorry." And I was. I hadn't wanted to put Brady, or anyone, through that, but it was the only way out I could see.

He placed his hand on my cheek. "I love you, Val. And I can't lose you. Please promise me, no more solo missions. I don't think I could take it."

He loved me? Where did that come from? Were we in love? Had I missed that too? I couldn't think about that now, but I knew he was right. It was time to make a choice. One I should've made a long time ago. I had to put my loved ones first, not the bad guys. What would Harrison have done without a mother? He'd have been scarred for life. That would've been on me. Brady. Mom. My sister. It was time I made a choice.

"I promise," I said.

He kissed me lightly on the forehead and squeezed me tight.

We both looked down at Damien's body. Part of me wished

he'd just die right there. The sound of boots moving, fast, and in formation, echoed through the hall. We separated as Jordan burst inside and scanned the room.

I raised my hand in a weak wave.

Brady said, "I shot him. He was on top of Val and had his hands around her neck. I didn't check for a pulse, but I cuffed him. We need to get Val and Sally to medical."

"We'll take care of this. We found Sally. She's with the team. An ambulance is on the way. Is there anyone else here?"

Brady said, "I didn't see or hear any movement other than in this room."

Jordan glanced over at me. "How are you doing, Val?"

"I'm okay. Thank you, Jordan."

He gave me a look. It was half scolding and half relief. He wanted to say I was reckless. That I'd been stupid. And he would've been right. He simply said, "I'm glad you're okay."

"Me too."

"The team and I will take care of this. You two go and get fixed up."

I nodded, and Brady and I walked out together.

It was time to put the Bear and all the bloodshed behind me. It was time to live life for the ones I loved instead of chasing monsters and nearly becoming one of their victims.

SIXTY

VAL

Every inch of my body ached. My head pounded. My face felt like it was on fire. My arms, my legs—everything hurt. The trek down to the trailhead parking lot felt endless, every step slow and painful. Brady was my crutch, both physically and emotionally.

It had been such a whirlwind of fear and trauma, but he never left my side. He took the slow, painful path down with me, never rushing, and never complaining. And through the pain, four words kept echoing in my mind, over and over. *I love you, Val.*

The sweetest four words I'd heard in a long time.

I hadn't said it back. Love hadn't even occurred to me in the chaos. I knew I cared for him, wanted to be with him, but I hadn't let myself think beyond that. Could we really be something? Did he mean it? And—did I?

As I limped beside him, each painful step making it harder to breathe, I already knew the answer. *Yes.* I stopped and turned to him.

"Brady?"

He glanced at me, instantly concerned. "Are you okay? What can I do?"

Always looking out for me. He always had, even when we were kids. Why hadn't I seen it until now? "I just wanted to say something."

His eyes met mine, searching. I smiled through the pain.

"I love you too, Brady."

A smile spread across his face, warm and real. He leaned in and kissed me—soft, comforting. "Good," he said. "Now let's get you fixed up."

I grinned, and I think I grinned the whole way back. When we finally reached the parking lot, it was no longer empty. FBI vehicles, sheriff's department cruisers, and flashing lights filled the space. They'd set up a mobile command post, and under one of the floodlights stood one of the best friends I'd ever had. Lucy.

Next to her, holding her hand, was her boyfriend Jonathan, his long hair pulled back, his eyes locked on mine the moment he saw me.

"Let's go talk to Lucy," I said.

Brady nodded, helping me along. As soon as Lucy and I made eye contact, she ran to me and threw her arms around me. I hugged her tightly, despite the pain, and whispered in her ear, "Thank you."

She clung tighter. "I'm so glad you're okay."

I nodded, sniffling. She pulled back, tears in her eyes. "Sally was here. They already put her in the ambulance. She's on her way to the hospital. I think she's going to be okay."

"Good."

"I thought you might be mad that I told Brady," she said.

"I'm not mad. You did exactly what you should've. I should've never gone alone. I should've told all of you."

Lucy shook her head. "None of that. It's because of you that we're all alive. You and Sally, you saved each other."

"I hope so."

"Where is he now? What's going on up there?" Lucy asked.

"The Feds took over. He's injured, but they're not sure if he's going to make it."

Lucy looked me over. "I'm assuming you're on your way to the hospital too?"

"I think I'll be okay."

Brady interjected, "Val..."

I looked up at him. My love. My protector. He gestured to my leg, blood soaking through the fabric. The reason I was limping. The reason I needed a crutch.

"Okay, okay, yes. I'm going to the hospital. I'll let them check me out."

"More than just check you out, Val," Lucy said. "You're bleeding."

"They'll patch me up. I'll be good as new."

"But you're not doing this again, right?" Lucy asked.

"No," I said, shaking my head. "But I think there'll be more dinners in my backyard."

"I sure hope so," Lucy added with a small smile. "But like, without a serial killer watching us, right?"

I couldn't help but laugh, and then wince. It hurt, but I didn't care. Jonathan walked over, his face tight with concern.

"Thanks for coming," I said.

"As soon as Lucy told me what happened, I came straight here. I wanted her to leave, but she refused to go until she'd seen you."

I reached out and grabbed Lucy's hand, squeezing it tight. "Sisters."

That's what we'd become.

"Well, thank you," I said to them both.

"We should get you to the hospital, Val," Brady said gently, ever the protector even when I didn't think I needed one.

"I suppose I have to go now."

"You do," Lucy agreed. "And I'm going to hold you to that dinner."

"You do that."

Brady helped me to his SUV and opened the passenger door with care, easing me in gently like I might break.

"I'm fine, Brady."

He gave me a look that said *you're not*, and he was right. I was bruised, cut, bleeding. But I *was* okay. On the drive, I called Mom to let her know I was safe and sound.

"Val?" she answered. "I'm so glad to hear your voice."

"I'm sorry I lied to you."

"Oh, honey. You know I could tell, right?"

"Mother..."

"Val, I need you to not do this again. You're going to be the death of me."

It became my second promise of the night. "I promise it won't happen again."

"Do you want me to come see you at the hospital?"

"No, it's late. Very late. Brady's here. We'll be fine. I'm going to call Harrison next."

"Okay. I know if you're with Brady, you'll be okay."

There was so much more I wanted to tell her, like what Brady had said, and what I'd said back, but it could wait. I glanced at the clock. Midnight.

Which meant it was 3 a.m. on the East Coast, where Harrison was likely sound asleep. I didn't want to wake him, but maybe, maybe this was an exception. I needed to hear his voice.

He answered immediately. "Mom?"

"Hi, honey. It's me."

"Everything okay?"

"It is now. We got him."

"I'm so glad to hear that," he said, sleepy but sincere.

"I don't want to keep you up, sweetheart. Just wanted to tell you that I'm okay. He can't hurt us anymore."

"Good to hear it, Mom."

"Now go back to sleep."

"Okay. Love you, Mom."

"I love you too." I hung up and set the phone down.

Brady reached out his hand and I laced my fingers with his and didn't let go the rest of the drive to the hospital.

SIXTY-ONE
VAL

As we approached the entrance of the hospital, Brady led me to the reception area of the Emergency Room and sat me down. He explained the situation and that I needed a wheelchair due to the laceration on my leg. I wasn't sure it was necessary but considering how my leg throbbed, I wasn't going to argue.

Within moments, a nurse in rose-colored scrubs wheeled one toward me. Brady helped me into the chair and then wheeled me to the check-in desk. The nurse, said, "It'll be a while before we can get you to triage, hang tight."

Brady looked like he was ready to argue, but I placed a hand on his arm.

"It's okay, Brady. I'll be fine. Plus, I want to see Sally. We need to check on her."

"But you're bleeding."

The nurse peered over the desk, "Let me get you something to put on that while you wait." She rushed out and returned on the other side of the desk with a large piece of gauze, and said, "Not too bad, but you'll probably need stitches. Go ahead and press firmly on it. We'll get you in soon."

"Thank you." I said. I turned to Brady. "Now, let's check on Sally."

Brady hesitated, but then asked reception, "Where can we find Sally Edison? She was brought in about twenty minutes ago."

Another nurse approached. "Are you family?"

"I'm with the sheriff's department," Brady said, as if the uniform wasn't a giveaway. "She was involved in a violent crime this evening. She's a victim, as is Ms. Costa."

The nurse nodded and typed something quickly before telling us where to find her.

Brady glanced down at me, "Ready?"

"Yes."

He wheeled me down the corridor. The hospital hallway was stark and sterile, buzzing faintly with overhead lights and distant monitors. When we reached the room, I saw Sally and she looked awful. Honestly, if it weren't for her bright red hair, I might not have recognized her.

Her face was swollen and badly bruised. An IV was in her arm. A nurse stood at her side, and a doctor in a white coat hovered nearby, reviewing notes. She looked over and gave a faint, weary smile.

"Hi, Val."

"Hi, Sally," I said gently. "How are you doing?"

"Apparently I'm a bit banged up," she said with a slur, probably due to heavy pain medication. I was glad for that. If she felt even a small fraction of what she looked like, she needed every drop.

Her speech was slow as she said, "How are you, Val? I'm so glad Brady found you. Did you get him?"

I nodded, swallowing the lump in my throat. "He did... But, Sally, don't worry about me."

"I'm glad you're okay," she said and then, "I'm sorry. I'm so sorry I didn't see him for who he was. This is my fault."

How could she think that? Sally had been a pawn in a psychopath's game. "It's not your fault, not even a little bit. If it's anyone's fault, it's mine. I should've known."

I should have known he'd try to get close, and with "Dominic" suddenly appearing in Sally's life it should have been an immediate giveaway. And it was my fault because if it wasn't for me, he would never have been in Red Rose County in the first place.

"No," Brady said firmly. "Both of you are wrong. This is on him. *This is his fault.* Not yours. And I'm so, so sorry this happened to you both."

Brady was right. As much as I took on the guilt, Damien Stokes had chosen a life of murder and destruction, not us.

"Did you see Lucy at the scene?" I asked.

She gave a faint nod.

"Me too. Jonathan came to be with her. She told me that when you're healed up we need to have dinner. I offered my backyard again, and she said—" I paused, debating if it was too soon for killer jokes. But I thought I knew Sally well enough and said, "As Lucy put it, without a serial killer watching us this time."

A tiny smile crept across Sally's lips. "It's a deal."

I placed my hand gently on top of hers and turned to the doctor.

"So... what's going on?"

He gave me a professional but calm nod. "We've completed her scans. There's some internal bleeding, several deep contusions, one broken rib, a fractured ankle and wrist. We'll be prepping her for surgery now. So—"

"Got it. We'll go."

He offered me a kind smile. "She's in capable hands. We'll take good care of her."

"Thank you." And then I remembered something I needed

to tell Sally, "One last thing. I almost forgot. I found the screw. Got him right in the eye."

Sally's eyes lit up and a satisfied grin formed on her face. "That's what I was going to do if I'd had the chance."

"I figured," I said, and I gently patted her hand. "Good luck, and I'll be here when you wake up."

Brady wheeled me back toward the waiting area. As we rounded the corner, a commotion surged through the emergency room doors. A person on a gurney, flanked by law enforcement, was being rushed through. My breath caught. The joy and relief I'd felt just a moment ago dropped into the pit of my stomach, replaced with a cold, sinking dread. *He's still alive.*

SIXTY-TWO

BRADY

The flurry of movement toward the entrance grabbed my attention. Surrounding the paramedics and a man on a stretcher was a sheriff's deputy along with Jordan and another agent. I glanced down at Val. Her swollen face was twisted.

Placing my hand on her arm, I said, "Do you want me to go see what's going on?"

Val nodded, her expression tight.

"You'll be okay on your own?"

"Yes, please, go."

With that I rushed toward Jordan, who had just retreated inside the emergency bay and was speaking with Kieran.

"Hey. What's going on?" I asked.

Jordan's face was serious. "After you left, we examined the body and we got a pulse. He's still alive."

My gut tightened. "Do they think he'll make it?"

He exhaled. "Paramedics didn't say. But unfortunately, most of the wounds appear superficial."

White hot rage bubbled inside me again. I should've gone for the headshot. Always the boy scout, I didn't want to kill him unnecessarily. But wouldn't the world have been better off?

The shoot would have been justified considering he had actively been trying to kill Val. But maybe that's just not who I am. I couldn't murder someone even when justified. Did that make me weak? How would Val see it?

I thought we would be able to put the Bear behind us and start a life together. Even in prison, the Bear could wreak havoc on Val's life. That didn't feel like justice. I looked back toward Val, worry creeping in again.

"How's Val?" Kieran asked.

"She's in the waiting room. She probably has a few fractured ribs, lacerations, and bruising. The worst of it is a nasty cut to her leg, but if there's no hidden injuries she should be fine. All things considered, she's in decent shape." I had to believe that she would be okay, I couldn't lose her. Not now.

"Good," Kieran said, visibly relieved.

Jordan said, "And how's Sally?"

"We just spoke with her doctor. They're prepping her for surgery now. Some internal bleeding, and a few broken bones, but they're positive she'll fully recover in time." She likely had months of physical therapy, not to mention months, or a lifetime, of working with a mental health professional.

Jordan said, "That's good to hear."

"Keep us posted on the outcome with the Bear. I know Val won't be pleased he made it out alive."

Kieran said, "None of us are, but we're the law. Not God. We don't make those kinds of choices unless we absolutely have to. Based on where he was shot, I'm guessing you agree."

I nodded.

Kieran continued, "We'll let you know his status when we get an update."

"Thank you. I'll stay here with Val until she's ready to go home."

Jordan gave me a steady look. "Good. As soon as we hear anything else, I'll come find you."

"Thanks," I said, meaning it. I turned and headed back to Val just as her name was called from across the room. As I reached her, I said, "Come on, let's go."

She looked up at me, reading my expression. "What did you find out?"

"I'll tell you once we're inside."

She gave me a look as if she didn't want to wait, but nodded. Right now, she needed to worry about her own health, not the prognosis of a sadistic killer.

SIXTY-THREE

VAL

The nurse had taken my vitals, asked a few questions, and said, "The doctor will be in shortly," before leaving the exam room. As I sat on the hospital bed, bruised, and bandaged, Brady sat quietly beside me.

Finally with a moment alone, I said, "What did you find out? Is he still alive?" I couldn't bring myself to say his name, or *any* of his names.

He hesitated before saying, "He survived. Most of his injuries aren't typically fatal, but he has multiple wounds so it's unclear. There may be internal bleeding they don't know about, but as of right now, he might survive."

I didn't like that. Not one bit. Why did he get to live, when so many innocent people didn't get the chance? Where was the justice in that? What was the point of it all if monsters like Damien Stokes got to breathe while his victims never would again? And if he survived, then this wasn't really over, was it? How could I live with that? Should I have ended him? I had the chance. I could've had the element of surprise and finished him off.

A middle-aged blonde woman in a white coat entered the

room and walked up to my bed. "Hello, Valerie, I'm Dr. Pinto. It's been quite the night from what I've heard."

"Yeah," I said, trying to smile. "Thankfully, it's almost over."

"Let's hope so," she said, then glanced at Brady. "Valerie, I'm going to do a quick exam and then send you for X-rays. Do you want the deputy to stay with you?"

We'd just exchanged I love yous, but we'd only kissed. I didn't want his first image of my body as bruised and battered after a harrowing ordeal. I was thinking more like dinner, wine, and lingerie.

I turned to Brady. "I think I'd rather you go."

Brady gave me that boyish smile. "You got it. I'll be right outside, Val." He gave my hand a quick squeeze before he left.

The next two hours were a blur of scans, stitches, and cleaning and bandaging wounds. The verdict was that I had no internal bleeding, but I had a cracked rib, a deep leg laceration, and a whole lot of bruising. My face, especially, looked like a horror show. But I'd survived worse. I *had* survived and so had Sally.

Lucy was safe. Harrison and my mom were doing well. And Brady was in my life. I was grateful, and I should've been content, but I couldn't stop thinking about *him*. The Bear was still alive. At least, he was the last time anyone had checked. The nurse wheeled me into the waiting room, when Brady came walking up.

"All done?"

"Yep. Did you find out how Sally is doing?"

"Yes, I spoke with one of the nurses. She's still in surgery. The doctor has addressed the internal bleeding and they think they've stopped it. They'll work on setting her bones next."

"Good. Did they say she's going to make a full recovery?"

"They did."

It was great news. We both knew it. Of course I was glad Sally would be okay. That we would be okay. But there was still that lingering dread. At the sounds of heavy footsteps, I glanced and saw Jordan and Kieran. I waved.

"I heard you're ready to head out," Kieran said.

"I'm going to wait for Sally to come out of surgery first."

Kieran said, "How are you feeling?"

"I'm okay. A little sore, but before you know it I'll be good as new."

Jordan and Kieran exchanged a glance. "But this is the last of your solo missions, right?" Jordan asked, his brows raised.

"For the third time tonight, I'm making a promise," I said, raising my hand like I was swearing in. "Solo missions have ceased. They're now part of my past."

Kieran patted my shoulder. "Good to hear."

"I heard he's in surgery," I said. "Is he going to make it?"

Jordan nodded. "He's out of surgery. They removed the bullet, repaired the damage, and bandaged his wounds. His eye is gone, but other than that he's going to make a full recovery."

"So... what's next with the case?" I asked.

"As you know, he's going into federal custody," Jordan explained. "It'll be up to him—whether he wants to go to trial or accept a plea deal. But I can tell you, and I think you know this, there's no way he will ever be a free man again."

"There's no way he's avoiding prison, Val," Kieran said. "No way he'll see the light of day again. He won't even get special privileges, unless..."

He hesitated.

"Unless he has other victims," I finished for him. "Victims we haven't found yet."

Kieran said, "Yes. If he gives up their locations, maybe he gets an extra Cup O' Noodles. But even then we already have enough to prosecute the multiple murders in Red Rose County. What he did to you and Sally alone would be enough for him to spend the rest of his natural life in prison. Not to mention, we've connected him to others and even if the physical evidence is thin, we've got enough circumstantial evidence to bury him."

I wished that was enough to allow me to sleep through the night, but I knew it wasn't. "He could try to contact me from prison."

Jordan didn't flinch. "That's always a possibility. But he'll never get to you. Or anyone you care about."

I nodded slowly, but deep down, I knew better. Serial killers don't always act alone forever. They find acolytes. Admirers. Copycats. People willing to do their dirty work from the outside. People who wanted to be like them. Unfortunately, there were a lot of sick individuals out there. Damien Stokes would never walk free again, but that didn't mean he wouldn't try to come after me with the help of a fellow psycho, but I couldn't dwell on that. I had too much to live for, too many people to love, to let fear control me. But I would remain vigilant and watchful, because until Damien was in his grave, I could never let my guard down.

SIXTY-FOUR

VAL

One year later

Our champagne flutes clinked, and I watched with a wide smile as Lucy and Jonathan shared a sweet kiss in front of all their guests. Lucy wore a gorgeous, fitted gown, and Jonathan looked sharp in a royal blue tuxedo. The ceremony had been beautiful, set in a clearing near their home, surrounded by trees and soft sunlight filtering through the leaves.

Sally and I had been bridesmaids. Lucy had insisted we could wear whatever we wanted, and we'd both chosen forest green, flowing tea-length dresses. We carried bouquets of wildflowers, just like Lucy. It all felt so natural, earthy, and deeply beautiful.

Lucy and Jonathan had found their happily ever after. I'd had no doubt they would from the moment they'd started dating. It had felt like fate. Their relationship had developed quickly, but from the start, they'd just clicked. I especially knew it was real when, after our last encounter with the serial killer, Jonathan had never left her side. He didn't want her to be alone. And I think that's what true love is, ensuring those we care about are never alone and they know they always have someone watching out for them. A partner. It was beautiful to see with the happy couple. I took a sip of my champagne and glanced over at Sally, who downed the rest of hers in one gulp.

"I'm jealous," she confessed.

"Of Lucy and Jonathan?"

She nodded, her expression soft and a little sad. "I'm forty years old, and I just don't think I'll ever have that."

"You will, when you're ready," I said gently.

Sally had healed physically from her captivity, an ordeal that had left scars far deeper than what anyone could see. She'd thought she was dating a lovely man, someone kind, someone safe, but Dominic had turned out to be a sadistic killer. It had rattled her to the core, shattered her ability to trust her own instincts. Honestly, if I were in her position, I wasn't sure I could trust again either.

Lucy and I had tried to reassure her by telling her that she'd sensed something was off within a week and a half, and that showed that her instincts were sharper than she gave herself credit for. I'm not sure she believed us, but she'd been in therapy ever since. She was doing the same grounding exercises my therapist had taught me. We both had meditation apps on our phones, and we'd started running together. It helped with the stress and the anxiety that came with the lingering trauma that clung on long after the bad guy was in jail.

I leaned toward Sally with a smile. "Well, until you meet him, or if you choose not to, you have Lucy and me. Forever. It is our solemn vow."

As I glanced at Sally, then over to Lucy, who was spying a look at us and smiling, I knew that in thirty years from now, we would still be friends, still gossiping over dinner, drinking wine, and sharing our lives. Just like my mother and her friends, Julie and Diane. They had stood by her through some of the hardest times of her life. And as if my thoughts had summoned her,

Mom walked over with Julie, both of them beaming from ear to ear.

"Are you two going to get on the dance floor or not?" Mom said, mischievously.

"We're just taking a breath, Mom," I said with a smile.

Mom was tough, one of the toughest women I'd ever known. With physical therapy, support, determination, and love, she was able to walk again, and take care of herself. And tonight, she was dancing at Lucy and Jonathan's wedding. With her best friends, and *Brady*. It was inspiring.

"Well," she said with a wink, "you'd better not wait too long. Otherwise, someone might steal your date."

Oh yes. *Brady*. My date, my love, and the best man I've ever known. It's interesting how much can change in a year. *Or two.*

Two years ago, I was an FBI agent hunting serial killers. My sole focus in life, other than my son, was tracking the bad guys, making sure they couldn't hurt anyone ever again. And then one of those bad guys had caught me. That one creep had let me go but not out of mercy, but so he could play a sick, extended game. For nine months, he'd tormented us. Killed four more people in my town and my mentor, Thomas Ingram. Then he'd kidnapped Sally. And then it came down to him and me. Fighting it out. Both of us surviving. That wasn't how I thought it would end. I thought he would've died in the attack. But I guess, deep down, he and I weren't anything alike. I couldn't take a life. Not even his. As much as I'd wanted to rid the world of his presence, I couldn't do it. Neither could Brady. He'd had a clear shot, but hadn't taken it. He'd just wanted to save me and do the right thing. That's one of the things I loved about Brady, one of the many things.

It's been a quiet year since then, and that quiet has been good. Harrison came out to Red Rose County to visit, and I flew out to visit him at MIT. Brady and I both went. He visited his daughter at college, and I saw my son. Both kids were delighted that Brady and I were finally together. Both claiming, with a knowing grin, that they "just knew" it would happen. *Oh, to be young again.*

I was so grateful for everything I had, and yet I couldn't ignore the milestone approaching. In just a few more years, I'd be fifty. It made me reflect. Think about what was next. Although I'd officially retired from the FBI nearly two years ago, it hadn't felt real until recently. But I knew my time in law enforcement was over. It was time for another generation to track the monsters. Time for someone else to carry that burden.

I thought I'd be bored without the job, especially since Mom was taking care of herself and Harrison was away at school. I had been wrong. Brady, Sally, and Lucy filled my time. Brady and I hiked and traveled. We visited family. It was a good life. If there was one thing I would change, it would be that Damien Stokes was dead. Instead, he'd taken a plea deal to avoid the death penalty. He was currently serving twelve life sentences. He would never get out of prison. As much as I wanted him gone, I knew I wasn't like him. I didn't have it in me to kill. But that didn't mean I liked the fact he was still breathing. There was always a looming threat that he could send someone after me, or worse, after my family. But so far, nothing. Not a letter or message, it had been total radio silence. All I could do was hope it stayed that way.

But I don't know if I'll ever fully relax as long as he's alive and maybe that's my cross to bear. There's always a bogeyman lurking in the shadows. Mine just happened to have a name.

Brady returned to the table, cheeks flushed, hair slightly tousled. "I barely escaped," he said, breathless.

Sally and I laughed.

"Is that right?" I replied with a chuckle.

"Your mom and her friends are very persuasive. I'm getting a great workout."

Brady had been far more amenable to my mother's demands

than I'd expected, dancing the night away with her and her best friends. He sat down beside me and gave me a light kiss.

Sally stood, placing her glass down with a smile. "Okay," she said, winking, "I'm gonna go talk to Lucy and leave you two lovebirds alone."

Brady said, "It's a pretty great wedding, don't you think?"

I smiled. "Yes, it was really beautiful. I'm so happy for Lucy and Jonathan."

"Me too." He snuggled a little closer, lacing his fingers with mine. "Do you think you'd ever wanna do it again?"

"Do what again?" I asked, my brow lifting.

He looked into my eyes and took both of my hands in his, suddenly sitting up straighter across from me.

"Would you ever want to be married again?"

I was speechless. Had I thought about it? Sure. Especially with all the talk of Lucy's engagement along with the wedding planning, the fittings, the bridesmaid dress, and the hair consultations. It had crossed my mind more than once. "I think... if it was the right person... I think so," I finally said.

"Yeah?" he asked, a sparkle in his warm brown eyes.

"Yes, I would like to get married again," I said, a little surprised with myself. I added, "but he'd have to be a really great guy. *Handsome* too."

Brady gave me a lopsided grin. "You know, I've been thinking a lot about this. And I'd like to get married again too. But only if it was to an amazing, tough, beautiful, spectacular woman—like *the most* incredible woman I've ever met."

I felt weightless, like if someone pinched me, I'd wake from a dream. How had I got this lucky? Then he let go of my hands and reached into his pocket. He pulled something out and held it up. For one of the few times in my life, I was truly speechless. It was a sparkling diamond ring.

My heart stopped. Was he really proposing to me, here, at

Lucy's wedding? Was that even okay? Would she be upset? It was supposed to be *her* day.

I thought, *Oh my. He's really doing this.* I glanced around, and that's when I noticed the eyes on us. An audience. He'd planned this, and they'd known about it!

My breath caught as I looked back at Brady.

His voice was tender. "Will you make me the luckiest man in the world and be my partner for life?"

I was so overcome with emotion, so filled with gratitude, that words failed me. He slid the ring onto my finger, and I nodded as we embraced. Part of me felt like we were in our own little world, just Brady and me, but then the cheers erupted, and clapping filled the air.

I turned and saw them standing around us: Mom, Julie, Diane, Sally, Lucy, and Jonathan, all beaming.

"You all knew?" I asked, wide-eyed.

"Of course," Lucy said, blinking back happy tears. "It was my idea for him to do it today!"

And just like that, with all the darkness we had seen, the sun was still shining, and the future was bright.

A LETTER FROM H.K. CHRISTIE

Dear reader,

Thank you for reading *Last One Alive*. I hope you enjoyed reading it as much as I loved writing it. If you're interested in exploring more of my books, or you'd simply like to say "hello", visit www.authorhkchristie.com and drop me a message. I love to hear from readers!

If you want to keep up to date with all my latest releases, just sign up at the following link. Your email address will never be shared and you can unsubscribe at any time.

www.bookouture.com/h-k-christie

You can also sign up for my newsletter where you'll be the first to hear about upcoming novels, new releases, giveaways, promotions, and a free eBook of *Crashing Down*, the prequel to the Martina Monroe crime thriller series. Sign up today at www.subscribepage.com/u7n7g8_copy2

You can also follow and reach out on social media.

Thank you,

H.K. Christie

KEEP IN TOUCH WITH H.K. CHRISTIE

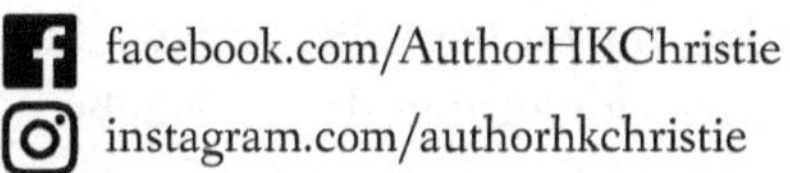

www.authorhkchristie.com

facebook.com/AuthorHKChristie

instagram.com/authorhkchristie

ACKNOWLEDGMENTS

To my amazing friends—Karen, Dusty, Barbara, and Trish—thank you for inspiring Val's fabulous new circle of girlfriends. As much as I adore my husband, life just wouldn't be as colorful (or nearly as fun) without decades of laughter, loyalty, and a little harmless mischief with you all. Writing thrillers doesn't always leave room for friendship tributes, but slipping in the Val, Lucy, and Sally scenes was my sneaky way of celebrating you.

I'd like to extend my deepest gratitude to the team at Bookouture, especially Helen Jenner and Ria Clare for helping bring this story to life.

And of course, a big thank you to my emotional support team. For Charlie, my little Yorkie Poo for always being by my side. Always. And to all of my friends, family, and husband for the endless support over the years.

Last but not least, I'd like to thank all of my readers. It's because of you I'm able to continue writing stories.

PUBLISHING TEAM

Turning a manuscript into a book requires the efforts of many people. The publishing team at Bookouture would like to acknowledge everyone who contributed to this publication.

Audio
Alba Proko
Sinead O'Connor
Melissa Tran

Commercial
Lauren Morrissette
Hannah Richmond
Imogen Allport

Cover design
The Brewster Project

Data and analysis
Mark Alder
Mohamed Bussuri

Editorial
Helen Jenner
Ria Clare

Copyeditor
Anna Paterson

Proofreader
Deborah Blake

Marketing
Alex Crow
Melanie Price
Occy Carr
Cíara Rosney
Martyna Młynarska

Operations and distribution
Marina Valles
Stephanie Straub
Joe Morris

Production
Hannah Snetsinger
Mandy Kullar
Nadia Michael
Charlotte Hegley

Publicity
Kim Nash
Noelle Holten
Jess Readett
Sarah Hardy

Rights and contracts
Peta Nightingale
Richard King
Saidah Graham

Dear Reader,

We'd love your attention for one more page to tell you about the crisis in children's reading, and what we can all do.

Studies have shown that reading for fun is the **single biggest predictor of a child's future life chances** – more than family circumstance, parents' educational background or income. It improves academic results, mental health, wealth, communication skills, ambition and happiness.

The number of children reading for fun is in rapid decline. Young people have a lot of competition for their time, and a worryingly high number do not have a single book at home.

Hachette works extensively with schools, libraries and literacy charities, but here are some ways we can all raise more readers:

- Reading to children for just 10 minutes a day makes a difference
- Don't give up if children aren't regular readers – there will be books for them!

- Visit bookshops and libraries to get
  recommendations
- Encourage them to listen to audiobooks
- Support school libraries
- Give books as gifts

There's a lot more information about how to encourage children
to read on our websites: **www.RaisingReaders.co.uk** and
www.JoinRaisingReaders.com.

Thank you for reading.